BEADS ON A STRING

BEADS ON A STRING

A Fractured Childhood

Cicely Mayhew

The Book Guild Ltd
Sussex England

The Book Guild Ltd.
25 High Street,
Lewes, Sussex

First published 2000
© Cicely Mayhew 2000

Set in Times
Typesetting by IML Typographers, Chester, Cheshire
Printed in Great Britain by
Bookcraft (Bath) Ltd, Avon

A catalogue record for this book is
available from the British Library

ISBN 1 85776 421 8

To Christopher
who encourged me to write it all down

CONTENTS

PREFACE

For my Grandchildren – and their Parents

Why do I have this urge to write it all down for you? You are very sweet and say politely, yes, of course you'd be interested, but why should you be? It's as one get older that one becomes more absorbed by the past, unless you're a proper social historian. It is also true – in fact it's a cliché – that the distant past is clearer to the old than last week or last month. And let's face it, I *am* old. Not middle aged, not elderly, but old. And at night especially, child-hood memories come sidling, then crowding back, most but not all of them pleasant, not all happy, but with a kind of insistence to be recorded. If they really are interesting to you, I shall be glad. Because, of course, they are in a way a part of you too. And if you're not very interested – well, that's all right too. I shan't mind. At least I'll have told you, take it or leave it.

My childhood was so different from yours and not just because it began 56 years earlier. To start with, I had lived in thirteen clearly remembered homes and been to seven different schools in two continents by the time I was ten years old, with yet another change of school to come and including a year without any school at all.

But memory is famously fickle. The times when we came to rest are etched indelibly with their attendant joys and sadnesses but in between are blanks. What happened in between? We must have moved, but how? These movements, these mechanics of life, have nearly all faded but the periods in between remain and come more sharply into focus as one memory stimulates another. So you won't be surprised that they come as fragments (sometimes as chunks!) but consecutive, like separate beads on a necklace, each distinct but linked by the thread which was my childhood. Later years diminish in definition. They are no less valued but fuse together more as the years pile up — with far less change of scene.

These are my memory beads, taking me back more than 60 years, when the world was fresh and new (if occasionally upsetting) and energy seemed inexhaustible in a vanished world.

INTRODUCTION

Something About my Parents

My mother

Mother had an adventurous life but it was not an easy one. Her childhood was quite as disrupted as ours, if not more so. From what I managed to piece together from scraps of conversation, she remembered seeing her father only once, when, as a small girl, she was the sole boarder in a dame school in Glossop at the turn of the century. There was a suggestion that he 'ran away to sea' — a habit of the time or a popular evasion? He appears to have been something of a black sheep of an otherwise respectable family — another Victorian phenomenon. Her redoubtable and courageous mother, my 'Auntie Mother',* thereupon emigrated as a young divorcee, to make a new life in South Africa. She succeeded, but while she was doing so, my mother was literally farmed out: in term time in the dame school, run by two kindly elderly ladies, and in the holidays at Cloud Farm, Simmondley, then a prosperous dairy farm, high in the hills above Glossop. Perhaps it still is. I walked up to it once with Mother in the Fifties. It hadn't changed much, she said. It was the home of the Retford family, of whom there were nine or ten girls and two or three boys, at least one of whom emigrated across the Atlantic. My grandmother was one of the youngest. The girls were locally famed for their long auburn

---

*She refused to be called 'Grandmother'.

1

hair and Mother's too was spectacular when she was young. At the Royal Academy of Music, her piano professor, forgetful of names, referred to her as 'the girl with the peculiar hair' – but not rudely. He just meant 'distinctive'. It was in fact an unusual dark chestnut.

At Cloud Farm the eldest girl in the family was Aunt Ann, the youngest was Annie! Did they just run out of girls' names? In those days there was work for the boys on the farm but not enough for so many girls and precious little choice for the surplus ones – it was either the mills or domestic service. They chose the mills. These didn't seem to have been the 'dark, satanic mills' of the industrial cities; they were on the edge of the Pennines and still in the countryside, like New Mills now, not far away.

Soon after Mother's return to Africa, I went to stay there with a cousin of Mother's, 'Auntie' Nelly, and her brother Joe. The old 'new' mills were just behind the house and being me, I had to explore. I remember a steep climb down to river level, gaunt stone walls open to the sky and the sightless eyes of broken windows, all overgrown now by trees, willowherb and scrub. It was the closest to a jungle that I'd seen since Kasanga. But I was still only ten; alone down there I found it frightening. I fled, imagining I was chased by a ghostly Something, and never went again.

I'm afraid that visit wasn't a success. It was too soon after losing Mother and I was still trying to settle in Sheffield. I was homesick, which may have encouraged the Sheffield aunts but was a bit hard on Auntie Nelly. She did her best but got fed up with my gloom and said so and I moped on.

But I digress. Whether it was there or elsewhere, I never got the impression that my great-aunts had too bad a time in the mills. Mother said that on high days and holidays, they had the use of the farm pony trap and went jaunting to Buxton. They certainly worked hard, but they scrimped and saved, some of them enough to leave the mills and start their own small businesses, while others married into other farms in the hills around.

All the same, when my grandmother emigrated, she was determined on a better future for her daughter, hence the dame school and music lessons – a perceptive move as it turned out. After the dame school, Mother went on to Mottram Grammar School. She was still based mainly at Cloud Farm but was shuttled round aunts

2

in other farms as need arose. They were kind without a doubt and Mother never complained in telling of this time. But they were also hard-working and busy, with little time to spare for entertaining a peripatetic niece in addition to their own families. There was no transport for outings, public or otherwise, except occasionally a milk float; there were rarely any outings at all. From an early age, Mother was accustomed to walking everywhere in the hills around Glossop. She must have had some lonely times but it was good training for later safaris.

She used to tell the tale of a rice pudding which she made in the cookery class at school. This turned out well. Flown with pride, she put a cloth over the basin and ran headlong a mile and more downhill to show it to the aunt of the moment, leaping from stone to stone as I used to do myself, so I know how you need to concentrate to keep your footing. She reached home to find her aunt at the stove.

'Look what I've made, all by myself!' she said proudly, whipping off the cloth to display – an empty basin. Splodges of rice pudding must have punctuated her path from school, no doubt to the delight of the local bird and rabbit populations. Her aunt knew a thing or two about children because Mother never recalled this incident without much merriment.

Eventually my grandmother married again and sent for Mother to come to her in Pretoria. Auntie Mother's second husband was an upright pillar of the community, a company secretary, I think, called Mr Law. Well named! It seems he kept clockwork punctuality, the house ran on oiled wheels according to his diktat and even the early tram down to the town centre would not leave until Mr Law was aboard. It is not recorded that he ever made it late. I got the impression of regard rather than warmth on Mother's side. But she had a stable home at last and, in due course, a stepsister, Dolly, our 'Auntie Wog'.

Whether my grandmother later reacted against the ultra-orderly routine of those days or whether it had been an attraction of opposites in the first place, I cannot possibly tell. But when we knew Auntie Mother, she was decidedly unconventional – a forceful merry widow with a robust approach to life. She was a fanatical bridge player and a keen racegoer. I remember her bursting into our house in Johannesburg one evening saying: 'Lily! I won the double! Sixty pounds!' Then as an afterthought, 'My skirts blew up... I'll *never* wear this again. But the double, Lily, the double!' What would £60 in 1932 be worth now? Quite a lot. Since she drew attention to it, I remember the undisciplined dress, a richly pleated brown number, Mother said georgette. Not one for a windy day, obviously.

Mother herself finished her schooling in Natal at a boarding school called Uplands. She was happy there and formed a lasting respect and affection for the headmistress, Mrs Colepepper, an early graduate of Newnham, Cambridge. I have a photograph of this lady. She does look impressive: authoritative, dignified and kind – not a bad combination. Piano lessons continued and in due course Mother came back to England to enter the Royal Academy of Music 60 years to the day before my daughter Judy, a coincidence which gave her great pleasure.

Once again she spent holidays at Cloud Farm, helping with the haymaking in summer, which she enjoyed but which scratched her pianist's hands woefully. In term-time she lodged in Gordon Square in Bloomsbury. She never spoke of romantic attachments but a book of poetry, the odd letter and an unnamed photo of a soldier she left suggest some who were interested in her! Whether or not she reciprocated I never knew. Perhaps the First World War interfered. In due course she got her LRAM and returned to South Africa and Uplands to teach there until her marriage. She kept her school hat ribbon to the end of her life. I expect it represented security and happiness for her. I couldn't destroy it now.

My mother's childhood could never be described as stable. If one grows up in such uncertain circumstances perhaps one is bound either to fold or to become more than usually self-reliant, independent and tough – and perhaps to take these qualities too much for granted in others. My mother was all of these things. She needed to be. She had a hard life and if I seem critical of some of her actions and attitudes – well, it's true, I was. But I hope I can now understand.

I met her two surviving aunts when I went on a 'keeping-in-touch' visit to Glossop during the war and again with Mother a couple of years afterwards. Aunt Annie was especially delighted to see her again. Her son now ran Cloud Farm, while she lived in a solid terrace house in Lord Street. By now rheumatism or arthritis more or less confined her to a sofa; she had become very heavy and could only move around with difficulty. But she still preserved the auburn hair of her youth (by fair means or foul). She reminded me of my grandmother, both in her looks and strong personality, and outwardly her robust spirits seemed to be undamped. In spite of this resolute cheerfulness, though, she had had enough of this life.

'Why can't I go, Lily?' I overheard her say to Mother. 'Why can't I just **go**?' But she would never have countenanced euthanasia.

Mother was in Africa again when she did die and I must have been abroad too, with the Foreign Office, since I never knew.

Aunt Edith was different. I remember her as white-haired, small, frail and hard of hearing. Her Victorian cottage in a row near the High Street had a real cottage garden back and front and inside, it was still lit by gas mantles, which you lit by reaching up, pulling a little ring and chain and applying a match. If you've ever seen one, you'll know what I mean. I stayed with her overnight on my first visit towards the end of the last war. She was sweet and kind; she obviously loved my mother – and I loved her almost on sight.

Unlike my grandmother, she retained her Derbyshire accent. The last time Mother visited her, she asked, 'How old are you now, Lily?'

'Fifty-three,' said Mother.

'Ee,' commented Aunt Edith, 'tha'lt go no better now!' Very true.

Surviving the hard winter of 1946–47, she tripped at home in 1949 and broke her thigh, which left her frailer than ever. Stairs were difficult. Like many others in her circumstances, she retreated to her one tiny room with a gas fire. She fell asleep one winter night with the fire, such as it was, still on. The pressure fell so low that it went out altogether; then at some point in the night the gas came on again. Aunt Edith never woke up.

I went up for her funeral, partly to represent Mother but also for myself. I think I know what a Victorian funeral would have felt like. I can see us now, a long black line following the coffin up the stark winter hillside. Senses were numbed through the service – it's gone. We went somewhere afterwards; a cold collation in a pub or tearoom. I was young, I'd never been to a funeral before. I was taken aback by the casual conversation and seemingly unconcerned tucking in to the sandwiches. I made my escape as soon as I could.

Aunt Edith's son ran a butcher's business in the High Street not far from Aunt Edith's cottage. Mother took me there, doing the rounds of her relatives before we went to Africa. I must have been nearly four. Quite suddenly, as I write, another memory stirs, a horrid picture. We were in their house, having tea. I expect I got bored by grown-up talk. Anyway, I wandered off, out into the yard. Did anyone realise, I wonder? For there I watched an ox being slaughtered. 'Humane' killing, I suppose, with a shot in the middle of the forehead; but only after the beast had been thrown to the ground and tied down. I can see again its eyes staring at me, rolling in terror. But I couldn't look away.

It's blank after that. Mother might have protested that I should have been shooed away – but I can't be sure. Perhaps I just wished she had. I must have partly blotted the memory out, otherwise I'd have been a vegetarian as soon as I realised what meat was.

That was a digression but it might be relevant. Aunt Edith's son and his wife were hospitable when I visited Glossop alone during the war. They invited me to dinner and it was quite a feast. But without knowing why, I was ill at ease as I never was with Aunt Edith herself. Perhaps it's fanciful but was it anything to do with that buried memory of horror when I had gone out to the yard, probably from that same room? I don't know – but it was odd. I did find the older generation, my grandmother's, more congenial and warmer than some of my mother's contemporaries, though.

Nonetheless, that same family took a hot dinner round to Aunt Edith every single day until she died. And when I went to dinner with them another relative was there, 'Aunt Ruth', I think. Aunt Ruth was mentally deficient – or handicapped – and could only smile and nod. She sat in a cosy corner next to the chimney piece and was cared for in their home day and night. Would it be the same today? Anyway, gauche as I may have been when I was there, I salute that family.

It was in the summer of 1934, when she brought Dick and me back 'home' for the sake of our education, that I first consciously looked at Mother as a person rather than just my mother. Then I saw that she was beautiful. She was smaller and slimmer than my father's family. Even I could appreciate her slender legs and neat ankles and feet. I recall her glee at being able to buy expensive shoes in the sales. With a size four foot, there was no problem and very little competition and she did dearly love expensive shoes – and a bargain. I don't think she ever wasted a penny. She told me later that Father used to congratulate her on this rare quality. She had far better dress sense than ever I achieved and kept that and her figure right to the end. And there was that hair – a cloud of burnished chestnut. That is how I remember her in my childhood and how I like to remember her now.

My father

My father was the youngest surviving child and only son in a family of six. There had been a small sister, Laura, especially beloved of my Aunt Rittie (Ruth); but she died of croup when she was two. I have never been sure what croup was – was it asthma? Aunt Rittie told me that she tried to write a poem for Laura and kept all her life a tiny wooden bat she used to play ball with.

The family lived in a modest but comfortable house in Filey Street in Sheffield, not far from the university in one direction and the site, later on, of Aunt Jessie's antique shop in the other. I guess that George, my father, was doted on as the only son as well as being the youngest. It seems he had an engaging zest for life and a sense of humour which kept the family entertained. He also probably benefited from the Victorian attitude to men as lords of the universe – and of their womenfolk.

My grandfather was an artisan/craftsman, while my grandmother was a Shaw from Ecclesfield, then a few miles north of Sheffield but now nearly engulfed. Her family was rather higher up the social scale of that era, and had known better days still.

7

There is a tradition that they were well-to-do landowners at one time but around the turn of the eighteenth and nineteenth centuries, the estate was inherited by a compulsive gambler – a not uncommon tale. This Shaw, having gambled away fortune and property, had nothing else to stake – except the family vault within the church. So he gambled on that – and lost again. Apocryphal or not, the fact is that up until the early years of the nineteenth century, Shaws occupied the vault; afterwards, they were buried in the churchyard outside.

I never knew my paternal grandmother. A photograph shows what would have been called a fine figure of a woman, with strong but not stern features, not unlike Aunt Emily but tougher. She was very much loved and it is clear that the whole family revolved around her. Twenty and more years later Aunt Emily would recall every detail of the morning when, going upstairs to see why her mother was so uncharacteristically late down, she found her dead in bed. She had died quietly in the night, presumably of heart failure. There had been no inkling of any weakness. They were devastated. Aunt Emily seemed to feel the shock as acutely as ever when she told us about it long afterwards.

It was probably their mother who ensured that as well as George, all the girls were well educated; three of the four became teachers, and all were well-spoken.

I have only a faint memory of the eldest, my Aunt Amy. I must have been about two and a half when I was taken to see her, very ill with what was then called consumption. I remember standing at the foot of the bed gazing at this grey, pale lady propped up on pillows, too awed and too shy to think of anything to say. Not long afterwards we were told that she had died. I registered it, as you see. But I didn't really understand. She left me a Rockingham tea service, and Dick a fine oak settle. I still have the tea service, although the magnificent teapot became a casualty of time, to my sorrow.

My father was a large man in every way. He was over six feet tall, with a complexion ruddy rather than tanned by years of tropical sun. As a small girl, I used to see his legs as khaki-clad tree trunks. They were the only part of him I could reach to hug if he was standing up. All the members of his family that I knew were what you might call generously proportioned except for my grandfather, who was much slighter. Father was very fair when younger and went white early, as did Aunt Emily. I used to wonder how old they could be.

I don't know when Father first went to Africa, except that it was before the First World War. With a first class degree in metallurgy, there were good prospects in a country where so much was being discovered so fast. Before setting off up-country, he met others far worse off – one of them a 'seafaring man' on the street in Durban who sold him a pearl for a song and a sandwich. Father had it mounted on a gold pin and sent it home for Aunt Emily, the sister nearest him in age and his favourite. It's one piece of family jewellery I still have. Most was stolen in a burglary, including a gold necklace of lovers' knots framing aquamarines which he had made for my mother.

That was after his success on what is now the Copper Belt, when he had met and married my mother and they went off into the wilds together to seek their fortune – and that is where Bead 1 begins.

THE FIRST BEAD

Beginnings and Crux Easton (1924–1926)

I have hanging on my bedroom wall an old sepia photograph of
my parents on safari – probably in what was then Northern
Rhodesia. It must have been around 1920, before my brother was
born in 1921. A long line of some 30 native bearers stretches
across the picture. The first group are carrying loads on their
heads, as the women of our gang taught me to do some ten years
later in Tanganyika – though my loads were much lighter! Next
comes what looks like a large baby bath, slung on poles between
two chaps and apparently being steadied as it went by a third. No
doubt it *was* a bath – the one and only one; it may also have held
fresh water. Next comes a litter, shaded from the sun and contain-
ing my mother. Astonishingly to me, as a child – and still – she
seems to be facing *away* from the line of advance. But perhaps this
was to gaze at my father, in attendance at the rear of the litter and
apparently shouldering a gun. Behind him, the rest of the party are
carrying four more containers of sorts slung on poles. They are
crossing an open space in the bush. The grass looks dry and short-
ish, with light tufts here and there, which might be cotton grass.
And there is a group of the ubiquitous anthills in the foreground,
rising up like misshapen sandcastles. This was a real safari, as I
knew it too, only a few years later. No conducted ride on *wheels*,
protected from all possible danger!

The companion photograph shows a snarling leopard cub: very
endearing, as the very young of all species usually are – even

10

human beings. The mother had been prowling round the camp and, being said by local villagers to be dangerous, she was shot. But my parents adopted the cub until they moved camp again. I always hoped it survived to a ripe old age.

My father was then, as always, prospecting and combining it with a spot of big-game hunting. He was successful in both. Countless pairs of horns *and* a rhino horn were sent back to England and mounted. They covered virtually every square foot of the hall and landing walls in my aunts' house in Sheffield. But only one pair of koodoo horns (I think) survives and I have it still. The rest were sold to help make ends meet in later years.

My father's prospecting also bore fruit – if that's the word. He was, as I have said, a metallurgist and he thought Northern Rhodesia was a promising area. He was right. He discovered some of the first copper in what later became the Northern Rhodesian Copper Belt. He used to tell how he had, single-handed, enlarged the British Empire. Coming across the northern boundary markers while out prospecting one day, he uprooted a few and 'relocated' them further north.

Unfortunately for the family fortunes, having struck not gold but copper, he was less canny. Soon after my brother's birth in Pietermaritzburg, with premature satisfaction rather than financial acumen, he sold out his concession for what was then the vast sum of £20,000 and brought his wife and baby son home to England. He planned to live the life of a country gentleman and to that end bought a small Queen Anne house with a large Victorian extension at Crux Easton near Newbury. We were always told that the first de Havilland Moth was built and tried out in one of our adjoining fields. (De Havilland's father was Vicar of Crux Easton at the time.) My father set out to enjoy a peaceful life, interspersed with bird's-nesting forays to the Camargue and Spain.

I therefore arrived in a nursing home in Newbury – and Crux Easton was the first house I lived in. Many years later, I gather Sir Oswald Mosley inhabited it for a time, until interned during the war. At some point, there was a fire in the Victorian wing and it was demolished – making a more manageable house for nowadays. I still have snapshots of the vanished Victorian facade with our old Dodge parked outside the door. We had a cook and maids from the village. They were reluctant to live in and would never stay overnight alone. The house was said to be haunted but where, how and by whom, never came into the story! Perhaps it was just that – a story.

All that is hearsay. But I do myself remember parts of this house surprisingly vividly. It was until recently the home of Lord and Lady Boyd-Carpenter and thanks to their kindness, I was able to visit it again with my husband a few years ago. So much was familiar. Their drawing room would have been our playroom. It's a lovely, well-proportioned room with a large square bay overlooking a small sheltered lawn.

'How odd,' I said. 'I remember a door there into the garden. I made daisy chains on the lawn.'

'Oh yes,' they answered. 'There was a door. But it was draughty – so we had it moved to the side.'

Their dining room I remembered as our kitchen, with cellar stairs rather dangerously near the door. Perhaps I was wrong. But no, it *had* been the kitchen; and the cellar stairs *were* too near the door, so they had been turned round to come up further away. In our day, the kitchen was down a long stone passage from the posh end – then the Victorian part. When the family was gathered in the drawing room and I disappeared from it, I was always told, I would have crawled at speed down this passage to the kitchen – for warmth, titbits and perhaps cuddles? Parents didn't cuddle much in my memory.

Most surprising to me, in the main bedroom upstairs I saw and recognised a small cupboard in the wall above the picture rail, well out of reach of prying toddlers. A splendid place to keep Christmas presents until the appointed time. As I looked at it 60 years later, there even came a faint echo of pleasurable anticipation.

Outside, the tiny church across the lane, with its eighteenth-century interior, is still etched in my mind. Not the whole, but the windows, largely plain glass but with a yellow stained-glass sun at the top. I hadn't consciously remembered them for what they were – but recognised them too at once.

Crux Easton is still unspoilt, with wide open views from the house, and barely a village at all. It represented the peak of the family prosperity. Relatives came to stay — and it was always, in my childhood, referred to as a golden age. And my goodness, how we would love it now! But my mother felt very isolated — as indeed she was. So when I was about three, and my brother pushing six, we moved to 6 Parsifal Road in Hampstead, with our nursemaid Florence — better known as Frollie — and a cook called Blanche.

This was really the home of my toddlerhood. This is the setting where I recall the excitement of new experiences crowding in. And of bewilderment and anguish at the unpredictability and — on occasion — cruelty of someone I loved and who did I am sure love me.

THE SECOND BEAD

No. 6 Parsifal Road (c1926–1928)

We can't have lived here for much more than two years but it was a time of awakening, of curiosity, of learning – memories now stirred, crowd so fast that I almost wonder if I remember something of every single day.

It was a solid red-brick house, Edwardian I should think, set back a bit from the road, with six steps up to the front door. My parents had been to Norway about the time we moved, and there is a snapshot of Dick and me on those steps. I am wrapped in a sealskin coat they had brought back for me – and look completely spherical.

Inside was a square hall and, on toddler scale, a feeling of spaciousness. Upstairs, my parents' bedroom faced the garden at the back, and my own, sometimes but I think not always shared with Dick, was at the front. I liked that. The glow from the street lamps was companionable at night – and traffic noises scarcely existed then. I remember watching the lamp-lighter come round with his long pole, lighting up those lamps one by one. I thought he must be *very* clever. And once at least, a muffin man came by with bell and a tray on his head. I did so want us to buy some but was told 'next time'. But it must already have been a disappearing trade – and I can't remember that he ever did come again while we were there.

A bathroom and a lavatory were across the landing from these two superior bedrooms, and up half a landing was a smaller room

14

which we occupied on occasion – probably when the house was full of visitors.

Up another half stairway were at least two large attic bedrooms. Here my father kept his precious birds' egg collection in a tall cabinet, each egg nested in cotton wool and carefully labelled. I used to love looking at them with him. It was only recently that I discovered from old letters that they'd been sold a few years later, together with his distinguished stamp collection, to help make ends meet. Poor father – he had so treasured them.

The back attic was our chief playroom. Here we could spread out our toys and didn't have to be too tidy. Dick was given a clock-work Hornby train set. I was as green as one of the engines with envy. But he graciously let me play with it, especially when we invented the game of crashes. All the rails were set in a large circle, then he started off one engine with the coaches, while I, on the far side of the circle, set off the other engine with the goods trucks in the opposite direction. Single track, you understand. I am ashamed to say that we found the inevitable crash most satisfying. Mother, though, was cross when she came up one day and found us at it! We were forbidden to do it again. 'It's want and destruction!' I thought she said. Which puzzled me not a little. *I* hadn't asked for a train set. Nor had Dick – it was a big surprise. I remember this because we discussed it when she'd gone. Grown-ups were sometimes difficult to understand. It was several years before I came across the word 'wanton' – and was transported back to the attic playroom and the ill-treated train set. And then I understood what she had been getting at.

On the way down the stairs the top flight was the scene of my first taste of triumph and power! Dick, being three years older and taller than I, had the unhappy habit, when in teasing mood, of pulling the corkscrew ringlets into which my hair would be carefully brushed each morning. His hair was not long enough and I was not tall enough to retaliate. But on this occasion we decided, for some reason, to pause and rest on the way downstairs. He, as usual, was in front as we sat down, so I was a couple of steps higher than he was. In front of and *below* me Dick's head of thick auburn hair was within my reach! A moment of realisation, a moment of exultation – and I bent forward, grasped two handfuls, leant back and pulled with all my might. Oh what delicious, evil delight! The grown-ups who came running to see what the hullabaloo was about must have seen my point, as there was no retribution that time.

In spite of this contretemps, we were very good companions in those days. Another time on the same staircase, he followed my experiment of seeing if I could get my head right through the bannisters. He could – but he couldn't get it out again. I felt deep concern then and went rushing downstairs calling out, 'Dickie's stuck, Dickie's stuck!' (Or rather 'Dickie 'tuck!' – I never could sound my esses; they were the bane of my life, especially with a name like mine. I would lie in bed at night practising aloud 'C stands for Cicely' but achieving only 'Tee tand' for' – enormous effort – 'Lishley!' in a shower of spray.)

My father's study was on the half-landing up from the hall. I don't know what he studied. I do remember waiting there for him to come home, and helping pull off his shoes and put on his slippers. One afternoon of high excitement he came home with a surprise birthday present for my mother and we were to share the secret and help get it ready. It was a miniature reference library from Asprey's. Of course I didn't know what that meant. But I saw eight small volumes bound in dark blue morocco, the leaves gold-edged, the spines gold-tooled. They all fitted neatly into a beautifully made little mahogany bookcase with curving ends edged in brass. I can check my memory now, because I have it still. Then, I just thought it was a lovely thing, as indeed it is. That afternoon our job was to help shine up the brass to a peak of glory. Which we did with a will. I wish I could recall its presentation – but alas! I can't.

Coming downstairs and across the hall to the right, perhaps two or three steps further down, was the drawing room. To me it seemed enormous. Large windows looked out to the garden and there stood my mother's Bechstein grand, where she frequently played – and less frequently sang. For every time she raised her voice in song, our splendid mastiff, Bill-dog (Highly Commended at Cruft's), raised his voice too – in protest or partnership, no one knew. It was a powerful but not a musical combination.

Dick and I were more taken with two large animal-skin rugs – a mighty polar bear and a tiger, both with heads attached. The polar

16

bear looked benevolent, the tiger snarled with open jaws and monstrous teeth and looked anything but, poor thing. The polar bear came from the Norwegian holiday, I learnt later. The tiger was presumably bought as part of fashionable decor, as whatever else he shot, my father never went to India and I knew from a very young age that there are no tigers in Africa. We loved to roll around on these furry rugs, stroking their heads (the tiger always from behind in my case – I didn't much care for the teeth), pretending they were real – and generally treating them as giant dolls. But we weren't in the drawing room that much. It was the age of 'children should be seen and not heard'. How often did that ring in my ears – obviously with little effect! In fact, I don't remember much conversation with my mother, other than similar admonitory aphorisms. 'Speak when you're spoken to and not before!' and 'That will do, Miss Butinski!' Requests to stay up longer were met with, 'There's always tomorrow'; interested speculation, probably on birthdays, as to how old any grown-up was, was invariably answered by, 'As old as my tongue and a little older than my teeth!' Which didn't get us far. I was thrilled when I was four at last! Why wouldn't grown-ups tell us how old they were on *their* birthdays? I never could understand this coy reticence – and come to that, I still can't. But persistence only got another, 'Children should be seen and not heard!'

The dining room at the front of the house was where my father read the morning paper – and teased us with riddles – 'What's black and white and red (read) all over?' Answer: 'A newspaper' – and so on. The HMV wind-up gramophone was kept there too – perhaps so as not to compete with my mother's piano in the drawing room. The only record I had was 'Three little kittens, Who lost their mittens' – I loved that. We had large family meals round what seemed an immense table. At Christmas dinner, as the monster pudding was served, my father pretended to find not sixpence but a handful of gold sovereigns in his helping. But I'd seen him take them from his pocket. Still, Dick and I were hugely delighted. It was indeed a sight; it would be even more now! When children weren't officially present, one would sometimes be hidden under this table, screened by the large cloth and listening with flapping ears. I was usually discovered; and anyway, it lost its charm after I heard talk about 'Oh, money!'uttered with palpable distaste. I recall no other words and understood nothing but there was an uncomfortable sense of something wrong. Now I realise that it probably heralded the end of prosperity.

Mostly, we ate with Florrie in a friendly sort of ante-room to the kitchen. This was half a flight down again from the hall and must have been under the study. There was a cheerful oyster-tasting there once, round about our bedtime. No oysters for us, thank goodness – but I remember my father swallowing what seemed a vast quantity with relish – and Worcester sauce? Why ever should that stick in my mind after all these years? There was also a (failed) attempt at butter-churning with some gadget, perhaps bought at the Ideal Home Exhibition. I looked forward to this with passion. The year before, Dick had been and there were all sorts of samples to be had – miniature loaves of bread, tiny packets of biscuits, pots of jam and so on, all perfect for dolls' tea parties. But alas! I fell sick of a fever, measles in fact, and was too ill to go. They brought me some nice things – but it wasn't the same.

At first, Florrie, Frollie to me, was always around. It was she who took Dick to school and me and Bill-dog for walks. Once I got slightly behind him as he wagged his tail. A mistake. I was so small and he was so big that it caught me on the side of the head and sent me staggering. I was rather proud of having such a dog – and quite right too. We weren't that far from Hampstead Heath but probably a bit too far for three or four-year-old legs. There was a park much nearer with tall pillars and iron gates, and there was a police station, blue lamp and all, past which I would be led if deemed to have been naughty! It inculcated respect for the law at an early age, I suppose – but I can't remember what my offences were. Answering back, perhaps – I was good at that! We may have had a different walk for each day of the week, because about this time I visualised the days quite distinctly. I don't remember Sunday clearly but Monday was just grey; Tuesday was a bed of tulips, Wednesday a pair of Wellingtons, Thursday, tall gates, Friday fried eggs and Saturday a large armchair. The associations of sound or image are obvious now, of course – unconscious then. One memorable walk took me, with my mother this time, to the

18

doctor's surgery to be vaccinated. My thigh was raked with a kind of fork and I did try not to screech. I remember the blisters coming up later – and everyone except me was very pleased! I don't think sweeties were dispensed on such occasions then. The nearest one got was drops of eucalyptus on a lump of sugar for a cold in the head. The doctor's house is still a doctor's surgery – I recognised it when driving by quite recently.

Sometimes I would go with Florrie to collect Dick from school. It was a small private school, called College Villas, on the Finchley Road. We and other nannies and parents waited in a courtyard, with a tree I think. I was in agonies of shyness, treading one foot on another and dreading anyone speaking to me. I went on being shy for years and probably over-compensated in the end!

When I reached four I joined Dick at this school for a bit. The first of eight schools! All I remember of this one is standing in the corner, and elocution lessons – no doubt to help me with my esses. I expect they did, since I don't think I had any trouble after we left Parsifal Road. I have no idea why I was put in the corner and I don't think I minded much. It was just something new. I think I started a cheerful hum or something, because I was fairly soon allowed out.

On one afternoon a week, there was a dancing class. We both went and were drilled in rows. 'Chassé and a step – hop!' is all I remember – would it have been the polka? I didn't like the little boy I was supposed to try it with but I loved my dancing pumps with the crossed elastic. I certainly didn't learn much dancing, then or since, which was a pity.

One fine day, we called at MacFisheries on the way home and lo! they had a big tank of goldfish for sale! To our joy, we were allowed to have one each. No one thought about a goldfish bowl, though, so two large jam jars had to do. I fell instantly and deeply in love with my fish but was afraid it might escape in the night. I had it by my bedside, and Dick and I, to make all safe, tied paper over the top of the jar. Of course in the morning, our poor little fish, starved of oxygen, were both dead. I was heartbroken. We decided we must give them a proper funeral, so we processed solemnly to the far end of the garden where there was a rougher patch with a few apple trees. And there, under one of these, we

19

dug a hole and laid the sad remains solemnly to rest. We covered them over and knelt to say a prayer. We had been taught the Lord's Prayer – and also,

> Gentle Jesus, meek and mild,
> Look upon a little child,
> Pity my simplicity,
> Suffer me to come to Thee.

But as neither of us had sorted out what a 'simply city' was, 'Our Father' (which of course we both knew by heart) seemed better. Which it was – and we recited it with great feeling. Nevertheless, I was in the dumps for a good week. I thought of another rhyme I knew by heart:

> One, two, three, four, five, six, seven,
> All good children go to Heaven.

'Do you think,' I said to Dick, 'our goldfish have gone to Heaven yet?'

We pondered this philosophical question seriously for some time before one of us thought of going to see. So we processed again and performed the exhumation. To our disappointment and disillusion, there they still were.

'Perhaps they need more time,' said Dick.

'Perhaps they weren't good enough,' said I. Or vice versa. Anyway, we didn't risk another exhumation and grief gradually dulled.

The rest of the garden wasn't inspired but it was good for children. A large lawn, edged with paths to push a doll's pram along, a climbable cherry tree near the house – and our splendid and gentle Bill-dog to play with. He even let me ride on his back – but this was rightly stopped as being bad for him. I had one much-loved and much-abused doll, unimaginatively called Blue-dolly. I was found belabouring her one day. I seem to remember doing it rather a lot. Why? 'Because she's talking silly nonsense,' I am reported to have said. Looking back, I think there may have been a bit more to it than that.

20

In that garden there also took place the wedding reception of my godmother, Auntie Betty. She was the daughter of the Vicar of Sandbach and had married the curate, Uncle Harry. In the wedding photograph, Dick stands as a page, I as a mini-bridesmaid, both dressed up to the nines in pink satin. Someone said to me: 'Oh Baygirl* you *do* look pretty,' to which I answered without a blush: 'I know' – which doesn't sound shy at all. Auntie Betty and Uncle Harry later went to Crewe Green in Cheshire to a delightful church opposite a long drive leading to the commodious Victorian vicarage on the edge of the Crewe Hall estate. Years later, I spent a lot of my school holidays with them very happily – they were endlessly kind and hospitable.

From Parsifal Road we went for holidays to Swanage and Studland. There are pictures of us on Swanage beach in rainbow-coloured rubber 'waders' and round hats – panama for me, grey felt for Dick. Dick built very fine sandcastles, I thought, and was outraged and hurt for him, one day, when a Horrid Big Boy came along and jumped on one he'd just finished. I wanted to help him build it again but he hadn't the heart. Donkey rides and ice-creams were to be had, pink and white, strawberry and vanilla, twopenny ones and threepenny ones. I remember the grown-ups were surprised at my preferring the white rather than the pink ones – I still do – and definitely, the threepenny ones! It must have been good weather, as I remember nothing of where we stayed but only the beach and sometimes forays into the countryside. Our car was a Dodge, in which my mother sat as if enthroned, and swathed in a motoring veil. A common game was to see who could (truthfully) first say 'I spy Corfe Castle.'

Back in Hampstead, we certainly had plenty of toys. Perhaps it was the ruthless way we played trains that prompted my mother one day to collect a large sack and say we had too many and they were going to the Salvation Army! I'm sure we were allowed to keep some – but I watched dumbly as the rest were shovelled into the sack without asking us which we really wanted to keep. It was in summer on the level patch of ground behind the house, before

*Baygirl was a corruption of baby girl which was how I was introduced to my brother. Baygirl stuck, and was eventually shortened to Bay.

a flight of steps went up to the main lawn. It was not the first injustice – there had been a worse occasion. But it was probably the first time I was conscious of it, as such. I remember very clearly saying to myself that the toys had been given to *us* and it wasn't fair just to take them away. Dick too was upset. But there! No doubt it was a good introduction to self-denial – or something.

Mostly, it was a happy time at Parsifal Road. Blanche and Florrie did not, I think, stay to the end, though Florrie nearly did. But it was in the mid-1920s and my father's copper-gained wealth, so apparent at Crux Easton and Parsifal Road at the beginning, evaporated, like many other fortunes, in the Depression. Children are quite good at accepting facts, however, and leaving the house did not memorably upset us. There is a blank. And then we were in Sheffield, staying with 'the aunts' at 39 Elmore Road, Broomhill – with Bill-dog but without Florrie. I missed her.

Before leaving Parsifal Road, though, I cannot hide that there was a darker side to our time there.

It was quite unconsciously when starting on this chapter, that I went first to my mother's bedroom. It is not the logical place to start but let it stand.

Children are innocent – not in a sentimental sense but literally. And small children ought to be able to stay so. However, one afternoon, Dick and I wanted the lavatory at the same time and raced in together. There we discovered, I certainly for the first time, that we were made differently. Perhaps he did know. I did not. But I remember laughing with *delight*. Not for long. My mother came upstairs and heard us. She went berserk. Aunt Jessie, who was staying, grabbed Dick and would not let her get at him. I was dragged to that bedroom, flung face down on the bed and thrashed mercilessly with a wooden coathanger. I remember crying out 'Stop, oh stop! I won't do it again, I won't do it again!' – though what I had done that was so wrong I did not know, nor was it then, or ever, explained. At last I fell off the bed – which stopped the blows – and lay in a sobbing heap on the floor. I do not know how long for. I was all of three years old. And I remember no comfort.

But children are realists. They accept. I suppose I did. I certainly still loved my mother. And I think I suppressed the memory at first, though perhaps with unconscious self-psychotherapy, I took it out on poor Blue-dolly! But many years later, I could still wake in the small hours and weep for that little three-year-old who was myself. As I grew older, I thought it was a wicked act which did great damage. I still do. But, too, I feel compassion for what could have lain behind it. My mother herself had no normal family life as a child – she never knew her father – and I don't think she really understood small children. I gathered that my birth was difficult and she would not entertain the idea of more children. But I can only guess. And it's better left.

There was another odd recollection. It was when I had measles and couldn't go to the Ideal Home Exhibition. During the night, I felt very bad and at last, was very sick. I never called out. Having been sick, I felt better and thought I'd better not! So there I lay till morning, the sick (if you'll forgive me) gradually drying on my neck. I can feel it now. I was still in a cot, so could not easily get out. In the morning I do remember concern. Why hadn't I called out? I was asked. Well, why? I can't imagine my own children not calling out – in fact, I know for sure they did. And quite right too. Was I afraid to? Surely not. But it was odd.

My father was always kindly. He seemed to like our company, liked jokes and spent time explaining things. I never remember anything from him but kindness. And I never saw him after the age of nine until I was grown-up with children of my own.

THE THIRD BEAD

No. 39 Elmore Road, Sheffield (Autumn 1928)

A smaller bead – like those on necklaces of bigger ones, only to separate each from the next. It was the brief interval between England and Africa.

I recall nothing of the journey from London, though I think it was by road. There's a vivid mind-picture of rounding a corner over a hill in the dark and seeing a mass of lights in the valley below. We were nearly there and in that dark, Sheffield's lights were beautiful. But I have no memory of arrival.

We stayed in Sheffield for three or four months, paying farewell family visits and unloading on my wonderful aunts, dear Bill-dog and the mass of horns and other impedimenta from my father's big-game hunting days.

We were there long enough, though, for us to go to school, especially as there was one next door. Eastville was a small private school where the big girls wore brown gymslips, much coveted by me. I remember sitting on a low, backless bench at the front (being one of the tinies) for Prayers – but nothing else *except* the fact, if you can credit it, that I was *always* late. It seemed to me that as I only had to get next door it took no time at all. Which was not true. Dick gave up waiting for me – and I never learned. It must have been regarded as a harmless idiosyncrasy in the end, as apart from a few minor scolds at the beginning, no one seemed to mind. And it was surely a good little school, because there I learned to read, painlessly and without even realising it. I just found I could. Of course we were read to a lot at home by my aunts, who were both teachers. Kipling's *Just So Stories* were favourites, particularly 'The Elephant's Child' – as an introduction to Africa, perhaps. No 'cat sat on the mat' or emasculated versions of children's classics for us, then or at any time. But lovely rolling phrases – 'the Precession of the Equinoxes', 'the banks of the great grey-green greasy Limpopo River, all set about with fever-trees'. And proper fairy tales – Hans Andersen (unabridged!) and later Grimm. This last had on its cover the sinister silhouette of a man with a sack of children on his back, and this did frighten me but I devoured the stories. At four, if I didn't understand all the words, that didn't matter – the sound of them was entrancing.

Apart from discovering reading, only one incident in Sheffield went deep enough to stay with me all these years. We went to visit my grandfather and the third aunt, Jessie, who ran an antiques business in West Street. We were in the front room upstairs, which was half sitting room and half showroom. We were probably saying goodbye, for someone produced two new coins to give to us, Dick and me. One was a shining new penny, which in those days was the size of a 50p piece; and one was a silver sixpence, about the size of today's 20p piece. Who was to have which? Someone suggested 'Ladies first – let Bay choose.' Now I knew perfectly well that the sixpence was worth more – I wasn't stupid! But I also knew that Dick longed for the sixpence and I loved my brother. So with genuine kindly intent I said I would have the penny. And everybody laughed at me for going for the bigger one and losing out. That, I suppose, was my first experience of being seriously unappreciated because at four, it *was* serious. Well it happens – and it's as well to make the discovery early on. But I've never forgotten it.

In due course, we got ourselves to Southampton – again memory of the journey has gone. All I recall is the station platform at Sheffield and my mother anxiously counting the cases and packages which were to go in the luggage van. There were 21!

We took ship for Africa on one of the Union Castle line, possibly the *Kenilworth Castle*. I liked shipboard life. I used to gaze over the rail, looking down into the sea, once we reached the tropics and the sun. The light rays shone down into the depths and you could *see* the water getting deeper as the rays converged. I didn't use this language to myself, of course, but was fascinated with a pleasurable frisson of fear as I imagined jumping over and chasing the light rays down and down and down. Luckily I had the sense to back off before I hypnotised myself! On an earlier voyage when I was two, I had been taken by my mother to see my grandmother in Pretoria. Mother awoke early one morning to hear me burbling and the cabin unusually dark. Then she saw that the porthole was blocked by a small pink behind and I was leaning right out, chanting something like 'Lubbly (or bubbly) sea, lubbly sea.' She shot across the cabin and hauled me back by the ankles. I only remember that bit but was obviously hooked on the sea from an early age. Astonishing to think of cabin portholes being openable at all these days, when all such risks are so scrupulously avoided. Perhaps too much sometimes?

On the later trip beef tea and water biscuits were brought round by the stewards to the steamer chairs at 11 o'clock each morning. I've tasted nothing as good since; and there always seemed to be a steamer chair free. How nice everybody was to a small girl, how invariably kind and polite. In the dining saloon, I was difficult, Mother said, always wanting what wasn't offered.

'Porridge, Bay?'

'No, bacon and eggs, please.'

Or if bacon and eggs were on offer it would be sausages – and so on. I suspect I was fazed by actually having a menu to choose from. But this is hearsay – family memories and teasing.

I remember little else of that outward journey and nothing of our arrival. Quite suddenly, it seems, we are in my grandmother's flat in the middle of Pretoria.

THE FOURTH BEAD

Into Africa: Pretoria (1929–Spring 1931)

Pretoria was the start of the years in Africa – the most colourful years of my life. So much has been written about Africa – about South Africa in particular – by journalists, politicians, polemicists, historians and real writers, like Alan Paton. So much has happened, so much has changed. All I can do is to recall the bright and happy world of a small girl over 60 years ago.

We must have arrived in Pretoria early in 1929 because I remember deep embarrassment when another child was brought to tea at my grandmother's flat and my (temporary) nanny boasted that I could read '... and she's not five yet'. There was disbelief, whereupon a novel of some sort was thrust into my hand – it had a red cover – and I was told to perform. Horrid!

There was something to do, something new to discover every day. And as I look back from the London of today, I am amazed at the freedom we had. Even in the middle of a busy city, five minutes' child-trot from Church Square, I have no recollection of being supervised or accompanied or even cautioned. We had an African nursemaid, Sina Mordesa, whose name I remember for its rhythm and because we loved her. We used to chant it at her and make her laugh. She bathed me and otherwise generally helped about the flat. But I would run alone down the stairs straight into the street, round the corner past the chemist's shop, and straight on to the busy road encircling Church Square, over it and into the square itself. The chemist's was well sited. Running at speed everywhere (walking being a stupid waste of time), I was accident-prone. Inevitably I fell on the pavement, grazing my left knee and right elbow. Kindly passers-by took me to the chemist, who bathed and bandaged the sore places. This was pre-Elastoplast, you understand. Two or three days later, rushing by again, I fell and grazed my right knee and left elbow. This time I took myself into the shop, emerging with both elbows and both knees bandaged. Arriving home with four bandages aroused amusement but no alarm. My wounds were tended, of course, and soon healed and I continued to charge into the square.

This was my playground. It was beautifully kept. I remember it as a smooth green oasis, divided into four, by wide paths which ended – or began – at splendid stone or marble steps with balustrades each curving down and round to shelter an ornamental pool and one or two palm trees. I generally stuck to the corner nearest home and spent hours playing there on my own, Dick, now eight, having started serious school all day. I had a kitten, Fluffy (what boring names I chose!), with whom I tried to share the fun, but she was unenthusiastic, especially when I tried to teach her to swim! Enough was enough for Fluffy. I managed to catch her before the road and went home with a very bedraggled pet. The experiment was not repeated.

Once or twice I ventured further into the square – and was ticked off for sitting on the wrong bench. *'Nie blankes'* it said. I hadn't seen. Sitting on the right bench towards the end of the year, I met another child of about my own age, and we got chatting. Naturally for me, about Christmas – and the presents I hoped for. She was *not* looking forward to it. What? Not looking forward to Christmas at five years old? Was this possible? She explained, with a resignation beyond her years, that the Christmas before, the parcels had all been there but turned out to be only her old toys wrapped up again. I thought her parents must be cruel and wanted to ask her to tea – but that didn't go down well at home. After all these years, I feel sad for the parents who might have been trying their best without money, perhaps without ideas, to produce *some* Christmas magic, even if it was bound to turn so soon to disappointment. Not clever people – but pathetic. ('Poor whites' were looked down on, an attitude absorbed unconsciously – but not shared — from odd phrases dropped in grown-up conversation.) I looked for my sad friend again with some idea of sharing my Christmas sweets but never found her.

After a while I went rather less to the square, and this is why. One of the palm trees by the steps had branches stretching right over the pool. Could I swing on one and edge right across? What fun! Something to cap Dick's tales of school when he came home. I jumped up and grabbed a branch. I started moving my arms along. There was a rending noise and I landed in the pool, branch and all. It was enormously long. Never did child leave square so fast! Up the steps I fled, across the road without due care — and was run over by a bicycle. The young man was most concerned but I wasn't hurt. Bumps and bruises were too common to worry about in my harum-scarum existence. I rushed on home unpursued and showed off the tyre marks on my thigh with much pride. But I avoided the square for some time.

Anyway, a term started when I too, like Dick, went to school. It was the Loretto Convent. I recall three things about it. The first was class-shuttling. Being five, I started in Standard III. But I could read and write. So up I shot to Standard I. But I was a freak among much bigger girls. So down I went to Standard II — and there I settled.

Secondly, it was here that for the first time, I fear I 'practised to deceive'. I was left-handed. The nun who taught us didn't approve of that and made me write with my right hand. 'Of course I could if I tried!' Well, of course I couldn't. This tall, forbidding nun would set us our writing exercises and then stalk up and down between the rows of desks. I worked out a system. I would clutch the pencil in my right hand, wrinkling my brow in thought while she was approaching, whip it into the left hand as she passed, write furiously until she drew nearly level from the rear, switch back briefly as she passed and switch again to left-handed mode as long as her back was turned. It worked a treat and no one gave me away.

Finally, there was a custom whereby from time to time we would be marched along to a small room, where we knelt down on a cold stone floor and prayers were intoned for what seemed a long time. No one ever explained why. I expect it was a chapel. Most children were probably Catholic and already instructed and the prayers may have indicated saints' days. But no one told me and it was a gloomy business, quite unlike my bedtime prayers.

I didn't stay at the convent long, because we left my grandmother's flat and moved out of the city centre and not far from Union Buildings hill.

But before we left, other memories of that flat nudge the mind. There were not enough bedrooms for all of us, so my parents and Dick and I had two bedrooms along the landing outside the flat proper. There was no front door to these. A staircase between them and the main flat led straight down to the street. One evening, Mother went to fetch something or other from the bedroom, when there came a shriek of 'George!' He ran out, I behind him – to see a large black figure run to the stairs and out to the street, just escaping my father's outstretched arm. As Mother had entered the bedroom, she saw a dark shadow duck down beyond the beds – and gave tongue. Nothing was missing, as I remember – but it was a bit of a shock. It also led to much talk, which I drank in as usual. It was not all unsympathetic. There had been a recent case in the paper where a native had been jailed for stealing half a loaf of bread. This enraged my relatives. Hard words were said about the Afrikaners and about the brutality of the Boers to the natives generally. The Boer War still surfaced from time to time! And there was brutality in plenty still to come – but we didn't know that.

About this time, we were very excited by a newspaper advertisement offering camels for sale. There were 30, no longer needed by the government and wanting good homes. Immediately it became Dick's and my dearest wish to own a camel. My father said he'd apply. We only had a dusty yard behind the flat, approached by an iron staircase from the kitchen. A pawpaw tree grew there and nothing else. We gathered old bricks and things from somewhere and built a mounting block – very unstable – and waited. I don't know how long it was before we gave up hope. I'm not even sure whether my father really did apply. What on earth could we have done with a camel in the middle of Pretoria? What on earth could we have done with a camel, anyway?

It was also in that flat that I heard for the first time one of the most famous records ever made. It was Ernest Lough and the

30

Temple Choir singing 'Hear my Prayer'. I was bowled over. From then on and for ever afterwards, I wanted to sing. Fifty-odd years later Ernest Lough joined the same choir as myself, the London Bach Choir – I need hardly say, a far more distinguished member than I. And bless him, he came to my seventieth birthday party.

One more new experience there. It was the one and only time that I was forbidden to read any book. The book was *All Quiet on the Western Front*. I did read it years later and don't think my parents need have worried. Nothing else was ever taboo – though it's true that some of the stuff in print today would not have been around. Nobody minded my studying form in the racing pages, however! My grandmother was a passionate racegoer and encouraged me to pick winners. Of course I knew nothing whatever about it – I chose horses by name. The only one I remember now was called Clove Hitch, perhaps because it was a lucky guess.

But I digress. We moved to a flat in a positive mansion called Entabene in a pleasant area of large houses, fruitful gardens, wide roads and peace, aptly named Arcadia. Our flat consisted of half the ground floor. I don't remember meeting any occupants of the other three-quarters of that house – it must have been very spacious. I am sure that it was fully occupied, because there were cottages within the grounds for the native staff. These dwellings lay up a drive behind the main house. Dick and I explored there, wondering if there were children we could make friends with. Language, we knew, might be a barrier – but as it turned out, it was not the only one. The cottages, humble enough but brick-built and sound, formed a mini village, shielded by a ragged hedge. We approached and paused. There were women chatting and indeed some children sitting playing games on a doorstep. But we were met with a frosty reception and were clearly not welcome. We backed off. My parents explained later that the people probably wanted to stay private, just like us, and we shouldn't intrude. So we didn't. But we thought it was a pity.

I can hardly recall the inside of that flat because we spent nearly all our time out of doors, except when we were asleep. The garden had orange and lemon trees and a fierce gardener who warned us off. There were not many flowers, I think; but there were lawns and a large tree in front of the house, where we celebrated Guy

31

Fawkes day – with one packet of sparklers! It was enough. There's a faded snapshot of us there, half blinded by the sun, with our Aunt Dolly, Mother's half-sister and known to us as Auntie Wog, and our newly acquired puppy, Mickey.

On the far side of the house there were also avocado pear trees, to Mother's delight. I hated them then – what a waste! Our friends across the road had pomegranates, which were much nicer. We picked them straight from the tree. They were sweet and juicy – most refreshing.

Behind Entabene a great mulberry tree dropped its fruit in profusion and beyond it a gap in the hedge gave on to a rough field with a straggly path leading to another road, where there were a few shops. No doubt the field was built over years ago but then it was our little wilderness. Once, we found a dead cat there and Dick decided to skin it! I can scarcely believe now that I watched with interest but I most certainly did. I was far less squeamish at six than I would be now. In particular I remember how satisfying it was when the fur peeled off neatly like a coat, which of course it was. We pegged it out in the sun to dry, but what happened after that? We did plan to make something with it, perhaps a little mat. I don't think that scheme came to anything; the skin probably disappeared.

As usual, we tracked around the neighbourhood in perfect freedom. Did our mother never wonder what we got up to? Among the nearby shops was a Woolworth's-style bazaar with sweets in open trays on the counter. My head barely reached up high enough to see them. Dick, with a better view and reach, considered the sweets were there for the taking. I jibbed at this. I suspect I was too scared and, anyway, I couldn't reach. I'm glad to say he was spotted after a bit and firmly checked but there was no hullabaloo.

Another time we went exploring near Union Buildings, impressive on their hill. They were and are beautiful as well as impressive, and the gardens below, not too formal, looked exciting if only we could have got in. We couldn't and were tired, hot and sticky long before we got home. We badly wanted a drink but had no money.

'Let's pretend we're poor children and beg,' said I.

'How?' said Dick.

I thought. 'We sit on the kerb and *look* poor,' I suggested.

Thinking it would help to look dirty too, I rubbed a bit of dust on hands and face. It worked – or did it? A kindly lady came along, surveyed us curiously and asked what we were doing. Piteously we said how thirsty and tired we were.

'Where do you live?' she asked. Whereupon we became diplomatically vague. It was a bit too near for safety. But she asked us into her nice cool house, gave us some very welcome lemonade and advised us to go home and not to make a habit of playing games like that! Kind but firm she was, and we felt a little chastened. We didn't try it again.

We discovered a children's playground, not too far away with the usual swings and roundabouts. There was also a climbing apparatus in the form of a metal ladder set horizontally with an access ladder at each end. A boy about Dick's age started walking upright across this ladder, then he slipped and fell right through, catching his chin as he went. There was a great deal of blood; I think he lost some teeth. I don't remember that he made a great noise. He must have been very stoical or mildly concussed. He was helped away and, we hoped, recovered. Even Dick, who had been bumping me on a too big see-saw, went rather quiet after this.

Another day, we wanted a dip in the pool there – but hadn't any bathing things. Dick, showing off a bit, suddenly dived in fully clad. Not very fully, since all he wore was a shirt and shorts. But it wasn't much more than a paddling pool and he banged his head horribly. I think we gave the playground a miss after this.

There was a good bakery not far away from home and one of our regular errands in the holidays was to go and fetch the bread. Fresh out of the oven, it was gloriously crusty and the smell was irresistible. By the time the loaves reached home, all the crusty corners and edges had been nibbled off. Mother never seemed to mind. Astonishing!

Across the road, in the house with pomegranates in the garden, lived the Sharps – two sisters, one called Olive, dark and beautiful, and a younger brother, Philip. I forget the name of the other sister. We were told they had come from India, where their parents still were. They were all grown-up and very kind to us children. Olive, I remember, looked after me once when Mother was away. I shared her bedroom and was much struck when she, a grown-up, knelt down by her bed to say her prayers as the most natural thing in the world. This was a pleasant variation on the Loretto convent style. We saw quite a lot of them but they were a tragic family. We heard with shock one day that Philip had been killed at a cross-roads on his motorbike. Dick described it all with the ghoulish delight of a ten-year-old ruffian but I was truly horrified. Olive and her sister returned to India not long afterwards. We heard later that both had died in a cholera epidemic. These things were by no means exceptional in British families in the then far-flung empire.

And there was school. I went to the Arcadia Government School and remember it still with affection although it was the scene and source of a hard lesson. School started at 7.30 in summer — until 2.30, leaving plenty of time for play. But while we were there, we worked. It was blackboard, chalk, and rows-of-desks education and none the worse for that. We children had slates. I rather liked the squeak of the 'pencils' on the slate. Learning by heart was taken for granted. The whole class learned their tables aloud together. We chanted each one rhythmically, starting piano, with a gradual crescendo to a fortissimo 'TWELVE TWELVES ARE A HUNDRED AND FORTY-FOUR!' We also practised mental arithmetic — as indeed we did when living with the aunts later as a parlour game. (It was only recently, in a local greengrocer's, that a lad jotted down the price of six or seven items and then turned to his calculator. 'It's three pounds sixty-two,' I said. He looked at me in astonishment. 'How did you know?' he said — really wanting to know.)

We had spelling competitions too, at which I reckon I had an unfair advantage, due to the amount of reading I did. I thrived in this atmosphere and was encouraged by our teacher — a Mrs Loxley, who was also the headmistress. Towards the end of one term, a prize-giving was announced. To my delight, my name was read out for something called the Progress Prize. Oh, I was so cock-a-hoop, even though I wasn't sure what 'progress' meant. But then came my downfall. One day, we were all supposed to bring one penny to school towards something to do with Prize Day — I quite forget what. I also forgot my penny. Why I was quite so overcome with embarrassment, I don't know. But I was — and scared stiff! Mrs L. came round the rows of desks collecting the pennies. As she approached me, her attention was distracted. Her hand was out for my penny and I put my hand in hers momentarily as if putting in my coin – meaning, I hope to bring it later but save an awkward explanation immediately. But she sensibly checked the money, found herself a penny short – and I was discovered. I had to bring my penny later, of course; but also, home was rung and my attempt at evasion declared. I was very ashamed, rightly so. It wasn't the end, however. Prize Day duly arrived with us all excited, especially the prize-winners. But when the turn of my class came and the prize-winners were read out – the Progress Prize went to someone else! My friends looked at me amazed. I pretended unconcern but I minded desperately. I never knew whether my mother had been told I'd lost the prize, or whether it was just decided in school. Either way, I do think it was very harsh not to warn me. *But* – the lesson was salutary and I've been grateful for that since. It set an uncompromising standard of truth and a clear distinction between right and 'not so very wrong' which is too often lost sight of. Ever afterwards, I found it impossible to tell a lie or even be evasive or inaccurate without correcting myself – sometimes in positively boring detail.

My reputation and my morale recovered and I left with good reports and good memories of a happy time when I learned that healthy lesson – and also that working hard can be enjoyable!

But the time was coming when we were to leave Pretoria and migrate to Johannesburg. I was sorry to leave Entabene and the school but we were already getting used to moving on.

THE FIFTH BEAD

Johannesburg (1931 and 1932)

It is a cliché but still curious how time moves differently in childhood. Having to wait for an hour can be torture — yet the days seem endless, especially in retrospect.

Long days in the Entabene garden, rambling around the gardens and the then unbuilt-on land at the foot of Union Buildings hill, Arcadia school and its ups and one dreadful down, avocado pears (ugh!) and pomegranates (delicious!) in the Sharps' garden across the road — we seemed to be there for years; and yet, by the end of 1931, we were already well established in Parkview, Johannesburg. This is a verifiable fact. I still read to my grandson *The Little Wise One* by Frank Worthington, 'Awarded to Cicely Ludlam, Standard 1b, Parkview School, for Merit' in 1931. I guess at the end of the school year, which I think went with the calendar then, if not now.

Johannesburg and Pretoria are not far apart. Is it still 36 miles?

Dick and I are riding in the dickey seat. We are laughing with glee as the wind ruffles our hair and we speed along at the dizzy speed of over 40 miles an hour! A dickey seat was like the inverted lid of a car boot fitted with two little bucket seats. Safety belts hadn't been dreamt of and at today's speeds the whole arrangement would be lethal — especially for children. We gloried in the ride. Auntie Wog had a long-term fiancé (it took them years to get married) and it could have been his car. He was called Bibs — I never did know why — and he was very amiable. Perhaps he was

36

driving us to Johannesburg while my parents took the luggage. We were never encouraged to talk of Jo'burg. That was considered *very* crude.

We arrived at Orange Grove – an indeterminate street of undistinguished houses. It was more of a staging post than a home and we weren't there long enough to go to school. All I remember of it now is the discovery of miniature golf, for which there seemed to be ample free municipal provision. We took maximum advantage. Then there were the sellers of watermelons, which Dick enjoyed far more than I did; and there was a minor but painful accident which happened to me inside the house. It was usual for there to be a gauze mesh door from the kitchen to the outside on self-closing springs, for insects were numerous and Flit and fly-papers the only defence. Rushing as usual one day, I didn't open this door properly and it shut, trapping my little finger. The pain was shocking and I couldn't free myself. Luckily Mother wasn't far away. She freed me, which hurt some more – and I was promptly sick. This went on all day. After the fourth time my finger was hurting less and I became intrigued enough to keep a tally. By nightfall it had reached seven. Mother wasn't surprised. 'Everything always goes to your tummy!' she complained, but in sympathy rather than exasperation. She was quite right. It did. Still does.

Although Orange Grove was planned as temporary we stayed longer than expected. My father was taken seriously ill with enteric fever and went to hospital. The grown-ups said he must have contracted it while coming home late one night and walking behind a sewage cart! What medical respectability this theory had, I never knew. We were also told that he couldn't eat anything, only drink. And a cautionary tale was told about a young girl with the same fever who pleaded and pleaded with her mother for just a slice of bread and butter, got it – and died as a result. All this we accepted without question and became very solemn. But strangely, I never felt any doubt about my father's eventual recovery and return. One's world didn't disintegrate like that – we thought. He did recover and we moved to rent part of a much nicer house at 58 Roscommon Road, Parkview.

It was commodious and comfortable, with a pleasant garden, smaller than that at Entabene but more private. The owners were a family called Birrell, with a daughter Nan, a little younger than myself. I don't think we were soulmates but we spent hours squatting together on a garden path playing made-up games in the dust with little sticks and the odd pebble! There was also a crazy-paving path which I thought quite beautiful, especially where the grass grew up between the cracks. How tastes change! Once we were settled, the Birrells left us to enjoy what was probably a short let.

So I lost Nan as a playmate but Dick and I found plenty to do together. We were near the Zoo Lake. I think it was the tram terminus up from town. I don't know what it is like now but I remember a very natural, almost rural setting, a clear expanse of water and the far side lightly wooded, with the odd track running through. We usually stayed on our own side just messing around, dabbling our toes and so on. One day we came to what looked like a large shack, quite close by. Imagine our excitement when we discovered it was a motion-picture house. We hared home and pleaded for a tickie each (a threepenny bit) and bought our way in for a matinee. What a magic world. They were silent films but a honky-tonk piano provided music, soft or rousing, soothing or scarifying as appropriate. Here we saw what was probably the first Nelson and Lady Hamilton film – *The Divine Lady*. At seven years old, I swooned with love and sadness. We saw *The Speckled Band* – rigid with fear I was this time, as the snake slithered down towards the pop-eyed heroine's bed. We were already wise to the danger of snakes – this was terrifying.

Less frightening was another film about derring-do on the North-West Frontier, then a popular heroic/adventure background. I quite forget the story. But there was a splendid peppery colonel, who demanded his coffee 'hot as Hell and strong as the Devil!' How we hugged this to ourselves as we scampered home to try it out; and how satisfying was the reaction until constant repetition dulled its cutting edge and it was discouraged.

Once and once only, my mother took me with her into town to the 'talkies', still a novelty. It was a much plusher cinema than our shack, the seats were more comfortable, the dark was darker – and I was bored to distraction. In vain did Mother shush and scold. 'But *why*?' I shouted at last in exasperation. '*Why* is that man biting that lady's ear?' At which I seem to remember she gave up and we left. Next time she went without me.

As in Pretoria, we were press-ganged into running errands to the shops, which were also near the tram stop and the Zoo Lake. We quite enjoyed this; there was often a tickie in it, and Dick especially was partial to sherbet with a stick of liquorice in the bag. On one particular day, we were to collect a large fish. We noted on the way to the fishmonger that the lake was being drained. In the process a large pipe had been exposed, leading from the surrounding pathway down into the sludgy mud which was usually under water but was now beginning to cake in the sun. A little further out, a fair amount of water was still there. This was all very interesting. We collected the fish, which was indeed a big one, I suppose about the size of 12-pound salmon. It was whole, undamaged and didn't look as if there was anything wrong with it.

As we passed again by the half-drained lake, 'Dickie,' I said, 'if fish die when they come out of the water, do you think they would come to life again if they went back in?' He wasn't sure. But there was that pipe . . . big enough for us . . . and water not far away . . .

'Let's see,' said he.

We crawled into the pipe, dragging the fish and reached the sludgy shallows. We held the fish by its fins and gently swam it to and fro for several minutes, until we had to admit failure. No, it did not come to life again. So back we went up the pipe. When we reached the bank, we surveyed each other and wiped each other down. Then we surveyed the fish. It did not look quite as it had! Perhaps the fishmonger would clean it up for us.

'You ask,' said Dick. Shy as I was amongst my contemporaries, I never lacked for cheek, so I did, while Dick hovered outside. The man looked at me and looked at the fish, so neatly wrapped, so recently. I explained that it had been in the water – all too obvious – and could he please clean it up and wrap it up again for us. He didn't say a word. Probably he was lost for one. But he took it, washed it and wrapped it up again. What a nice man. We took it home and had it for supper – except for me. Everyone knew I didn't like fish.

Soon, school began. This time, it was Parkview Government School to which we both went, though we didn't see much of each other due to the difference in our ages.

39

My fourth school at seven. It was a bit difficult at first. In the long break, for instance, team games were all the rage. This naturally involved picking teams. But I was new and such talents as I had were unknown. I would wait in agony hoping not to be the *very* last to be chosen. 'Oh well, we'll have her!' was the ultimate humiliation. (I was reminded of it years later as an evacuee – but that's another story.) Happily, this initiation period didn't last long. They were a friendly lot and I had one trick which proved popular. I could stand on my head, on any sort of ground, for an almost indefinite period – certainly counting up to 100. At home my father actually encouraged me to show off by doing it in a wing chair while belting out 'Hearts of Oak' at the top of my voice. This was my breakthrough at school and soon I was even invited to a birthday party!

I was excited but nervous as I still didn't know anyone well. Mother dressed me up nicely – one did wear party frocks in those days and she always made sure I had nice clothes, most of which she made herself. *But* she didn't come with me. It was quite a long way from home and by the time I reached the address, I could hear the party in full swing behind the tall hedge fronting the garden. I simply could not pluck up the courage to open the gate and go in alone in front of them all. After a few miserable minutes, hoping someone else might turn up, I turned round and went sadly home.

My mother did come with me to have my photo taken by the brother of a friend of hers – a lovely, sweet-faced lady called Nan Savory. These were the days when the photographer set up his apparatus on a tripod and one had to keep quite, quite still with a fixed smile, while he disappeared under a black cloth for what seemed an age until there was a flash and all was done. I still have that portrait, which was sent home to the aunts. I look very cheerful – and I have a fringe with a 'step' right in the middle. Mother wasn't one to waste money on professional cuts for seven-year-olds. I don't think many people did and, on the whole, I think they were right.

It wasn't long after the aborted birthday party that I made my first close friend. She was called Winifred Till – and she lived at 22 Kildare Avenue, where I loved going to tea. She was in my class and we moved up together.

My aunts had sent out from England *The Book of the Flower Fairies* (still reprinting). Winifred and I loved it and shared it and vied with each other in learning the songs off by *heart* – not 'rote'. Such a lot of nonsense is talked nowadays about the evil of 'learning by rote'. We did it for fun. We learnt every poem in that book. Winifred's mother didn't believe we had at first – but we soon convinced her. To this day, I treasure passages of poetry and prose which I was set to learn at various schools, as well as some which I learnt by myself from sheer love of the language.

Being interested and having a good memory helps enormously with school work at that age. Winifred and I were well matched and used to compete to be top with a third little girl called Anita Segal. (I thought it was Seagull – such a pretty name!) I don't remember other children by name – except the twins, Cyril and Cecil. Prematurely spotty, poor lads, and not very popular. Nor was one of our teachers in my first class. One afternoon I was nearly goaded to open rebellion. It was a history lesson, I suppose. The Boer War came into it, embellished with a diatribe against the English, more venomous than objective, as even I could tell. The English were a disgracefully mixed-blood race! Look at the Saxons, Danes, Normans etc. It was an extraordinary foretaste of Nazi (or apartheid)-type doctrine, delivered to a class of seven- to eight-year-olds! It was the first time I consciously felt bolshie. And I might have erupted, so cross was I, but was saved by the class nosebleeder. This useful child produced a nosebleed at least once a week and had to go up to the front, where there was room to lie on the floor with a cold key down her back. That afternoon this performance effectively put a stop to the indoctrination, which I never heard again – at least at school.

It was also from Roscommon Road that I was packed off regularly to Sunday school. I enjoyed this but regret to say I can remember none of the teaching – only the colourful attendance stamps. We had special little books with a space for each Sunday and every child who turned up was given the appropriate stamp depicting some Bible scene. But the real glory came with the bigger, finer stamps which went in the spaces entitled 'Never absent, never late during the first (or second, third, etc.) quarter of the Church's year'. Now *there* was something to be proud of – though

41

that was probably not the right response! I know I earned one – but then we moved on from Roscommon Road, and were too far away. Something of the teaching must have gone in though, more effectively than that of the cold convent, and laid a foundation of faith which has never deserted me.

Before we left, I reached my eighth birthday. I don't remember any celebration or cake – though I dare say there might have been. I do remember my birthday card from England. It was the shape of a figure of eight and showed a very smart golliwog in striped trousers and a red jacket standing on a springboard about to dive. I thought it was wonderful – and there were no exaggerated inhibitions about 'political correctness' to spoil it for me. Even more exciting, it heralded the arrival of a large tea chest also addressed to *me*! Inside, safe and sound in most careful packing, was a life-size baby doll with a complete wardrobe, knitted, crocheted and stitched by my loving aunts, especially Aunt Emily, who was a notable needlewoman. The doll had a most beautiful china face and I adored her at once. I christened her Snowdrop, though the aunts later told me they had thought she had the look of a baby boy and had provisionally called 'him' Billy. Although there was an upsetting accident years later and I had to mend her head, her face is still unmarred. Apart from the year in Tanganyika, when she was safer packed away, she has never left me. She came to represent continuity – and much as I have wanted to give her to two of my granddaughters since, I couldn't bear the thought of possible accidents while I am around! Very many years later, when the original wardrobe was falling to bits, I took her to Harrods for some new clothes. A bonnet hid her china hair – and I was complimented on my beautiful baby!

We left Roscommon Road and spent the rest of our time in Johannesburg at 34 Emmarentia Avenue, our own new bungalow, the last house of a recent development. Open land lay beyond, and behind our house but not so close as to disturb, two or three other houses were going up. Across the road was a golf course, bisected by a small but picturesque ravine with a stream at the bottom. Beyond that again, rough ground stretched up to a reservoir and a plantation. Ample scope for adventure and mischief for which South African school hours – and marvellous weather left us plenty of time, not to mention inclination! We were still within walking distance of school but it was quite a long way. Our route led us along a rough lane between the backs of gardens. Over one wall was a prolific grenadilla plant, called passion fruit in this country. Whatever its name, there is nothing more refreshing at the end of a school day than to pluck one or two, nibble a hole and suck out the pippy juice. I don't think the owners of that garden or anyone else ever picked them; perhaps they didn't even know what bounty was there out in the lane.

Our puppy, Mickey, had come with us to Emmarentia Avenue and soon we attracted four or five more dogs. I really don't know why. Certainly we loved them and played great romping games with them, and they with each other, as we all tore about the open spaces surrounding the house. We didn't know where they came from, and eventually one, an Airedale, never did go home at the end of the day. We tried advertising but no one claimed him. He seemed quite happy but in the end he contracted distemper and died. We were very upset at this and agreed with our parents that we should discourage others. Mickey was enough. All dogs needed grooming and ticks were a constant problem. I couldn't cope with that but Mother did a bit and Dick was rather good at it, cuddling Mickey between his knees and drowning the beastly things in a basin of Lysol.

The golf course was strictly private, so naturally, an irresistible attraction. The stream in its little valley was especially delightful. Here we could make dams and pools, sail home-made boats and generally mess around to our hearts' content, out of sight of the actual golfers. After a bit we got more venturesome. Walking through the rough, we found the odd golf ball, received with great pleasure by a golfing friend of my father's – from another club, of course. Well, that was all right. But then we noticed how many balls, checked by the branches, came to rest amongst a row of willow trees straddling the nearside fairway right up to the little ravine. Lurking just below its edge, Dick began to mark where a ball landed and would then dart out to grab it before ducking back out of sight. We watched the golfers search in mystification and thought it hugely funny. I was too scared to join the forays but watched and admired. Inevitably these depredations were eventually spotted. There was shouting and cursing from afar; and one day Dick was nearly caught. He saved himself with Tarzan-like agility by seizing a willow branch and swinging himself over to the far side of the ravine, where I scrambled up to join him. 'Where do you live?' shouted the justly enraged golfer as Dick swung out of reach. 'In a house,' replied Dick. Oh how witty I thought he was! We legged it off as fast as we could – in the opposite direction to home, I need hardly say.

There we discovered the reservoir and an assorted group of other children, mostly boys. We played around and swam – surely not allowed. But this was in all innocence. No one wore bathing suits, including me – and this was in all innocence too. Dick was already very good with his hands and had made a large model steamer, which he brought up to sail – or rather pull along the edge by a string. It balanced well and he was very proud of it. But one day, he and I went on to investigate the plantation. As it seemed fairly dense, and the fence took some negotiating; he left his steamer in the grass by the fence, carefully marking the place. When we came back, it had gone. I remembered his ruined sand-castle on the beach at Swanage and I felt the same hurt and rage. Poor Dick. He had spent hours on that model. Our parents had admired it and I remember that my father came back again with us in case it was there after all. But it wasn't. And I'm not sure we visited the reservoir again.

Nor did Dick try to make another, although there was a carpenter's bench and various tools across the yard from the kitchen. He also 'found' a plane in one of the unfinished houses. I think he genuinely thought it had been discarded. We used to go and play catch on the building site in the evenings after the workmen had gone, tearing along the scaffolding and the half-built walls. I can't imagine why we didn't come to grief. Nor could the foreman, who came in search of his plane and warned my mother of the dangers. He must have been remarkably forbearing.

We were outside most of the time but not quite all of it. Dick would often be tinkering at the carpenter's bench and I might be helping in the kitchen. But it was pretty uninspiring: cleaning currants for cakes – no 'washed and ready to use' in those days; or chopping mint for mint sauce – no bottled stuff either. A more dramatic experience was my mother's attempt to cure my swollen glands. She didn't 'believe' in doctors but swore by iodine. She duly painted my neck with iodine for two or three days, with no result. Losing patience, she then applied the rest of the bottle. It was like knives round my neck – like an execution. I shrieked and she was actually a little mortified. But the glands took fright too and apart from a prettily iodine-tinted neck, I was fine and went back to school next day.

Apart from these occupations and, in my case, playing with Snowdrop, we had our stamps to keep us busy. Father encouraged this hobby and was a great help, as well as supplying most of our stamps. It was possible in those days to build up a large collection of 'British Empire' only – and within this limitation, and with the help of Stanley Gibbons' catalogue, we became quite knowledgeable. It wasn't only our philatelic, but our geographical knowledge too, which benefited. Father always showed us where the various countries were on a large map of the world, what their capital cities were and so on.

We went on two holidays while we lived in Johannesburg, the first since Swanage. We were all together on the first one, which was in a hotel in the country, with tennis courts and whole orchards of apricots. Mother seemed to spend a lot of time on the tennis courts. Father took Dick and me around and one day he was told that we could eat as many apricots as we liked. There was a glut. I didn't like apricots much but how could one spurn such an offer? Dick loved them and laid a bet he could eat more than me. Up got the old competitive spirit and I stuffed and gorged. I made myself disgustingly sick and disliked the wretched fruit for years. Even now I much prefer them tinned.

This was about the last time we were all together as a family. I was eight and Dick just eleven.

The other holiday was on a farm, miles into the veldt, called Summer Rose – but my father was not there. The farmer's wife had been at school with my mother and the two of them seemed to spend a lot of time sewing Cash's name tapes on to navy blue school uniform for the daughter, who was about to go to the same (boarding) school. I don't suppose it was really *all* the time. I expect they just enjoyed gossiping. Meanwhile Dick and I ran

45

wild as usual. There were donkeys about. We were allowed to borrow a couple one day but there was only one saddle. Dick challenged me to a race to the next farm – but he chose the donkey with the saddle! I had only ever ridden a donkey on the beach at Swanage. This was a bit different. A donkey's back is not broad and accommodating. It is like the steeply pitched roof of a house. And if you have ever tried to ride one bareback, you will know what I mean. It wasn't as if either of us had ever had a riding lesson in our lives. Why the mokes went at all, I don't know, but they did. Long before we arrived, I wished they hadn't! Dick won, of course. And I don't remember how we got home. I can't believe I 'rode'.

A minor hazard came from the bats at night. Do bats really make a beeline for women's hair? I still don't know but it was a widely held belief. It didn't worry me but Mother had long, thick hair. Dick was woken by her calling frantically one night, 'Dick, Dick, there's a bat in my room!' But at 11 he was getting tough. 'Well, put your hat on!' was all he said, and went to sleep again.

We missed my father. He must already have gone ahead to Tanganyika, to make further efforts to recoup the family fortunes. I am saddened now to think of the worry he and my mother must have had during this time in Johannesburg and Pretoria, trying to get some business off the ground in the inauspicious climate of the early 1930s. And grateful in retrospect that none of this worry was allowed to filter through to us or disrupt our happiness.

Back briefly in Johannesburg, Sina Mordesa was still there to help, but not living in. I remember her arriving one day with a badly scratched cheek. She said she had had to get through a barbed-wire fence because of the 'Amelitas'. I have no idea if this is the right spelling. They were yobs, tearaways, brigands – whatever you like – and dangerous. She told us where they were and warned us against them. She also taught us a Bantu insult of such appalling potency that she said, if ever we used it, to be at a safe distance to start with and then *run*! She refused to translate – and I'm still none the wiser. I can still say the dreadful oath but I'd be afraid to ask any respectable person its meaning now. Maybe she was just teasing but we certainly didn't think so at the time. We were very fond of Sina.

Before we left Johannesburg there was another dreadful contretemps with my mother. I was in the workshop with Dick and trying to emulate him. He began to tease, as boys will, but *would* not stop. Nowadays I'd say he was deliberately 'winding me up' and he succeeded. Finally, I flung whatever it was I was holding at him. It missed, of course, went across the gap, through the kitchen window and narrowly missed my mother.

'Who threw it?' she demanded.

When she heard it was me, she didn't ask why or wherefore, whether it was meant for the kitchen window or her or anyone. I was dragged to her room, punched, thumped and when I fell to the floor, kicked. Shoes then had pointed toes. Am I likely to forget? I managed to crawl away into a wardrobe cupboard and there lay sobbing on the floor. She sat down on a chair and started sewing! Dick came along soon. I think he was concerned and perhaps felt partly responsible.

'Where is Bay?' he asked.

'Where she should be,' I heard my mother answer.

I don't know how long it was before I crawled out. Dick comforted me as best he could. I still can't begin to understand my mother's behaviour on this occasion. No doubt I was at fault, but not so much as to justify such a reaction. Dick was also partly to blame, had she thought to ask but I never knew her to raise a finger to him. I think he was her favourite – but poor boy, the tables were to turn against him quite soon and I never begrudged that at all. And though as I write all these years later, I cannot help being shocked, I know I loved my mother through it all.

I don't remember much in the way of endearments – they came more from my father. But I have no doubt that despite any adult worries in the background, I was a happy child and that the occasional harshness was balanced by an unusual degree of freedom and tolerance for our escapades. Perhaps Mother just didn't know about them! Which was itself a kind of freedom.

THE SIXTH BEAD

To Tanganyika (1932)

Once again I have forgotten the upheaval of removal from Emmarentia Avenue, though it must have been considerable. Nor can it have been much fun. Any toys I had, my stamp collection, my beloved Snowdrop – for safety, all were left behind, probably wisely, since we were heading for the back of beyond.

Even worse than that, Dick and I had to say goodbye. He was going to Rhodes Estate Preparatory School in what was then Southern Rhodesia – again probably wisely from an educational point of view as he was now 11. But I was going with my mother to rejoin my father, while he was off to boarding school for the first time and without home holidays to look forward to. He was to go instead to a distant connection, Aunt Anna Dures at Shabani. She turned out to be wonderfully kind – but at first she was a stranger whom he had never met. And I'm not sure that anybody explained the whys and wherefores to him.

Our family was never to be united again and Dick and I never regained the close companionship we had enjoyed. At first he wrote pathetic letters, begging me to write; but they took so long to arrive that he thought they'd been ignored. Later as the first homesickness subsided, he wrote more cheerfully about midnight feasts of sardines and condensed milk (sic!) and happy holidays with Aunt Anna and her terriers, Whisky and Soda. I suppose it relieved my parents. I was glad too – I was even a bit envious of him having Whisky and Soda.

My mother and I had boarded a train with our own little bedroom (i.e. couchette), which I thought quite delightful. And we steamed north from Johannesburg, heading for Beira on the coast of what was then Portuguese East Africa. It was a long train journey but the passing panorama defied boredom. Mother said we would cross the Limpopo River at some point – so there I was, glued to the window to catch the first and longest possible look at 'the banks of the great grey-green greasy Limpopo River, all set about with fever-trees'. I was not disappointed. I can see the river now – but not the fever trees. And it *was* great, grey-green and greasy (with mud not fat!).

We arrived at Beira and must have stayed a night or two. I recall a boring day on a beach, with crowds and beach huts. I don't think I had a proper swimsuit and there were too many people. Nothing else remains. I know we voyaged up the coast in another Union Castle ship, the *Dunluce Castle*, but like others before it, this transition journey remains vague. I had begun to be sad at leaving, so often, places which had become familiar and people I had come to know, so perhaps I just switched off during the process until new sights and sounds were there to be explored.

Well, they were ready and waiting at Dar-es-Salaam – and that was not forgettable.

THE SEVENTH BEAD

Dar-es-Salaam (1932)

We stayed at the New Africa Hotel. I loved it. I loved the high, high ceilings, with lazy fans stirring the heavy air and an impression of lofty, squared pillars framing doorways and a grand staircase. Everything seemed lofty – including the dignified, white-robed staff, softly padding around on bare feet, as I did too, whenever I could. I used to waylay the head waiter nearly every morning to get a preview of the day's menus; food was a major preoccupation! And I liked a cloistered passageway down the side of an inner courtyard where it was always cool.

In bed at night, we were enveloped in mosquito nets suspended from the ceiling and tucked in tight all round. I used to jump in as fast as I could and close the gap at speed lest mosquitoes followed, for they loved me. I had been recognised as a succulent morsel from the moment of my arrival in Africa. And let there be the tiniest hole in the mosquito netting – they would find it. It is amazing to think of the days of itching one small insect could inflict on one small girl!

In the daytime, the menace was less. What wildlife I remember best was on the beach, which in the early morning was covered with sandcrabs, from small down to minuscule, coming to the surface in little whorls of wet sand. It must have been just as the tide receded, for later on, when the sand was dry, they seemed to disappear.

My great challenge lay in the coconut palms – and in particular

50

in a group which grew just across the road from the hotel. I used to watch the native boys, no older than myself, shin up them by hand and toe. Perhaps I felt some pique as what would doubtless now be called my 'tree-climbing skills' had been well thought of by the gang back in Johannesburg. Then, with a mixture of triumph and disillusion, I discovered the toeholds! There they were, cut neatly all the way up the trunks. Very plainly to be seen on travel films on TV nowadays – but a revelation to me then! There was now no question in my mind. Up I must go – and if possible get a coconut. All one had to do, it seemed, was to embrace the trunk and walk upstairs!

So up I went. Very fine too, for the first 20 feet or so. But eight-year-old arms and legs, unaccustomed to this particular form of exercise, get tired. I missed the friendly auxiliary branches of 'proper' trees to rest on. The ground began to seem a very long way down. Another 10 feet and doubt grew. Could I make it to the top? Disastrously, I looked up, clinging tighter as I did so. This caused the top quarter of the trunk (which I had *just* about reached) to sway a fraction. And *this* brought down a shower of dusty fibres into my eyes and panting mouth. I knew when I was beaten – and had the sense not to look *down*. Going down tired was rather more testing than going up fresh but I did make it safely to the ground; I can't think how. The coconuts still mocked me from the top of the tree – but I told myself I loathed them anyway. This wasn't just sour grapes – or coconuts! Dick and I had each been given one in Johannesburg several months earlier. He bored a hole in the shell and drank the milk, which he said was delicious. So of course, I had to too. It was quite horrid. Then he ate all of his and said it was lovely. I tried to keep up – and felt extremely sick. I still dislike coconut.

What my mother was doing while I was up the palm tree, or indeed anywhere else, I have no idea. I have no recollection of ever being supervised or watched over, which left me very free. And it must be a tribute to the security and stability of society there and at that time, that she apparently never worried and no mishaps befell me.

I have other memories of Dar-es-Salaam which do include my mother. We went for occasional walks together in the early evening along a coast road to a second bay. We arrived one night as the full moon rose, the palms stood out so sharply against the silvery water and, across the bay, the land was a mysterious mass of steadily darkening shadow. We went on to the sand, which was soft and silvered too, and there we gathered cowrie shells by the light of the moon and I thought I'd never seen a place so peaceful and so beautiful. I still have several of the shells.

There was another expedition by day – in a rickshaw, a rather old and shabby one, nothing like the ones I so loved later in Durban, with their magnificent Zulu 'drivers' in towering head-dresses of 'horns' (elephant tusks) and feathers. The Dar-es-Salaam rickshaw was a scruffy affair but we went along at a spanking pace to market. Mother was looking for some citrus fruits to take with us upcountry, for vitamin C, I now realise. We scoured the 'market' – a colourful dusty square, with a few makeshift stalls and groups of cheerfully gossiping natives squatting on the ground. We tracked down a heap of limes, small, green and hard; but Mother thought the price exorbitant and after some brisk, good-humoured bargaining, I think she admitted defeat. I don't think any limes came with us.

Another day, I went with her and a friend to visit a mosque. 'But what is a mosque?' I asked, and was told it was a kind of church. I was intrigued, even more so when we shed our shoes before starting up what seemed like a very long stone stairway, winding upwards and out of sight. I don't know now what I was expecting to see round that corner because I was stopped in my tracks as I came level with a deep window embrasure about halfway there. There was no beautiful ornament, no mysterious symbol standing on the sill – but half a cabbage and a chipped white china plate! To say I was disappointed would be an understatement. I was dumbfounded and definitely shocked and I can't remember anything else. Thank goodness, I have since seen the Blue Mosque in Istanbul – and above all the austere wonder of the Dome of the Rock in Jerusalem. The forlorn cabbage in Dar-es-Salaam remains a mystery.

But our time there was nearly over and soon we were getting our luggage together again and boarding the train to Dodoma. It was like most long train journeys, especially in very hot countries

— dusty, dirty, cramped and boring. Even the scenery seemed dull for that part of the world, apart from some fields of what looked like giant pineapple plants — most uncomfortable and prickly-looking. I was told it was sisal.

But then we reached Dodoma. And there to meet us was my large and beaming father. How pleased we were to see him — and have the business of luggage and transport looked after. I was tired out — but remember, even at that age, what joy a bath can be!

The next day, we were to leave railways and roads behind and start for Mbeya.

THE EIGHTH BEAD

Mbeya and into the Interior (1932 and 1933)

The next day we set out by lorry – the three of us in front and all the luggage and the stores which my father had been collecting strapped on behind.

There was no road for most of the way, only a blazed trail through lightly forested country. We drove as best we could from one blazed tree to the next and hoped to reach a rest house before nightfall. The 'blazes' were patches on tree trunks where the bark had been sliced off and they showed up quite well. I have only the vaguest recollection of a basic wooden hut which must have been the rest house; after a day bumping along in a lorry I was half asleep before we arrived.

But during daylight there were wonderful glimpses of wildlife. There were several different birds, small and beautiful deer (okapi perhaps?), which my father identified for me, with the occasional more exciting spoor; and once, we thought, undoubted signs of elephant. Larger animals seemed to be shyer but was it possible there were once porcupine? I recall most clearly passing through a wide glade suddenly dividing the trees. There on the edge a group of antelope flickered away into the shade at our approach but a flock of guinea fowl carried on feeding unconcernedly as we passed. They stuck in my mind partly because I thought they were pretty and partly because mother said how good they were to eat. I was deeply shocked.

There was one disaster for me. I had a little blue-spotted parasol with a wooden handle ending in a knob. I was very fond of it and *very* proud. But it got in the way in the confines of the driving cabin and I was persuaded, much against my will, to let it be tied on the back of the lorry with the rest of the luggage. In vain I pleaded that it would slip out. 'Nonsense,' I was told, 'of course it won't.' But of course it did. I was heartbroken. I always did have a tendency to ascribe to inanimate things feelings more sensitive than any human being. I wept for my poor helpless parasol, with all those fierce animals about after dark! I was comforted with the news that another lorry was following a day or two behind us, and would no doubt see it and pick it up and we could leave a message at the next resthouse to say whose it was. My parents were very resourceful – and I suppose I was soothed though I can't help feeling I must have been very naïve, even for eight, to put my trust at all in such a tarradiddle! And, of course, I never saw the parasol again.

Apart from that episode, the whole journey was a great improvement on the train, if less well-sprung! And at last we drove over a final range of hills and looked out over the wide plain where Mbeya lay.

Before I embark on the rather jolly time in Mbeya, I should explain what we were doing in Tanganyika at all. My father was a geologist and metallurgist and was hoping to repeat his earlier success on the Copper Belt, this time hunting alluvial gold in the rivers of the Tanganyikan interior. He was a freelance prospector. The procedure was to scout around for a likely-looking river, identify a likely looking stretch of it – and then stake a claim. To do this, poles were stuck in the river bank to mark a fixed distance, possibly a hundred yards. On the poles was a notice which became official once the claim had been registered with the nearest district officer. At least, that was how I understood it worked, when I went out 'prospecting' with my father later. We, and the few others like us, were no part of the colonial administration, habitually referred to by Father as 'the Boma stiffs' – Boma being the district office compound.

While we waited to start this precarious life, Mother and I stayed at the Mbeya Hotel and Father went ahead to stake a claim or two and get a house ready.

I wonder what Mbeya is like now. Then there was little more than a native village and an Indian store about half a mile away, and the hotel. I rather think a Scottish doctor lived in a house standing on its own about halfway between the two. As for the hotel, I remember a main single-storey block, with a corrugated iron roof and a verandah running its length. This was where the public rooms were. At right angles to it, a similar wing of bedrooms faced the approach road; but demand had already outgrown this and new bedrooms had been built, each one a separate little house of brown mud bricks, forming two sides of a square, with the main hotel building making a third. There were also a separate bath house, memorable for water so soft that one could produce a most impressive foam bath with ordinary soap and some brisk stirring. The fourth side of this bare earth 'quadrangle' was bounded by a decidedly mucky stream, used for washing (!) a variety of utensils, clothing etc. – none too salubrious and best not enquired into too closely.

Mother and I shared one of the huts on the far side, well away from this stream and near the main block. It was solid and comfortable I think, but I was not given to bothering much about such things.

There were not many people in the hotel but they were all friendly. The great excitement, indeed the only event each week, was the arrival of the two regular planes – could they have been on a modified Cape to Cairo route? Every Thursday and Friday evening, we would pile into the available transport – at most, two or three vehicles of sorts. I was usually on someone's knee. We would drive the mile or so up the dusty track from the hotel to the large, rough 'field' which served as the airport. There we would stand and gaze fixedly towards the high blue mountains in the north until someone shouted, 'Here it is!' and the rest of us strained to see the small biplane gradually getting larger as it approached. I had excellent eyesight in those days and was no end proud when I spotted it first, as I often did. I was never sure where they came from or where they went. I was more interested in the pilots! When the plane landed, the pilot was escorted ceremonially to the hotel for the night and the same procedure was gone through in reverse the following day. I don't remember any passengers – perhaps it was just a mail plane. Or perhaps I was too besotted with the pilots. There were three of them, all Italian, arriving in rotation. One, known as Casabianca, had curly fair hair and blue eyes and completely bowled me over. But he ignored me. Another short, fat, stubby one was much less handsome, alas! but kinder. Through him, I was once actually allowed on the plane and carried off a small packet of cotton wool, presumably for earplugs, as a souvenir.

There were no companions for me but I don't remember minding that. As usual, I attempted to adopt any dog around but there weren't many of those either. The hotel manageress had a very staid and distinguished Scottie; there was an Alsatian, reputedly fierce but always polite to me; and there was a black stray whom I dearly loved and who seemed friendly until one day he jumped up and bit at my face, narrowly missing my right eye. I like to think it was only in play but Mother was alarmed at what might have been and I avoided him thereafter.

One dramatic event, frequently disastrous for local farmers, but vastly interesting to me was a swarm of locusts. We were alerted by the wives of the hotel staff that it was coming. Mother said, 'Stay inside,' but I said, 'No, I want to see what it's like.' She didn't follow me! It was horribly fascinating. There in the distance, a black cloud blotted out the sky. It grew larger and louder and came lower and faster. And then we were in the midst of it. Great 2–3-inch-long creatures bashing into one's face and hair. I saw that the native women had made little fires and to my amazement were plucking the locusts out of the sky, pulling off their legs and roasting them to eat! This was something I did *not* imitate. The mass passed at last. It must have been a big swarm and judging by its lack of height when it (literally) hit us, I expect it landed quite soon, with the usual devastating effect. Having been in the middle of it, it is not difficult to imagine. But what it is to be a child and 'the world so new and all'. I would take cover like Mother, now!

What I did enjoy doing on that earth quadrangle by the rooms was practising jumping; I rather fancied myself as a long-jumper. The stream on the far side varied conveniently in width, so starting at a narrow part, I worked up to the wider ones and at last reached

57

the widest bit of all. Here a plank bridge had been laid. Could I spurn this and jump across? Remember, that stream was no pretty babbling brook! Never mind, I took a good run and leapt. I made it. But my landing foot began to slide back towards the water. Wildly I planted the other foot in a heap of ash dumped there. But it wasn't a heap of ash. It was a heap of red-hot embers with only the thinnest covering of ash. Two chunks wedged inside my sandal and I shrieked and hopped in real agony. Luckily Mother was in earshot and rushed out. She was very good at this sort of thing. My sandal was off in a trice – and true to her independence of doctors, she coped. That is, she swooshed a whole bottle of the powerful disinfectant Lysoll all over my poor foot – which I suppose stopped any infection and excluded air, which helped a lot. Then my foot was swathed in bandages and I hopped around, rather enjoying the attention it aroused. 'Look before you leap' has had an added potency ever since. The scars are fainter now but they are still there.

Shortly after this, my father arrived to escort us to the first house of our own in Tanganyika. There were three in the end – Kasanga, Etebbe and Chakula – all known by the names of the rivers nearby where my father had hopes of gold. Our address remained PO Mbeya throughout, though each was quite distinctive in its surroundings and its memories.

'ARCHITECTURAL' INTERLUDE

Before I venture further into the interior, it may be a good idea to describe the sort of houses we lived in for the next year. They were all what might be called 'home-made homes' and all on the same pattern, built of elephant grass and tree trunks with baked mud floors. Mother's description was very apt — hollow haystacks — with one or two interior subdivisions.

I thought them great fun. And given the labour, trees one is allowed to cut down and ample supplies of elephant grass — I could make you one tomorrow. *And* prepare and smooth a beautiful mud floor and even put a sheen on it.

The main ground plan of all of ours was a simple rectangle. It didn't have to be. People with plans to stay longer in one spot, like the Scharrers, perhaps, at Kasanga, could add on a room or two at an angle or build verandahs. We stuck to the bare essentials.

So, having cleared a level piece of ground, the first thing was to mark the outline, rather like marking out a tennis court. Then a double row of nice straight tree trunks of even height was 'planted' round this perimeter, the outer row staggered, so as to make a more solid screen. And, of course, a space was left for the entrance, either at one end or near the end of one side. Less stout divisions were needed as room dividers inside, so only one row of trunks was used. In our houses the living room, immediately inside the entrance, took up rather more than a third of the whole space. It led through to the 'master bedroom'' and, through that, past a similar 'wall', was a much smaller room—my bedroom. But a section of this was half cut off as a store room. No cupboards, but a shelf made by laying long poles across a series of forked sticks to form a framework for bound bundles of elephant grass. A crucial detail was to remember to set the legs of the forked sticks in pans of water – the sort of heavy affairs used for panning gold. If you failed to do this, anything remotely accessible would be covered with ants in no time at all. I still can't happily leave any food uncovered!

Having established the framework of the house, the fun began. Large bundles of uniformly trimmed elephant grass were firmly tied together and then secured to the rows of tree trunks on both sides of outer and inner walls alike. An outer door was constructed in much the same way – tight bundles of grass tied on to a wooden frame. The 'hinges' were strips of oxhide tied to the particularly stout trunk which framed the door. The grass, of course, was dried and remarkably strong. We didn't bother with windows, which made everywhere apart from the front room a bit dark; but at least there were no curtains to make. Light came through the door and filtered through the gap between the tops of the walls and the roof. This was pitched and constructed very much like a thatched cottage roof in England – only there were no ceilings.

When all the building was done, it was time to get busy on the floor. It would already have been roughly levelled and made good after all the tree trunks had gone in. I was able to 'help' with this final stage at our last house, Chakula, to my huge delight. The other houses were ready for us when we arrived, thanks to our splendid gang. But at Chakula, we slept in a tent at first and I was really in on the fun. First, any bumps were levelled and hollows filled. Then the floors were well tamped down with any weights or heavy implements available – or even stamping feet. And *then* we made the floors wet – one great big oozy sea of glorious mud. I suppose children nowadays don't go in for mud pies. They don't know what they've missed! Having made the mud, we swirled and spread it as smoothly as possible. The boys of the gang were brilliant at it. I probably just got in the way, but how I enjoyed it! Finally, it all had to be dried out before we could move in. You might think the climate dried it all pretty quickly but in fact we had to use the heavy gold-panning pans again, filled with red-hot embers to finish the job (shades of the Mbeya Experience!). The pans were moved around periodically, until the whole floor throughout the house was dry. One actually could then, with a very careful rag, get the surface up to a dull sheen. But we also bought the mats which the native women made by sewing plaited bands of dyed grasses together.

Our only conventional furniture consisted of two or three folding, upright camp chairs, a card table and my camp bed. My parents' bed was again home-made. A wooden framework filled with interlaced strips of oxhide was supported on forked sticks planted in the floor, and the mattress was a home-made straw palliasse – well covered with material. They *said* it was comfortable – but I think I was lucky to have my camp bed ... we all, I need hardly say, had mosquito nets, which were regularly examined for the slightest hole or tear and promptly mended.

Any other furnishings were provided by packing cases, tastefully draped with pieces of cretonne – until, that is, we got to Chakula, when Mother, who was very inventive, saw no reason why the forked-stick-and-pole framework shouldn't also provide a proper dining table and banquette. So a packing case was cannibalised and reconstituted into a flat board and laid on such a framework; and a grass-upholstered seat was constructed round two sides of it. Very prickly it was too, till Mother managed to find some remaining scraps of cretonne to make a little frill along the edge.

She also devised an oven, when the craving for home baking grew too strong. This, I think, was as early as Kasanga. She found a petrol jerrycan, had one end removed and scrubbed it out. Then she mounted it on its side on stones, and got the cook to pile ashes under, over and up both sides, put a rudimentary loaf inside, a tin plate and more hot ashes over the open end – and instructed him to keep them hot. This he did most faithfully – and behold, we had home-baked bread. Labour-intensive, no doubt – but labour – and cheerful labour too – was not in short supply.

Other buildings were always separate from the main house, for obvious reasons. The hen house would have been noisy and smelly and the kitchen potentially lethal. Open fires and grass

61

houses do not mix without disaster. So the kitchen was always at a sensible distance away. Like the house, it was built of poles and grass, but with open sides, a flattish roof and just enough in the way of walls to protect the fire from unwelcome winds and rain — in the rainy season, that is. The fire never went out. Wood was plentiful and collected by cook and houseboy and Adam the water-carrier as needed. At Chakula, Adam used to sleep by the fire, curled up on the floor. A good spot, because it could be quite cold at night, high up as we were. We ourselves would sit by the doorway in the evenings, retreating further back as it got colder, and Angerari, the houseboy,would bring a pan of hot ashes from the kitchen to warm our toes.

Near the kitchen, there would be a reasonably secure store-house. Kasanga was the only house where it was actually inside the main house, perhaps because my parents had not yet realised how entirely trustworthy our people were.

There was no plumbing, of course. The bathroom was a tin basin on a cabin trunk against one wall of my parents' bedroom. And one didn't fuss about the water not being hot enough. Every drop of water had to be carried up from the stream; to expect it hot as well was asking too much, though we probably had it heated for hair-washing and things like that.

As for the loo — that was *very* separate too! It was a deep, deep pit with a plank seat which called for a firm grasp of the edge by a small girl. The whole was modestly enclosed in a grass shelter, with an open entrance, no doubt for freshness, but a further screen in front for privacy. All very delicate and discreet. There was, of course, neither toilet paper nor flushing. One poured Jeyes Fluid into the pit instead — and though the 'toilet roll' can't possibly have been a telephone directory, since there weren't any, it was something very similar — probably a catalogue of some sort. These sordid details are not to shock you — just a further demonstration of how possible it is to do without almost everything we so easily come to think of as essential.

So, having tried to describe the common features of the houses we lived in, let me go on to tell you about the different places in which they were built.

THE NINTH BEAD

Tanganyikan Homes (1931–1933)

Kasanga

Kasanga was a sort of halfway house between the 'sophistication' of the Mbeya Hotel and our later two dwellings.

In the first place, we had neighbours. Not only that, people dropped in on at least two occasions! And I had a playmate – human not canine. We were surrounded by forest – but not lush tropical forest, which might have been claustrophobic. We were always, I think, around 1,000 feet above sea level. The trees seemed immense but the undergrowth was manageable. Our neighbours were called Scharrer and their daughter Jean was about my age. We got on very well. There was a narrow path beaten between our houses, which were about a couple of hundred yards apart. Jean and I would meet roughly halfway, where we made ourselves a little camp – and concealed in the forest edge, played 'mothers and fathers', sometimes in ways which would have horrified our parents, especially my mother!

The Scharrers' house was rather smarter than ours; I think they had been there longer and got more ambitious, though our own was quite substantial. I used to go over to them quite a bit. But it's fixed in my mind chiefly on account of meeting 'Friday' there. I never knew his real name, where he came from or where he lived. He would arrive out of the blue – perhaps usually on a Friday? – and the Scharrers were very kind to him. Even at eight, I could

63

sense there was something wrong and felt uncomfortable in his presence – *for* him, I hope, rather than at him. He was a small but thickset man, habitually unshaven and dressed in stained old khaki shorts and shirt. My father never wore shorts. (Maybe that is why I still think adult males look better in trousers – except on the football pitch!) 'Friday' tried to be friendly to me – but I was shy and embarrassed by him and shrank away. From snippets of grown-up talk, I gathered that he drank heavily whenever whisky was available, had had little success, lived alone – and had, in the usual phrase then, more or less 'gone native'. He was a tragic figure, I can see now; a failure in his own eyes as well as everyone else's, with no hope in the future. I was at the Scharrers' house one day when I heard that he had been found dead, alone in his shack. No one went into details before me, which was quite right, but I suspect he drank himself to death. Poor 'Friday'! To my present sorrow, then I felt little more than relief at not meeting him any more.

Whether it was the presence of Jean I don't know, but for the first time I took little interest in the local dogs. They lived in the native compound. (I should explain that our workforce was a gang of, I think, anything between 20 and 40 chaps and a foreman. They either moved around with us or were re-recruited locally if numbers dropped. They lived with their wives and children, just far enough away for mutual privacy, in smaller versions of our house.) The dogs were scavenging types, not very attractive even to me. But what put me right off was seeing them feed on wide flat dishes of – solidly congealed blood – like red junket! Revolting!

Needless to say, they couldn't compete with the bushbabies. The hollow grass walls of our house did harbour a bit of wildlife but less than you might suppose. A bushbaby was the only visitor I remember actually seeing. In bed one night I heard a rustle, and looked up to see an enchanting little face gazing at me from the top of the grass wall with his great round black eyes. A bushbaby! He must have crept in under the 'eaves'. I fell in love. He came more than once. If I was very lucky, he would edge along the top of the wall and look down at me in bed. I could just make him out from the lamplight coming through from the living room. My dearest wish was to catch and tame one as a pet. But of course they were too shy for that and I never did.

Kasanga too was rich in insect life, especially so because of the surrounding forest, I expect. I was warned about ants from the start. Not civilised British ants, you understand. These were larger and had pincers, which they knew how to use. A couple did crawl up my leg once while I was playing with Jean in our 'house' by the path. I wittered and pranced and danced like a dervish but Jean was very clever and got them off! A more fearsome species were soldier ants, so called because when on the move, they would literally form dense columns and march inexorably forward in a straight line, devouring everything in their path. Horrid! If seen, avoid! Maybe these warnings were exaggerated a bit for my safety. I must check up on the entomology. Then I accepted what I was told.

Other insects attended our suppers. We ate in state on folding chairs at a card table inside the front door and our food was brought by the cook-boy from the kitchen. (Sorry about 'political correctness' but that was what he was called – and called himself with some pride.) There is no twilight in the tropics; one moment it is light, the next it's night. We needed light to see to eat and we had a hurricane lamp. It was a mixed blessing! It took only moments for what seemed like the entire winged insect population of the forest to discover us. We and the cook called them 'doo-doos'. Dinner was quite an adventure. The moths fluttered in our faces, singed themselves on the lamp and fell into the soup. It says a lot for the excellence of our cook's soup that we went on drinking it. It worried me at first, picking so many wriggling creatures out of my soup, but one adapts and, in the end, I used to pull my chair back from the table and eat in the outer shadows. I could cope with the odd doo-doos who followed, and they weren't quite so clever at falling on to solid food. One night, before my retreat to the shadows, I started counting. 'No, no,' said Mother, 'it'll only make it seem worse.' I did, though, out of curiosity. I picked them out of my parents' soup as well as my own – and then the next course – but gave up when I'd reached 200!

It was at Kasanga that I most often went out prospecting with my father. We went on forest walks, inspecting new stretches of

65

known rivers or looking for new streams which might be worth working. We trod very narrow paths – probably animal tracks – through the trees. I was trained always, but *always*, to keep my eyes on the ground and never on any account to tread on any twig or small branch lying across the path. Why? Because ten to one it wouldn't be a branch or twig at all but a venomous snake intent on trapping smaller prey. It couldn't *eat* a human, of course – but its bite could be fatal. I also knew what to do if bitten. We carried purple crystals of permanganate of potash with us. In case of need, one made a cut in the flesh above the bite (i.e. nearer the heart) and inserted these crystals. That was the only remedy we had. Fortunately perhaps, it was never put to the test – though I think my father had used it and survived. The head-down drill became a habit which lasted for years and rendered me round-shouldered by the time I got back to England. Then two good schools took my 'deportment' in hand.

I wandered quite a bit on my own, as I was so used to doing. My parents must have known it was not a dangerous area for wild animals – apart from the snakes. I think it was here that I remember the tallest trees and, on the ground below, the prettiest things. They were dark brown and glossy, the shape of slightly flattened acorns and, like acorns, they had cups – but these were the brightest orange. I gathered a few and still have four. They are mahogany beans. Perhaps I might ask Kew if they could still be viable!

Two or three times, I came across the abandoned pitch of some earlier prospector. One had a garden, where whoever it was had grown vegetables. The house was just a pile of logs and rotting grass, but a few plants of French beans and maize survived nearby. This really was a find; we hardly saw fresh produce. I started a garden of sorts near our own house – and had success with the beans. Goodness, I was proud! It was just about then that we actually had visitors. How enchanted they would be to see my bean plants, thought I. But they didn't seem so keen; they and my parents were enjoying the rare pleasure of a bit of conversation. It was too frustrating. Finally, I pulled up a bean-bearing plant by the roots and took it inside. Then they had to admire it.

That plant was never the same again, but the next and only other time I recall visitors, I was able to provide about a spoonful of green beans each. Mother was delighted. I don't remember the people, how far they had come or where they were going. It must have been near my ninth birthday that February, though, because these kind, if forgotten, people gave me a present – a tin of Cadbury's chocolates. Everything like that had to be in hermetically sealed tins to survive the climate. In spite of this the chocs had a 'bloom' on them but that didn't stop me. They were the only chocolates I saw that year.

Soon after this, we were on the move again.

Etebbe

Etebbe (not to be confused with Entebbe) was our next house. This was on rising and much more open ground. The hen house and kitchen were further down the slope, and a little further still and to the right was the cluster of the compound. Some things have faded about each of our houses, others stand out as if it were only last week. Mother's gramophone must have been with us throughout but I can't remember it at all at Kasanga. At Etebbe, she used to sit in the doorway, enjoying the splendid view, and play her few records. My favourite was Beethoven's Minuet in G. Then there was a recording of 'Cherry Ripe' and a splendid one of the 'Volga Boat Song. I don't think 'Hear my Prayer' had survived – I could never have forgotten that. We had the wind-up HMV gramophone, from Parsifal Road, no doubt a bit scratchy by now but all we had. Some of the gang always came crowding round the door at the end of the day when it started up, Adam our water-carrier in particular. He was a big, beaming man, not over-bright, as I found to my great cost later. But his delight with the gramophone was a treat. He never failed to peer into the recesses of the soundbox to try and see who, what mini-man, was making all that noise.

I don't remember any sign of the fruits of our gold-hunting labours at Kasanga – perhaps there weren't any! But at Etebbe, although I can't visualise the river which must have produced such fruits as there were, I do remember Nelson – the gang fore-

67

man. Nelson was small and lithe, with a battered felt hat which he wore all the time, an engaging grin, and more than passable English. He could write it too. He was very highly regarded by my father and implicitly trusted to go off prospecting on his own, with a small team. Sometimes a runner would come back with a pencil note addressed to 'Honourable Sir George Ludlam' and reporting progress – if any.

The rest of the gang operated nearer home. At the end of the week, they would queue up at the door of the house, where Father sat at the card table with a small pair of scales. Each man brought his finds, which were weighed and entered on his card with the appropriate payment. Mostly, the finds were small, sometimes only flakes of gold or even small accumulations of gold dust. But it all counted – and occasionally, amid enormous excitement, someone produced a veritable nugget – that is, a solid piece about an inch long! When there was enough, it would be packed into a small Navy Cut tobacco tin. Mother then stitched round it a cover of meracani, the coarse natural cotton which many of the natives also used for clothing (presumably it was American cotton). When stitched tightly round the tin, it was easy to write on and address in indelible ink to the Bank of England in London. At regular intervals, our runner would take it and any letters and walk the 30 to 40 miles over the mountain range to Mbeya Post Office. There he would send it on its way to England, collect any mail for us, plus any essentials we needed from the Indian store – and walk back again. He was totally honest; nothing ever went astray.

The native people we knew throughout my time there were very good to me. I couldn't communicate much as I wasn't there long enough to learn more than a few basic words of Swahili and I wasn't encouraged to invade the privacy of the families in their houses. The men, of course, were out all day. But the women and children stayed at base and always seemed to be happy and joking. Mother constantly held up their marvellous carriage as an example to us all, especially me! It was partly due, she said, to the custom of carrying loads on their heads, like buckets of water. This I did think I might try. The women smiled indulgently. I could *not* manage a full bucket of water, even though I was shown how to fashion a little rag pad, worn forward on the head to stop the bucket digging in. Whatever I did practise on, I managed to get the knack and walk, oh so carefully, without disgrace. I could still carry four books on my head for years afterwards – it would have helped to counteract the round shoulders if I'd stuck to it but would have seemed a little bizarre in Sheffield High School! The women also showed me how to plait the wide strips for making mats and baskets, using flat strands of dry grasses dyed in soft vegetable-based colours. I managed to make quite wide bands, using up to a dozen strips of grass at a time. I never actually made them up into anything but my friends accepted them, so I like to think they were of some use.

There was no Jean and there were no memorable dogs here – not even a bushbaby. So I fell back on the poultry. The hens were boring. But there were two roosters, which I christened, with my usual dazzling originality, Greyneck and Greenfeathers. Greyneck was an altogether nicer bird than Greenfeathers. He was old and modest, with a friendly personality. Greenfeathers had personality too. Even as cocks go, he was inordinately conceited, strutting about, flaunting his tail which was indeed a splendid furl of dark glossy-green feathers. His voice was strident and he would invariably try to crow down poor old Greyneck. But he was young and proud and I could not bear the thought of eating him! This became a real threat, out of the blue. A message arrived by runner that someone my parents knew would be passing close. Hospitality was a matter of course. But what to feed them on? The hens had been laying away. With plenty of eggs and vegetables plus what was in a tin or two, Mother could think of something. But there were no eggs. Greenfeathers would have to go. My distress was painful. I proposed finding some eggs, and struck a bargain. I began a desperate search. I can't think how long it was before I saw a bale of straw leaning outwards from the (straw) walls of the hen house. I peered into the recess. I couldn't believe my luck. There were over a dozen glorious eggs – all fresh too, as it turned out. All the hens must have been taking it in turns to lay there. Greenfeathers was reprieved – but I have no idea what we did have for dinner!

I seem to have stayed closer to home at Etebbe, except when I got the itch to climb to the top of a steep, tree-clad hill almost next to us. It was a challenge like the coconut palms of Dar-es-Salaam. And again I failed. Again I started up in fine style. The ground was rocky underfoot but an agile child can use rocks as steps. Onward and upward I went. Then two things happened at once. I remembered hearing my parents saying the night before that Nelson had reported baboons in the neighbourhood and that I had better not stray too far. They had a reputation for hugging stray humans to death. Can this be true? I ask myself now – and I asked myself then. I looked up to see how far I had to go to the top. The trees at the top were swaying, quite violently, and there was no wind ... I turned round and sped headlong down again, jumping from rock to rock like a scared goat. I wonder if there really were baboons there. I certainly convinced myself, that nice hot day, that there were.

In the end, my memory of Etebbe is not happy. I don't know if I can convey the grief which came to me. Probably it will seem exaggerated. Probably if I try too hard, it will seem mawkish. So perhaps a bald narrative is the only way.

It's obvious, I think, that I was fond of animals. After all, what other friends had I? So I was intrigued and delighted when quite near our house one day, I saw the earth move and stir. Before my eyes, a little snout appeared – and there emerged my first mole. Adam was passing near. I called to him to look and share my delight. He looked. He picked up a heavy stick and hit out at the mole. I shrieked at him to stop; I jumped up and down in horror. He thought I was cheering him on! He hit it and hit it, he turned it on its back and hit it across its little white tummy. It writhed and writhed – and so did I. But it died, of course, my little mole. And I couldn't stop him and I couldn't bear it. I'd given it away to this brutal, horrible man. I rushed indoors sobbing. I still do when I think of it. Mother must have coped, seen the remains removed and the little molehill levelled, because I saw no sign of it again. I kept well away from poor stupid Adam. I realised he'd thought he was pleasing me. It made it worse. How *could* he think that!

I suppose there's always a lesson somewhere. My parents certainly helped and I dimly saw, even then, the importance of being able to *communicate*, of understanding each other's meaning. My grief and my horror were very real. I couldn't forgive Adam for a long time. To this day, I cannot begin to understand those people, good, kind people very often, keen naturalists very often, who can take pleasure in killing wild things for fun. After this, I was not sorry to leave Etebbe and move to my favourite Tanganyikan home – Chakula.

Chakula

It was a happy time at Chakula. It started well with the making of the mud floors and our sophisticated dining-room 'furniture'. As well as these delights, the house, though the smallest of the three, was cosy and seemed lighter. There was no separate room for me through my parents' room, which was larger here. It didn't worry me. I slept on my camp bed in one corner and the 'bathroom' as usual was there too – the tin basin on the cabin trunk against another wall! This had its hazards. One day, having sponged myself down, I picked up my cotton frock – and out dropped the most enormous spider. I let out a mega-shriek. Tarantulas were things I was warned to beware of. I was certain sure that this must be one – but it had scuttled off before Mother could check. My mosquito net was tucked in even more securely at nights after that!

It was not just the house I liked. The surroundings were lovely. We had built on a little plateau, sheltered behind by a gentle grass slope. In front, the ground sloped down towards the outbuildings – kitchen and hen house – and at the bottom of the slope, enviably near the small river, the gang had built their compound. We were not in wooded country like Kasanga and the views stretched further than at Etebbe. We were surrounded by a series of hilltops near enough to be interesting but far enough away not to loom at us. They were not densely wooded but the trees grew right to the tops, so that the light shone through them, making them seem like lace edging. There were some villages hidden from sight amongst these hills, and at dawn, you heard the first cock crow, then all the others answering, village to village, hilltop to hilltop, until the sun was fully up. I loved the sound. I believe there are some who find crowing cocks irritating. Extraordinary – we don't hear them enough nowadays!

71

It must have been walking upstream towards the hills, that my father discovered a natural swimming pool. There was a waterfall, quite a high one, and it had gouged out a pool in the rock at its foot. Surrounded by trees, it was a beautiful spot and I was very happy to plunge in, just remembering to shed my frock. A lovely wallow; but it was very cold, probably very deep, the banks were steep – and I think it wasn't considered very safe for me, so we didn't go swimming there again.

The proximity of villages meant that a version of itinerant salesmen sometimes came to the door, selling chickens (Greenfeathers was safe!) and eggs. But best of all was the honey man. He wore a ragged blanket and brought honey from wild bees in whisky bottles. He charged 50 cents a bottle, roughly sixpence – or 2.5p in today's coinage! Mother wanted to give him more but he wouldn't always take it. Goodness knows what risks he took to collect it. The bees usually nested high up in the trees and were said to be fierce as well as wild! The flavour was quite distinctive and I never met its like – until I bought some Tanzanian/Tabora honey from Traidcraft, took one taste – and was wafted straight back 60 years to Chakula. Honey made a nice change from marmalade, of which we had a store. It was tinned IXL brand from South Africa, and very good too but too closely associated with getting my daily dose of quinine down. Modern prophylactics against malaria were unknown. I had to take a truly bitter pill of Howard's Quinine every single day. Buried in a spoon of marmalade it was just manageable.

But there was no recognised medicine against 'jiggers'. These were nasty little insects which liked to get into people's toes and make themselves at home – and lay their eggs. They lived in the dusty earth, of which there was plenty around. I wore sandals most of the time but they were very open – and a jigger duly attacked my big toe. Mother's answer was a bread poultice – as hot as I could bear and then a bit more. Well, it worked. The wretched thing was extracted, the inflammation eased and I kept extra careful watch over my feet from then on.

Excitements were not wanting. The gang had had a good couple of weeks when Father decided they ought to have a treat and bought an ox for the compound. We wouldn't have intruded on the compound party but I did watch a great bonfire being built and the ox slung over it. It smelled very good. Then the dancing and the drums and the splendid rhythmic singing began. I watched from the shadows, too shy anyway to go nearer. It was a very good party indeed and went on long after I was in bed.

My own excitement was finding gold! I'd watched some of the boys panning the stream at the bottom of the slope in front of the house and I wanted to have a go. So Father got one of the smaller pans for me. He warned that that bit of the stream had been well worked over; it was unlikely that there'd be anything to find – but hope springs eternal . . . and anyway, it was a pretty stream to mess around in. So I scooped up mud and water into my pan in the approved fashion – and panned, as I'd seen it done, swirling it all round and round, until the stones and mud were gradually separated by the ridges round the pan, and you were left with fine black sand, which should – if you've done it right – collect in the hollow on one side. Well, I had and it did. And believe it or believe it not, there winking up at me was a tiny speck of gold. Was I thrilled! Casting the pan aside, I leapt up with my gold on one finger and started haring up the slope to show my parents. I was wearing a woollen skirt which had worn into little balls, as wool will. In my haste, I dropped my gold on to this receptive surface – and search as I might, it was never seen again. Never mind – I *had* found gold and my parents did believe it!

Then there was the Great Kitchen Fire. That was the day the wind changed unexpectedly and the kitchen did indeed catch fire. What a conflagration! Adam and Angerari – he who brought hot ashes to warm our cold evening toes – with great courage, dashed in and out between the flames, flinging out pots and pans and pieces of meat – anything movable and savable. Mother's white shoes, newly blancoed, had been drying off near the fire. She was frantic. 'Angel-face, Angel-face,' she shrieked, 'my shoes, oh my shoes!' She never could get her tongue around Angerari – and he was *very* good-looking! He was also a real hero, he made a final valiant dash and rescued them. Altogether it was a convincing demonstration of the wisdom of building kitchens well away from houses; and also of the advantages of wood and straw structures. A kitchen as good as new rose literally from the ashes in a couple of days.

All that time in Tanganyika I had no toys and only one book. Where that came from, I have no idea. It was a thriller, beginning with a horrific account of the slaughter of an isolated white family. The one survivor escaped by hiding in a pile of mealie husks and eventually made his way to safety – not before falling into the hands of a fierce tribe, controlled by the Magicians of Charno. One magician was robed in black – and was evilly disposed. The other, robed in white, was friendly – but had to pretend not to be. Tense moment followed tense crisis. I forget the detail. It was gripping all right and I read it again and again. Otherwise, there were occasional magazines sent out in parcels from the aunts, with sewing thread for Mother, too, and various thoughtful and unobtainable extras. There was one magazine called *The Little Animals' Friend*, which had a correspondence column. Realising the rarity value of my address, I wrote. Sure enough, my letter was published and a couple of months later, I got a letter from New Zealand. But we left soon afterwards so I never followed it up.

Time was marching on and my parents began to worry about my schooling. Mother attempted to teach me something but could only think of three Latin tags:

> *Lapsus linguae* – a slip of the tongue
> *Multum in parvo* – much in little
> *Festina lente* – More haste, less speed (freely translated!)

I copied these out in careful copperplate – and that was it! Without books, there was little more she could do. It became obvious that steps would have to be taken. So, sadly, we left the house by the Chakula river – and with a few of the gang (leaving the rest in Nelson's charge, I expect, until my Father's return), we set off on the long walk back to Mbeya, to Dar-es-Salaam, to South Africa and Durban and Amanzimtoti, to collect Dick and finally to embark for 'Home'.

THE TENTH BEAD

The Long Way Home I (1933)

The Longest Walk

There come into my mind fleeting glimpses of longer walks during that year. There were the prospecting forays with my father around Kasanga, following forest tracks to likely-looking streams. And there were exciting plunges through vast acres of elephant grass much taller than myself, on narrow paths worn by local people on their journeyings – and by who knows what animals. I always went in front, Father behind so that he could see possible danger – and see me. Not that I ever remember a crisis, but anything *might* have been lurking in the dense grass. We each had a staff, Mother too. Just like Little John and Friar Tuck, I used to think. Father had a 6-footer, Mother one slightly shorter. Mine was cut to my size by one of our gang. It was nicely shaped into a knob at the top and the upper 12 inches were decorated with a criss-cross of pokerwork. Very smart and I wish I still had it. We held them horizontally in front of us to push aside the elephant grass when it grew too close and high.

I cannot now place these walks with certainty. There was more than one and of course they were part of our house-moving. But the walk from Chakula to Mbeya is as distinct as if it were yesterday. It marked an end – and I suppose a beginning. But it was the end I was more conscious of. Nevertheless, I enjoyed the walk. Who could not?

We followed the route of our faithful mail carrier, who did it in a day each way. With Mother and myself in the party, we were slower. The bearers suggested a litter – at least for me – and were very willing to carry it. But Mother was a doughty walker and to me it was a matter of pride to keep up. Like the Dar-es-Salaam coconut palms and the hill at Etebbe, I wasn't going to be beaten without trying. This time, I succeeded. Many years later, I read an account of a safari into the interior from the coast somewhere near Dar-es-Salaam. It was during one of Burton's explorations a century before. It corresponded in virtually every detail with my own memories of how we travelled in 1933, even down to the customary loads carried by each bearer – 35 pounds. There had been almost no change in the century between. What an unbelievable contrast took place within 20 years of my own experience! And today, I believe it's a tourist area, with holidaymakers going on 'safari' on wheels! 'Safari' indeed! I count myself truly blessed to have seen it as I did, before such things were dreamed of.

On this last safari of mine, the path started from behind the Chakula house and bore left, rising fairly gently and steadily – and steadily and steadily and on and on and on and on! I expect we stopped for a picnic bite, but at some point I stopped admiring the view and just concentrated on keeping going. I remember best arriving at the overnight spot recommended by the bearers. It was a marvellous choice, a plateau just at the head of a waterfall which they called the 'sucking pig' – there *was* a sort of sucking noise as the water hit the bottom but we couldn't see what caused it. It was dark suddenly, as always in the tropics, and the stars were out. By then, I was most healthily tired and as soon as the tent was up and the bedding unrolled, down I flopped and fell asleep to the sound of the waters.

We woke at dawn and made an early start to allow for a rest during the heat of the day. And soon we were on the heights of the Mbeya range, as we knew it. Do I remember 8,000 feet? I can't be sure. (And once I start checking facts, my memory will become overlaid. These are the memories of a child.) What I remember is blessedly level ground, a restful stroll compared with the day before. We had left the tree line, and the surroundings were amazingly like high downland or the Pennine foothills of my mother's own childhood. Suddenly, she went into raptures at the sight of clumps of purple flowers. 'They're Michaelmas daisies,' she said – and there was no one to contradict her.

So on we went at a measured pace, resting over midday, and finally, in the cool of the evening, coming down and into Mbeya again – but not to stay more than a night or two this time. Again I couldn't fail to sleep from healthy exhaustion.

But all too soon we said goodbye to my father and left again by lorry, up the track past the airfield, into the hills to the north and the blazed trail to Dodoma and so back to Dar-es-Salaam.

All I remember, all I cannot forget, is my father standing there waving, getting smaller and smaller, in front of the hotel, and myself twisting round and waving back until I could see him no longer. Mother was to return at the end of a year but I was not to see him again for over 20 years.

THE ELEVENTH BEAD

The Long Way Home II (1933–1934)

Mind and memory are blank. We left Mbeya as we had arrived over a year before, by lorry and blazed trail. We must have done. But though I remember so much of the journey out, of this return there is nothing – only the gradually dwindling figure of my father, waving goodbye outside the Mbeya Hotel. I don't know who was driving. I know nothing about it. I suppose if I wanted to conjecture or invent, I could say I was too upset at leaving Father behind. But the whole point of this saga is to record the impressions of the child I was, with absolute truth. I'm sure it wasn't happy but that journey is blotted from my mind – until the point when I see myself back in Dar-es-Salaam, in the market with my mother.

Ever since my seventh birthday I had been given sixpence a week pocket money, an admirable custom. In Johannesburg I spent to the hilt. But beyond Mbeya there were no shops and saving was easy. So I went with Mother to Dar-es-Salaam market feeling rich and able to buy presents for the aunts in England, who had sent so much out to us. I bought carved ivory animals, beautifully coloured, and a small round ivory box with a lion's head 'engraved' on the lid. I have them again now. But the most extravagant present, secretly negotiated, was an ivory brooch, carved into a wreath of forget-me-nots and delicately painted. It cost all of four shillings and sixpence, a considerable chunk of my savings. It was to be a surprise for my mother, whom I was so soon

78

to lose – for 13 years, as it turned out, though neither of us knew that then. I found the brooch among her things when she died. The colours have faded now but it still conjures up that market scene so vividly – the kind Indian stallholder, head bent down to mine in collusion. And the sense of recent and impending loss. Nothing else of that second visit to Dar-es-Salaam remains.

With scarcely a pause, it seems, I am on board another liner, Union Castle again, I am almost sure. There is a storm. I am alone on the promenade deck. There is a corner seat glassed round, as far forward as you can get, and I am kneeling on the seat and watching through the glass. The ship plunges down a green seething slope. It feels almost vertical. I look up and see a wall of water rising right up above my head and the ship. We can't climb to the top of that, I think. We don't. We appear to climb and then plunge straight through the wall and emerge into another trough. Down we nose again – and there's a smashing and a crashing of all the china in the world, you'd think. And I am *not frightened*! Not a scrap. If I were there now, I'd be terrified out of my wits. And somebody is. With every other passenger down below, my Mother has suddenly realised that I am not! An anxious steward appears on the deck. He lunges towards me, grabs my arm and hauls me inside . . .

I imagine there was some relief that I was still on board but I don't remember that either. The storm blew itself out at last and in due course we arrived in Durban.

We stayed a short while at the Grand Hotel on the front, where I met grapefruit for breakfast for the first time – and along the road, my first dentist! I didn't care for either. What I longed for was a rickshaw ride. In those days the rickshaws were very smart and drawn by splendid Zulu warriors in full rig, with great feather and horn headdresses. Oh, they were grand! But I never got my ride. I believe the rickshaws have gone now – and tourists go to a tourist Zulu village, where they obligingly dress up and do a war dance. But it's not the same. Genuine Zulu war dances were tremendous. They were mighty warriors.

We very soon moved down the coast to Amanzimtoti – and the Amanzimtoti Hotel, where we were to live until the end of Dick's last term at Rhodes Estate Preparatory School. Most unfortunately, this also meant that I could fit in most of a term at the nearest school, Warner Beach Government School. My sixth school. I had to go by train two or three stops down the line. I hated it. I'd got out of the school habit, but besides that, I knew no one and no one wanted to know me! And all I learned was the Welsh national anthem, 'Land of my Fathers'. I liked that all right but how bizarre! This was Natal, of course, with closer associations with Britain than, say, the Transvaal. Apart from the occasional pleasure of belting out that splendid song, this was the only one of my eight schools which I actively disliked. To make matters worse, I arrived back at the hotel one day to find that my mother was not there! She had gone away for a few days to see her mother in Pretoria and to meet Dick at the end of his term and bring him back. I felt deserted and devastated. She hadn't thought to explain any of this to me. She just asked the hotel manageress to keep an eye on me. Which that nice woman did – and very kindly too. She was a great comfort, especially at bedtime. But she was busy, naturally, and during the day I was left to my own devices and the hated train and school. It probably wasn't for long – but it felt like it. Child psychology wasn't yet fashionable!

Otherwise, Amanzimtoti was lovely. The hotel stood above the river estuary only a short distance away. There were pineapple fields over on the right – sixpence for a big one, a 'tickie' (three-pence) for a little one, sold on site. Beyond the pineapples was the station, a small country halt. There were no other buildings to speak of then. Behind the hotel a dusty track led through lush growth to a sandy cove, where the rollers, surging in from the Indian Ocean, were big enough to surf on without any board. Very exhilarating. It called for careful judgement of course, for the timing was crucial. Once, I got it wrong. I was plunged under, pounded, rolled and buffeted till my ears were bursting and I was at last tossed up on to the shingle. In that, I was lucky. But in fact my ears were damaged, which led to trouble later, fortunately manageable. I was a bit less enthusiastic after that. At least I knew better than to go into the sea on an ebb tide, unlike a grown man I once saw there, struggling to get back up the steeply shelving beach, against the underpull of those vast waves. He was no more

80

than 2 or 3 yards from the shore but lifeguards had to throw him a lifeline to get him safely out.

Snakes were still a hazard but the only one I actually saw, apart from small grass snakes, was a green mamba hanging dead over a branch of a tree by the track to the hotel. It must have been at least 6 or 7 feet long – and why left there? I shuddered and passed on.

I enjoyed the hotel – the comfort and the freedom I had. Having a menu to choose from was a tremendous treat after our good but limited diet of the past year. I specially enjoyed the accompaniments. I chose pork, not for the meat but for the crackling and the apple sauce, lamb for the redcurrant jelly – and so on.

Our bedroom was on the first floor, overlooking the estuary and opening on to a (roofed) verandah. I was allowed to have my bed moved out there to see the stars. Very nice it was, except for one night. I woke suddenly to the sensation of someone silently feeling me from my toes all the way up towards – my neck? I was rigid with fright. Until the purring started and the hotel cat snuggled up under my chin.

All the time, I was looking forward to seeing Dick again. I would love to have been there to meet him off his train from school. At last he and Mother did come – and there was a stranger, in his neat grey suit and wide-brimmed round felt hat. I didn't know what to say. We were both shy at first and he had been only with other boys for over a year. But there was plenty to do together and we relaxed quite soon. It was a good place to rebuild companionship. He introduced me to fishing. We would sit on the bank of the estuary with our 'rods' and our string and our safety pins. The water was teeming, mostly with small striped fish. We put our catch into buckets, where they died. I had to persuade Dick to bait my pin – and take off any catch. The whole thing was not and never became my idea of fun. It was much more pleasant to be taken in a boat and explore upriver where there were reed-beds full of birds and curious nests, until the banks became jungly and monkey ropes dangled from the overhanging trees.

We made one delightful discovery: a grassy bank on the way to the estuary, which by daylight looked just that – a grassy bank. But after dark it was jewelled, tiny diamonds studding the turf. They were glow-worms, of course – so small, so insignificant by day –

and so beautiful by night. We'd never seen any before and I have never seen any since.

All good things come to an end, they do indeed.

At the very beginning of 1934, Mother, Dick and I returned to Durban and took passage for England. Not this time by the Union Castle line, but in a small passenger/cargo boat, the *Umvoti*. We steamed out of Durban harbour in relative calm and found, as others have before and will again (unless everyone flies) that round the Bluff, the ocean swell really asserts itself! We were all good sailors, though.

Our first port of call was Capetown and there was time to go ashore. I only remember Adelaide Street, wide and tree-lined; and above us Table Mountain with its 'tablecloth' on – but no time to go up. It was back to the ship and then we were really on our way.

There were only a dozen or so passengers on the *Umvoti* and we were the only children. The others were elderly – or perhaps that was just the perspective of a nine-year-old! Elderly or not, they were so kind and forbearing. I hope we didn't pester them. The ship's company devised all sorts of entertainment for the passengers and they too always remembered the two children. There were deck sports; they rigged up a canvas swimming pool; they even re-enacted the old ceremony of 'Crossing the Line', complete with Father Neptune coming on board from the sea and a willing victim to be shaved and ducked. And there was the sweepstake, guessing the distance covered each day – or was it each week? It was a six-week voyage but I don't remember ever being bored. And, of course, I always loved just watching the sea and a very occasional flying fish – I forget where. What we miss by flying!

We had one special friend on board – the second officer. He was very good-looking and, what with the uniform and all, of course I fell for him. He was also exceptionally kind. You would think he would want to relax when not on watch or chatting up the adult passengers in the line of duty. But no. We would sit on the step of his cabin, while he told us stories of days at sea under sail (during his apprenticeship) and under steam. He told us how ships in bottles got there and would have made us one but didn't have the right-shaped bottle to take a square-rigger. He did make us a model, though, and mounted it in a cigar box. Dick kept it, of course, but I didn't grudge it him. I think even then I realised subconsciously how much more he had missed out than I had over the last year or so. The little ship has come back to me now – SS *Medway*, Outward Bound. It is one of my most evocative things. I wonder if our second officer survived the war. Perhaps it is better not to know. I hope he did.

One day we were told that we were passing the point where we would be able to see the distant coast of Africa for the last time. Dick and I felt very solemn about this. Africa had become so much part of us. This really was goodbye! We found a quiet bit of deck and, standing side by side facing that hazy coastline, we sang 'Sari Maree' (Maray?). It was the South African national song, then, if not exactly an anthem. We could think of nothing better to mark our farewell.

Our next port of call was Tenerife. No vast hotels or timeshare then, just a small town at the foot of a large hill. We didn't go ashore but boats came out to us with things to sell and amazing young boys, who dived like bronze arrows from our deck for coins thrown into the sea from the same deck – and retrieved them. What an astonishing feat!

My tenth birthday came as we approached the northern latitudes in mid-February. All the passengers said 'Happy Birthday' and one, a particularly kind old man, found me a little present. It was a bit young for me but I was very touched.

At last we entered the English Channel and steamed up to call at Dunkirk before entering the Thames Estuary. One of the passengers, Mr Drabble, escorted us all three ashore – which was nice of him, as I think he was really more interested in Mother! In the town centre he showed us marks on buildings where shells had struck in the First World War, still called the Great War. (It was only six years later that Dunkirk was to figure again in war history.) More cheerfully on this outing, he led us to a café and introduced us to hot chocolate in the French manner. How delicious it was on a cold and clammy day.

It was another cold and clammy day, and foggy too, when we finally entered the Thames to a cacophony of foghorns, our own included. We slowed almost to a standstill – and finally did stop altogether. We were delayed for 24 hours, they said. At one point, Dick and I watched pop-eyed as another ship loomed suddenly out of the fog and moved across our bows, missing us by a few yards. How lucky that we weren't moving too.

At last, we docked at Tilbury, Dick and I on deck again to watch all the bustle. 'Mother,' we called out, puzzled, 'there are some ladies on the quay waving and waving.'

She came to look. 'Yes, of course,' she said, waving back. 'It's your aunts, Ruth and Emily.'

And so we really had arrived.

THE TWELFTH BEAD

No 39 Elmore Road (Summer 1934)

We stood awhile at the quayside, watching the cranes emptying the hold, until one swung out our own 'Not Wanted on Voyage' luggage and dumped it (fairly) gently on the quay with the rest. It all got sorted out and Mother did her usual count.

Then time and memory dissolve until we are back with the aunts in Sheffield. It was early March. How different from Africa.

It is hard to think of that summer without emotion. We were brought up to be proud of the British Empire, far-flung and prosperous and, so we believed, benevolent. Run a check over events since in many of those areas once coloured pink on the world map – and perhaps we weren't so deluded. But for the families who served that empire or, as in our case, went adventuring under its protection, there was a price to pay in the sacrifice of normal family life. There was no swift, affordable air travel to keep in contact. After the happy years in Africa, home for Dick and me now and until we were grown-up was not with our parents but with the aunts. How lucky we were to have them.

They were both successful in their chosen career – teaching in what were then called council schools. To them, it was a vocation. Auntie Rittie was headmistress of Heeley Bank Infants School, Auntie Emily, senior mistress at Springfield Road Secondary school. They were dedicated to the children they taught, in and often out of school hours. Classes were large but discipline was far better than nowadays; numbers did not seem to be a problem.

Children expected to sit still and listen and learn – and parents generally supported teachers.

Their combined incomes had enabled them to live in some comfort, and a strong pound even allowed occasional holidays abroad to Switzerland or the south of France – Nice, no less, before the tourist explosion and package tours swamped it. Otherwise they favoured the beauties of North Wales, especially Morfa Nefyn. Their home at 39 Elmore Road, Broomhill, was a substantial, detached stone-built house, just round the corner from the top of Moor Oaks Road, which dipped and then climbed up steeply from Whitham Road, the main tram route down to the city centre, via Weston Park, the university, and in West Street, my Aunt Jessie's antique shop.

There weren't all that many rooms but all of them were spacious, well-proportioned and superbly furnished, for my aunts had excellent taste and a good source. Virtually all the antique furniture and many of the pictures came through Aunt Jessie, who was a shrewd and respected dealer. Today their value would be phenomenal. I recognise similar pieces singled out for special notice in National Trust properties from time to time. As children, we took them for granted but we did unconsciously absorb a lasting appreciation of fine furniture. I have some bits now but most had to be sold after the war to eke out their non-inflation-linked teachers' pensions.

It was into this comfortable and well-ordered world that, already in their fifties, they welcomed two children at or approaching that most tiresome stage of life, adolescence, and made over to them their home and their lives.

The house was on three floors plus a semi-basement. At the top, there was a good front bedroom, a less good one at the side – and a splendid boxroom. I've hankered after one like it in every house I've lived in since. The bathroom was oddly sited halfway down to the first floor, where two very large bedrooms and a smaller single one all looked out to trees across the road or down the hill behind. During that summer, Mother and I shared one of the large bedrooms, the aunts the other and Dick, of course, had the single room. The top floor was empty.

On the ground floor, as well as an outer and an inner hall, were

My Father, just graduated

My Mother, as a student at the Royal Academy of music

The early one of my parents, recently engaged

The statutory infant portrait of myself and brother at Crux Easton, 1924

Me at my best. Swanage 1927   Parsifal Road - dressed up for my Godmother's wedding

Summer 1928 at Sandbach. Aunt Emily, Mother and Uncle Harry in the background

Summer at Sandbach. Dick and myself with 'the aunts' Emily and Ruth, my Godmother and Uncle Harry

The garden at Entabene, with Dick and Micky the pup. c. 1930

Father, Dick, myself and Micky at 34, Emmarentia Avenue, Parkview, 1932. The last snap of us all together

P.O Mbeya
T.T.
31st Jan 1952.

Dear Grandad and Auntie JESSIE
I hope you
are very well. The kitten must be
darling little thing, but a wee bit naughty
One of our hens lays her egg in my bedroom
and she never misses a day. A bat
came in while we were having dinner
last night, and a stoat the night before.
Altogether we have four woodland friends
but the prettiest of all is a little bush mouse
mouse, with a very furry tail and a nice
smooth grey and brown coat. Then there
are the bush-babies, but they stay outside
and do not come in to visit us. The
4th one that visits us is a big rat,
so I am not very short of friends in the
night, am I. Lots of love and kisses
from
XXXXXXX
Cicely
XXXXXX

P.O. Mbeya
Tanganyika Territory
Januay the 10th 1933

Dear Auntie Rittie and Emily

I hope you are very well. Thank you ever so much for your lovely letter. It was so nice that instead of going to bed that night, I wanted to stay up all night reading it. I am longing for my Birthday to see what the little books the case of needles and the jigsaw map are like, and Mummy has promised to give me a tin of cherries. I am sure Mummy will be very pleased if I give her some needles out of my case. (when I get it) as she is getting rather short of them. How is Billy-Boy I hope he will recognise Dick and I when we come back, for we have changed rather a lot. Your shool must look very nice with all the decorations, especially Christmas trees.

I am sure I will love the Schoolgirls Diary judging by what Dick's was like

Lots of love and

kisses from

Cicely

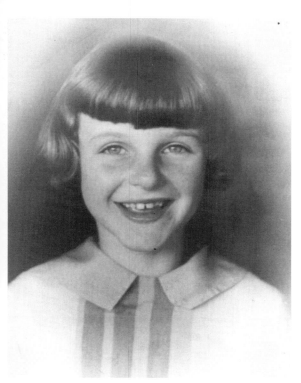

Just 8 at Parkview, home
haircut plain to see

Stanage Pole, Redmires - the day
before Mother left, September
1934

Taken for my parents

Return to Parkview, 1997. The golf course of our childhood raids, just opposite 34, Emmarentia Avenue. Jim Malenawi from Soweto drove me there

the drawing room, the dining room and a very modern (1930s!) kitchen/breakfast room. A curiosity of the house was that, being at the top of a hill, the drawing room looked directly over a small front garden, but the dining room behind it, and the kitchen were one floor up above the backyard. Cellar steps led down to an enormous food larder and a large coal cellar below ground level, while the original big kitchen was well lit with a window and back door opening on to the yard. It still had a food lift, hooks — for hams? — in the ceiling, a disused range and a shallow stone sink under the window. I rigged up a bar from those hooks to practise gym tricks, like hanging upside down by my legs. It was *not* a good idea. One day the hooks gave way and I fell on top of my head. I wasn't quite knocked out and Dick was there to pick me up but I was probably lucky not to have been badly hurt. We didn't tell anyone — but we did dismantle the bar.

Later, the shallow sink under the window was excellent for newts, while the asphalt yard, shaded by neighbours' trees and with a small stone store, open on one side, suggested rabbits and guinea pigs to our pet-crazed minds. All in good time.

Upstairs, our back windows looked out over houses down to a reservoir and the main road. At night, one could lie awake and listen to the trams clanging and ringing their way down to the city — or groaning and clanking their way up towards Broomhill and Crookes Junction. Very companionable they were.

It was an urban view but a very open one, looking over to other comfortable houses at the front, and the tree-sheltered garden at the corner house where my piano teacher lived. I hardly remember ever seeing any cars, parked or otherwise!

Well, we soon settled in at Elmore Road. I had been longing to see Bill-dog again, and there he was. He hadn't forgotten us but he couldn't see us. He had gone blind. Some time earlier he had somehow got upstairs right to the top of the house, into the back bedroom — and fallen out of the window on to the stone steps down to the yard! Miraculously he survived. No one knew how it could have happened but it might have contributed to the blindness. He still loved his walks, knew his way around the house and the surrounding streets and was as good-natured as ever. He was a splendid dog, the loveliest I've known.

But in setting the scene, I become aware that I am procrastinating. I am avoiding stirring up that summer of 1934. In many ways, it was a happy time – but always with sadness looming. It was a beginning and an ending. We were by now conditioned to change and to accepting things as they were and must be. What else could we do?

The first thing was to arrange about schools. There was little point in our starting before the summer term. But then, after some discussion, Dick was to go to King Edward VII school and I to Sheffield High School. Both were within walking distance – at least, by pre-war standards – and close to each other. Mother was to stay over the summer term to see us settled before going back to Africa.

I didn't want to think about that. We lived in the present. We explored the neighbourhood, which had quite a few unmade-up, almost countrified lanes and spaces still. And there were fascinating back lanes between high walls offering short cuts between roads. They were called 'jennels' – elsewhere, 'ginnels', I believe. I wonder how safe they are nowadays.

On Sundays, we walked further up hill to St Thomas' Church, Crookes. During the week we took the tram down to the city centre and got familiar with such delights as Boots' Bargain Basement, and one of the big stores, Coles', opposite the black cathedral and next to the Cutler's Hall. Further up Fargate the air was filled with the aroma of roasting coffee from Davy's. I disliked coffee then – but the smell of it roasting was wonderful. Further round the corner, near the Grand Hotel, a small shop was one of two Thornton's, home of Thornton's Special Toffee long before it expanded nationwide. Coles' Corner was the standard meeting place and it was at Coles' that we bought my school uniform and, as a rare treat, an ice cream.

My uniform was a brown gym tunic and yellow girdle, beige square-necked blouse, a brown blazer with the school monogram in yellow on the pocket and a panama hat with a yellow hatband. There was a brown reefer coat and a beret for winter and, of course, brown walking shoes, brown house shoes for indoors and brown galoshes for wet playtimes. What sensible things galoshes were! They're hardly known now. I thought my uniform was frightfully smart. I'd never had so many new clothes before – and all matching too. Just as well I liked it, as the money wouldn't stretch to any other new clothes. Mother made me what I can see now was a beautiful blue coat for Sundays out of a remnant of heavy-quality satin – not the horrid, shiny stuff. She had found it in a spring sale, I think. But I refused to wear it! She worked hard at it – and I wouldn't wear it. I was in that silly self-conscious stage. I suppose I only felt safe from mockery in my school uniform, looking like everybody else. I am sad about it now – but I knew, too, about mockery.

I had started at the High School full of bounce. It was my seventh school so I was used to being a new girl. Anyway, it couldn't be worse than Warner Beach. Also, after my bookless year, I was positively thirsty for reading and learning. (Perhaps *depriving* children of school for a year might be worth an experiment!) So off I went. I'd missed two terms of French but the rest was not too demanding. The teaching must have been good and I've no doubt that, knowing my background, they were out to help. The classroom presented no problems.

Outside, things were a bit stickier. I discovered for the first time that I had a South African accent. This was considered very funny – and was duly mimicked and laughed at. However, I was blessed with a good ear and in due course I subconsciously adapted to what I heard round me. But for weeks my life was made, perhaps not *miserable* but definitely uncomfortable, by a child I will call Molly Wolverton. She was chocolate-box pretty, rosy-checked, with shining dark hair which was *always* tidy, unlike mine. Her clothes were immaculate too, horrid child. And she would not stop sneering at me and making fun. Most of all, she mocked my South African accent. At home, I was advised by Mother and the aunts, 'Don't rise, dear!' Nobody would have called it bullying – and even at ten you were expected to learn to cope. So, 'Don't rise, dear,' they said, 'and they'll soon get tired.' (They said the same when Dick teased me.)

So I tried not to 'rise' but it wasn't easy. Nor did it seem to work. The day came when I had had enough. Our form room was in a First World War army hut, with cloakrooms at the end, and here I was goaded too far. Being summer, we were wearing our panama hats. Molly had a new one of obviously superior quality and was showing it off, twirling it round and round on her finger as she taunted me and mine. I 'rose'. I grabbed her beastly hat, I threw it on the floor and I jumped on it. Oh, the satisfaction! And oh, the wailing and the shrieking that went up! It brought our form mistress to the scene – and a clamour of explanations.

To my astonishment, everyone united in my defence. 'It's all Molly's own fault,' they said. 'She's always horrid to Cicely. She won't leave her alone!' The teacher listened. She told Molly to pick up her hat and stop making such a fuss. She said nothing to me, and that was the end of that. I never had any more trouble. I found I did have friends and was very happy at school from then on.

At weekends at home, we sometimes went for family expeditions. We took a tram, then walked to the bottom of the Manchester Road, where the Hallam Tower Hotel now stands. There we would get a bus to the terminus at Lodge Moor or Rivelin – and were in glorious country. We explored Wyming Brook and one special day, we walked on from Lodge Moor over the moors past Redmires (where the aunts had had a family holiday cottage when younger), right up to Stanage Pole. There's a brown snapshot of Dick and me standing windswept by the Pole itself, with Mother balanced a little lower, holding my hand. I have her copy. Unusually for her, she had written the date on the back – *2nd September, 1934.*

If we'd felt really tough, we could have gone further, negotiating the Edge and eventually arriving at Hathersage in the valley below. A Robin Hood fan, I thought of Little John's grave and wanted to go on – but it really wasn't practicable. Still, it was a magic day. It got Mother reminiscing about her own childhood walking in the hills around Glossop. She must have covered miles. I felt closer to her that summer than ever before – or since, alas! I loved sharing a room with her. There was a night when friends arranged a theatre – or was it just a dinner? Anyway, it was a night out. I came up at my bedtime as she came out of the room, ready to go. I looked up at her on the landing; she was wearing a silky frock in tiny squares of dark red, black and fawn. Her hair was a soft cloud around her face and I thought she was beautiful. I said so, loving it and loving her looking so happy. I have not so many memories of her looking happy. She had had, and was to have, so few nights out for so many years.

However, that summer, she did make the most of all the concerts and recitals that Sheffield could offer. She must have felt starved of music after being limited to the four records which were all we had in Tanganyika. And no wireless either. She also wanted to encourage any musical talent I might have – I was always chirruping away to myself whatever I was doing. So she took me along with her to a performance of the Messiah. I don't think I appreciated it as I do now. We sat at one end of the curving gallery in the City hall – or perhaps the Memorial Hall next to it – with a good view of the platform. I'd had a brief explanation of what the Messiah was but all I remember now is my complete bewilderment at the outset. Why was this man singing to us all: 'Come for tea, come for tea'?

Another time Rachmaninov came to Sheffield. Mother hurried to book seats for us near the front, with a good view of the keyboard and Rachmaninov's hands. I have never forgotten those hands, pale and tapering, thundering on the keys. Nor my first hearing of the C minor Prelude, which he played as a finale. Powerful it was – ffff – and I went home positively inflated.

After the schools broke up, we went on a traditional seaside holiday to Prestatyn. In 1934, there were no holiday camps or caravan parks. It was a pretty little town, running down to the sea and backed by a wild and beautiful hillside. We boarded in a modern house, right on the upper outskirts, with a rough field in front and the hill behind us. I don't remember anything else about the house myself but I don't think the grown-ups rated the cooking very highly!

Dick and I were outside all the time. Usually, we walked down to the beach but it was a fair way, and if there was a spare twopence we could ride down in one of the open-topped 'toast-rack' buses. We were rather more impatient to get there than the grown-ups, which was all right, provided we could be found. There was no pier or promenade or obvious landmark to meet by but Auntie Rittie sported a very fine bright yellow holiday blazer. You couldn't miss her arrival on the beach, so all was well. Except for one day. I hadn't learnt to swim properly (still haven't) but that didn't stop me wading in for a wallow *just* within my depth. I was always trying to see if I could swim after all, so I thrashed around happily for some time, until, looking shorewards for the yellow blazer, I found myself a hundred yards at least further down the coast from where I had gone in. Nor were my feet touching the sand. Panic lent power. I struck out frantically for the shore and managed to get out of the current which had carried me along and find a foothold. How fortunate that that current ran parallel to the shoreline and wasn't too strong.

I was much more cautious after that and thought I might prefer riding to swimming – but riding lessons really were out of the question. Instead, we concentrated on Dick's latest craze – and at that time, mine too – entomology. The field in front of our holiday house was rich in wild flowers. Ragwort, I remember, bore a remarkable number of those black and yellow striped caterpillars and there was a whole range of butterflies we hardly see now – fritillaries, peacocks, burnets, chalk blues, tortoiseshells and crimson emperors. There was no wholesale use of pesticides then.

We all went one afternoon for a glorious walk up the hill behind us and over the top, where there was said to be an eleventh-century Saxon church. It was a steep and longish way but the wild flowers everywhere, plus the services of a very knowledgeable botanist guide in Auntie Emily, beguiled the time and the miles and we did reach the little church. It was very plain and simple. I remember being shown the wooden pegs in use before nails came in. Could I have dreamt it?

The long, idyllic days came to an end, we packed up and sent the heavy luggage home 'PLA' – i.e. Passengers' Luggage in Advance. The charge was two shillings (10p!); the luggage was collected the day before you travelled and delivered to your home address on your return. And the trains ran on time and were clean, in spite of the smoke outside.

The new school term started and the day for Mother's departure grew nearer – and arrived.

It was very early morning. We took a taxi, the aunts, Dick and I and Mother, down to the old LMS station. On the platform we chatted in that forced, trivial way one does. To this day I hate seeing off and being seen off.

The train came in, the luggage was loaded. Mother was very calm and collected. But suddenly it hit me. My mother was going away. Any minute now, she was *going*. As she kissed us and said: 'Be good,' and got on the train, the whistle blew. I fled from the rest of them. I took off and pelted as fast as I could to the very end of the platform to get the last possible sight of her, tears streaming down my face. As the carriage passed, she was leaning out, no longer cool, her tears streaming too. We waved until the train went round the corner and she went from my sight for 13 years. It was never the same again.

It felt like the end of everything. I just stood there. My aunts waited a bit, then came and gathered me up and comforted me as best they could. But they had to go to another day's teaching and we had to go to our schools too. Dick must have gone first; he was probably more stoical. Anyway, the days of our closeness were fading. I went alone, trying all the way to stop crying by telling myself I wouldn't have been seeing her anyway while I was at school. I was well beyond caring what I must have looked like. But if I still find tears now — and I do — they are mostly for her.

At school they were understanding. No one asked questions and there were the usual distractions. I actually liked lessons. And at the end of the day, some neighbours' children, who became great friends, waited for me and we came home together. Once in Johannesburg, I had been worried in case Mother should die. Perhaps it was after my Father was so ill. 'Don't worry,' I remember her saying. 'At your age, you'd soon get over it.' I was affronted at the time. Now I told myself that at least she wasn't dead; she was going to be with Father, which was right... And, of course, I did get over it. One does. In those days, hundreds and hundreds, if not thousands of British children suffered the same sort of experience — and worse, far worse, was to come in the war. We at least had the care and love of Auntie Rittie and Auntie Emily and that must have cheered Mother too. I very much doubt whether I can possibly do them justice, but I will try.

THE THIRTEENTH BEAD

Getting Used to it All (1934–38)

We lived at Elmore Road for over six years – far longer in one place than ever before, or indeed for several years afterwards. I've since learned that our aunts had not originally expected Dick as well as myself, as he was already established in an excellent school in what was then Southern Rhodesia, from where my parents hoped he would go on to Oxford via a Rhodes Scholarship. But he'd already been left behind once and my mother hadn't the heart to leave him again – and render her family even more fractured than it already was.

Was it the best decision? I'm not at all sure that it was, even from Dick's own point of view, who wanted it. But it was done and my aunts accepted it gladly and did their utmost to make it succeed.

The three years between Dick and myself now made an enormous difference, both in our individual experiences and in our relationship with each other. That, which had been so close, foundered. It wasn't really surprising. I was still a child; Dick was growing up, and it made everything more difficult for him than for me.

He entered a new school at 13, at least two years behind in Latin and French. At first he seemed to them almost alien in outlook, in background and, no doubt, in accent – as I found too. And he was less naturally gregarious than I was. I think the lack of stability in our peripatetic lives and the virtual loss, yet not loss, of our

94

parents made us both insecure and unduly anxious for approval – but perhaps I was better at hiding it and, being younger, was better able to adapt. (Actually, neither of us ever quite got over this weakness!)

Then, too, I wonder how long it took Dick to recover from the sense of rejection he undoubtedly suffered at being packed off to boarding school in the first place.

Altogether, life was pretty tough for him in and out of the classroom. The teens are difficult enough anyway, and with no father and no resolute mother around, it was not surprising that he compensated at home. To quite a large extent, he took his frustrations out on me! Our aunts were very patient and long-suffering. I wonder if he realised it.

They did their best to understand when he was moody or unreasonable – or downright horrid. And they did their best to help me understand too. It was not easy! I was perplexed and upset at the loss of the close companionship we had once enjoyed. Luckily for him, Dick did make one friend at school fairly early on. After that, I was right out. For the first time, I remember the sour taste of jealousy.

Quite soon, perhaps propitiating him rather too much, the aunts agreed to Dick taking over the nicest room at the top of the house as well as his bedroom. It was furnished quite comfortably and he filled the remaining space with glass cases of butterflies and stuffed birds, so beloved of the Victorians. They came through Aunt Jessie's antiques business and, as it turned out later, could have been the death of him!

So now he had two rooms of his own, while I still shared a room (and a bed) with Aunt Rittie, with precious little space to put anything. Not much fun for her, one would have thought. Not much fun for me. So I staked a claim to the remaining room at the top of the house. It wasn't as pleasant as Dick's 'study', facing as it did the wall of the house next door, but it would be a room of my own. Once the idea took root, both aunts did all they could to make it nice and wondered why they hadn't thought of it before. They christened it my boudoir – which I rather fancied! At first its situation was a bit of a disadvantage after dark. There was no light on the top landing. I had to get up that last flight of stairs to bed – and

I didn't like the dark. It became a bit of a performance. I used to stand at the bottom of the flight, start singing 'Onward Christian soldiers' at the top of my voice and rush up as fast as I could, singing all the way and slamming the door behind me. Safe! I grew out of that mini-phobia eventually.

The door was a shield and a defence in another way. It opened inwards, straight opposite the projecting chimney breast and just clearing it. Dick, I'm sorry to say, could be a bit of a bully. But I could escape. Tearing upstairs and bracing myself between chimney breast and door, my drawbridge was up! The door held firm. Mind you, I did my share of goading. I gleaned from my reading the taunt of the curled-lip sneer and perfected it in the mirror. Then I would put it into practice to most satisfying effect, and run. Auntie Rittie once said I really should *never* look at anyone like that! So it obviously worked and after all, it was my only weapon.

The aunts got home after we did and were often not there to keep the peace. Anyway, after coping with large classes in tough schools and then tramming and bussing home and climbing a steep hill – who would have wanted or felt up to sorting out tiresome teenagers? Luckily, in between our squabbles, we had our separate interests and managed to rub along.

Dick's glass cases, as I said, could have been the end of him. One day, he was up there rearranging them, I was downstairs doing my reluctant piano practice and the aunts were not yet home. Suddenly there was a crash, a shout and pounding feet down the stairs. I went out to find Dick near collapse on the bottom step, blood pouring from a horrible gash in his arm. 'Get help,' I think he said, but I didn't need telling. I flew over the road to our friends and neighbours, the Meekes. It was Gwen, the elder daughter, who came running. She can't have been more than 14 or 15 but she was the very epitome of competence and level-headedness and thanks to the Guides, she knew some first aid. She found the pressure point and applied a tourniquet, while her mother rang for an ambulance. Dick had severed an artery. He lost a great deal of blood and was in hospital for several weeks. The Meekes very probably saved his life. And I reflected, after the panic was over and we knew he would get better, that I did care very much what happened to my brother, after all! That was nice to know!

As if that drama weren't enough, Aunt Emily took a tumble not long afterwards as she was carrying a tea tray downstairs. The tray shed everything, and she dislodged a picture from the wall. She got a nasty scalp wound from the broken glass and was obviously shaken. Again I was the only one at home and found her lying where Dick had flopped, her head bleeding profusely as head wounds do – but I didn't know that. Over to the Meekes again I fled and again they coped and I set about sweeping up the broken glass and china and mopping up the blood. Aunt Emily kept remarkably cool. She was taken off and patched up and was in bed for a while but did not have to stay in hospital. She made no fuss. They were stoical, my aunts! Things *don't* always go in threes, thank goodness; there were no more accidents like that.

The Meekes were wonderful neighbours and friends, so were their next-door neighbours, the Monypennys. Gwen and Sylvia Meeke, one older and one younger than I, and Margaret Monypenny all went to the High School. I was in and out of their houses and always made welcome – even sometimes on Monday washdays! The Meekes' house still had its 'washus' at the end of the garden, solid and stone-built, with a copper in the corner and a sink and a mangle under the window. The fire was lit early in the day under the copper, the bodger was at hand to squash and squish at the boiling whites – and the rest of the day was suds and steam and red hands and pegging it all out on lines across the garden. Washdays really did take all day. I found mangling rather satisfying but can't claim to have been the slightest help, and soon the novelty wore off.

When I was ill in term-time – not often, luckily – Mrs Monypenny would come over to see me. She taught me how to relax most effectively, well before it all became so fashionable. 'Feel the air between each of your toes,' she would say, 'and then work up slowly and let every joint melt.' It worked!

Less successfully, she recommended a highly regarded medicine called Fennings Fever Curer. It smelled ghastly but I was persuaded at least to *try* and, having been accustomed to stomach the unpalatable but necessary in Tanganyika, try I did. It came straight back – explosively! Poor Mrs Monypenny! She never flinched, merely remarking with unfailing good humour that

97

it probably didn't suit me. And cleared it up. *And* came again!

It's sad that when I went away to school and we left Sheffield during the war, we lost touch with these good neighbours, though Auntie Emily and I did visit Mrs Monypenny once many years later. Theirs, I think, was a house with the happiest and most loving atmosphere I have ever known.

Back in those days, though the aunts might be late, we never came home to an empty house. At first, there was Mrs G. who came daily, cleaned and made beds, left a hot meal ready for the evening and some tea for us. She always stayed till one of us had got back. She was a good gossip, very chatty and always arrived with a neat suitcase carrying her working slippers. Unfortunately the suitcase burst open as she was leaving one day, spilling out not just slippers but several little parcels of this and that. Most embarrassing. At least it solved one of the aunts' puzzles – how were we managing to get through quite so much tea/butter/eggs/bacon etc. all of a sudden? Auntie Rittie was the family manager and kept meticulous accounts in a Boots Home Diary. So Mrs G. left by mutual consent and was replaced by Edith Longbottom. Edith was a tremendous worker who simply loved washing lino floors, which she then protected with what she called 'the Brussels'. These were sheets of newspaper meant to keep our muddy feet off until all was nicely dry. I can't think where the name came from. Her other unforgettable characteristic was her way with jokes. She 'did enjoy a good laff', so much so that whenever you told her a joke, she would tell it back to you all over again in detail, carefully explaining the point! I collected a great fund of feeble jokes at that age and enjoyed trying them out on Edith.

A regular routine soon developed. We would all leave the house betimes, Auntie Rittie first, as she had furthest to go. Dick and I walked, of course, though rarely together, sometimes escorting Aunt Emily to her tram at the bottom of the hill. There was no bus or tram to our schools and, anyway, it was only a mile or so, through pleasant enough roads, ending for me along an unmade lane, Melbourne Avenue, with very large houses and long gardens to one side and a market garden on the other. Dick's friend Marrian lived on Melbourne Avenue, so did his headmaster. The avenue led past a back gate into our school grounds and there were no cars. It was very peaceful. No one came to school by car in those days, even if there was a car in the family.

Back home in the evenings, blessedly free of TV (or deprived, depending on your taste) we spent the time after supper and homework playing ingenious parlour games with the aunts. They had an endless store. Our mental arithmetic developed amazingly. (I read the other day that it's 'coming back' in schools.) So did our spelling. When these palled, there was rummy, German whist, pelmanism with playing cards, Kim's game – a memory game like Pelmanism but more difficult, using several different objects on a tray instead of cards. There was also a dice game called beetle, which could be a hilarious success at parties.

On Mondays, the BBC offered Ronnie Waldman' s *Puzzle Corner*, including a Mystery Voice, which we *never* guessed. Our wireless was not 100 per cent reliable but served us pretty well. You can buy replicas now from Past Times, 1930s curiosities, no doubt with up-to-date insides. If we'd hung on to ours, I expect it would be quite valuable. But you never know, do you? On it, we listened to the bulletins on George V's last illness. I remember hearing the last one: 'The King's life is drawing peacefully to its close'; and when the end came, influenced no doubt by the aunts I did feel a genuine sense of bereavement. Later, we listened to the famous – or infamous – broadcast of the Coronation Review of the Fleet in 1937, where the commentator, Commander Woodruffe, got stuck in an alcoholic groove and kept repeating 'The Fleet's lit up ... and ... and the Fleet's lit up' – and precious little else. In my innocence I took some time to grasp what was wrong. The aunts didn't know whether to laugh or look shocked. As a broadcast, it was unforgettable. It seemed to go on and on for an extraordinary length of time before it was cut off.

On winter evenings, we sat round the dining-room fire. This was free-standing (apart from the flue at the back), a shining black oval open stove with a domed roof. Now there's a confused description – but, being unable to draw, I can't think how else to describe it. It was beautiful in itself and very cosy. We still play Scrabble on the little oak drop-leaf table we used then, another find in Boots' Bargain Basement.

On Friday evenings, it was back to school for Guides, with

Gwen and Sylvia and Margaret. Guide uniform demanded black shoes – so my weekday regulation brown shoes got blacked instead, which with black laces, quickly switched, served very well. They were 'browned' and the laces changed again for Monday. Money didn't stretch to two pairs of walking shoes – and why should it, when it wasn't necessary? Afterwards, I came back to a late supper after the others had finished. Once it was 'a very nice new kind of tinned meat; and there's a salad ready', on the kitchen shelf. I found the tin and cut two or three generous slices; I didn't think much of it, it tasted like sawdust to me, but I was hungry and ate it up. Oh dear! I'd missed 'the nice new stuff'. It became well known as Spam. What I had eaten was another novelty: early Chappie – tinned dog meat, in fact. Ugh! But there was no after-effect.

Saturdays saw the aunts turning their attention to matters domestic. Auntie Emily was a fanatic with the Hoover. Even Auntie Rittie, the soul of patience and forbearance, was heard to mutter uncharacteristically, 'Can't she leave that thing alone?' But Auntie Emily couldn't. Even after Hoovering, she would stop three or four times on the way upstairs, to pick up the tiniest thread or speck of fluff. I can see her at it now.

Then there were 'the errands'. It was usual for daughters – or nieces – of the house to 'do the errands' on Saturday mornings before being free for play. This meant the weekend shopping in the local shops at the bottom of Moor Oaks Road. There was a grocer's where butter was still cut off an enormous block, sugar came out of a sack and was made up into neat blue paper bags, bacon was sliced to order, 'cooking' eggs were a shilling a dozen (meaning 13) and plastic wasn't seen or heard of. (Greengrocers, where they happily survive, have changed far less.) There was a baker's at the corner for bread. A lady-like proprietress, Miss Birk, did sell cakes too but ours were always home-made. In fact it was a matter for reproachful comment if, on the rare occasion one was invited out to tea, one was offered 'bought cakes'! Coffee mornings were unknown. In the culture of the time, one did one's work in the mornings, domestic or otherwise, holiday or not. I still found myself strongly disapproving of social coffee mornings after I married. Charitable ones are a bit different.

100

Sometimes Dick came on the errands too. The weekend was pocket-money time and we liked to make it go as far as possible,so we bought our favoured magazines between us. We regularly devoured the *Magnet* and the *Gem*, especially the *Magnet* featuring Greyfriars and the Famous Five, with Hurree Jamset Ram Singh and Billy Bunter among others. I suppose the more absurd of the 'politically correct' would disapprove of both these popular characters now. But they *were* popular! There was also the *Hotspur*, which, if I remember rightly, went in more for futuristic fantasies of space travel. Dick enjoyed that more than I did. More improving was Arthur Mee's *Children's Newspaper*. Perhaps the aunts provided this. I used to approach it rather as a duty – then found myself getting interested, duty turning to pleasure. It often happened; still does, come to that!

After the errands, I couldn't miss visiting the sweetshop, just opposite where the road from school came out. If I had a copper to spare during the week, I would occasionally call in then, but it was mostly at the weekends. The shop's sterling feature was the Halfpenny Tray. It was actually a glass case with two shelves, standing at one end of the counter, and nothing in it cost more than a halfpenny. You could get four aniseed balls, liquorice 'shoelaces' (loved by Dick, loathed by me), marshmallows, rather spoilt by coconut coating, packets of Wrigley's chewing gum (plain or spearmint), and flat strips of hard, delectable toffee. If really in funds, the big counter had Cadbury's twopenny filled blocks of eight squares of chocolate, or Fry's Crunchie and, at some stage, the Mars Bar made its bow to our world, a sophistication of sweet delight! – all at twopence – less than 1p in today's money. Sometimes the errands took us further up to Broomhill and Crookes tram junction. Here were the post office and the Yorkshire Penny Bank, and shops which sold pikelets and oatcakes and muffins and crumpets, not to mention potted meat, freshly made. I passed the tripe shop with eyes averted but we became pretty good customers at the pet food shop. On the way back we could get dandelion and burdock to quench our thirsts. It must be related to Coca-Cola but is infinitely superior. To me, Coke tastes like mouthwash by comparison. I've never been able to understand its success. A triumph of PR over judgement, I guess.

101

And there was Peel Street. It ran parallel to the main road in Broomhill. Coming back from games it could be a short cut but no one took it. In an otherwise comfortable suburb, it was a street of poverty with a reputation for hostility. I didn't understand it. I remember the raggedness of the children playing in the street and the warnings to avoid it – but not, I think, from my aunts. Children like these were the children they taught. It was probably my friends at school who said, 'Never go along Peel Street!' But I was by nature contrary, curious – and willing to be friendly. So I did go one Saturday on my way back from the fish and chip shop near the far end, while my friends went the long way round. There were quite a few Peel Street children about. Most stopped and stared but I don't remember the expected barrage of catcalls, though there may have been a few. Near the end of the street – it wasn't very long – I stopped and said 'Hello' to two or three girls of my own size. I can't say we had a conversation and they were obviously surprised, especially as I would have been wearing my school clothes. I hadn't many others. But it was an amicable exchange and I hope I shared some chips! I emerged unscathed, not that one expected violence then...We were far from being rich – but I remember it as a taste of the very definite fissures in society at that time.

Back at home, the aunts would be being housewifely, enjoying the contrast with school. They were both good cooks and they cared tenderly for their lovely furniture and ornaments. There were plenty of ornaments! Some lived in the boule cabinet, which it was my job to dust every weekend and where I was very pleased to see the ivory animals I had bought for them in Dar-es-Salaam. Every ornament which wasn't under cover, so to speak, was carefully washed before Christmas and again at Easter every year. It was quite a ceremony.

The aunts always liked to observe the traditions of every season as it came. Marmalade was made when the Seville oranges came in in January and February, eggs were laid down in water-glass in the cellar in spring; Shrove Tuesday wouldn't have been Shrove Tuesday without pancakes. In summer, there was the Vicarage Strawberry Tea and, later in the year, we were entertained on Guy Fawkes Night by the Manders, Mr Mander being the aunts' solicitor and a very good friend to us all. Mrs Mander sang in the Sheffield Philharmonic Choir and all four, the Manders and the aunts, enjoyed regular bridge evenings together. They had three sons around our age and built very fine bonfires on a spare piece of ground beyond their garden in Park Lane. It was tremendously exciting, I thought. And there was bonfire toffee and moggie – West Riding dark sticky gingerbread. At home, come Advent, we stirred the Christmas pudding and wished. I wished for my parents – but with resignation rather than hope as the years went by.

On Sundays, we still went up to Crookes parish church. I don't recall a Sunday school but do remember a Crusader class, further away in Fulwood run by our dentist, an old family friend of the aunts. I'm sure we were well instructed, but what stuck were the choruses, which we sang lustily – I still do, sometimes! 'I will make you fishers of men,' etc., nor do I remember being bored by the normal services. I was duly confirmed but fear I have no memory of the service. The aunts and Dick all came to support me but what overlays any other memory was our return home. No one had remembered the keys. We were locked out. Eventually, Dick managed to wiggle loose the grating across the coal chute. It was a tight squeeze but I could just get through – in my white silk confirmation frock and all, to land on a large pile of 'best Derby Brights' – and let them all in. I had a bath but the white frock was never the same again.

It was about this time that I began again to say my prayers regularly every night, as we had been taught to do when very small. Perhaps the confirmation classes did bear fruit, perhaps it was having the privacy of my own room. But I also had a dream, centred on Crookes parish church. In it, I was sitting alone in our usual place towards the back, when a great light shone out from the star fixed high up to the left of the east window and a voice sounded: 'You are among the beloved' – and I woke up. Well, what do I make of that now? I truly don't know. Perhaps I had been learning off by heart, for scripture homework, Isaiah Chapter 6: 'In the year that King Uzziah died, I saw also the Lord, sitting upon a throne, high and lifted up and His train filled the temple [and a voice said] "whom shall we send and who will go for us?" ' etc. As you see, I know it still. Perhaps some dreams do have spiritual significance, as the ancients believed, but surely most don't — and how do you tell t'other from which, especially when you're 12 or so? I never told anyone about this dream but it affected me powerfully — and confirmed what became a lifetime habit of prayer. I couldn't manage without.

Then, I used to pray 'for a happier home life'. I know it, I remember it — but was I really that unhappy? I can't think so. Or if I was, I'd no business to be. My major worry was fear of any of my relations dying. I would pray earnestly, either that I would die first, or that no one close to me would, before I was 21. By then I thought I would be old enough to bear it! Perhaps this reflected grown-ups' worries about my grandfather. Perhaps it also had something to do with not having my parents around, where I could keep an eye on them. I didn't want to lose anyone else.

Grandad was a fine old man. He was in his late eighties (exactly how old one *never* asked!) and lived with Auntie Jessie. I liked visiting him. We didn't talk much but I liked the picture he made, sitting in his rocking chair by the fire, his shock of white hair gleaming in the rather dark room and sipping his tea. He always had it laced with 'a sup o' summat', i.e. rum. And he was the only person I ever knew who habitually took snuff. Somehow, without saying much, he just exuded goodwill. The aunts told us that he'd lost both his parents from 'consumption' very young and had been brought up by his grandmother. She, when he was naughty, used to tell him that if he wasn't good, Boney would get him. That's the sort of thing that telescopes time!

One winter Grandad did die. He was in bed, in a tiny dark room again, when I went to see him for the last time. It didn't look very comfortable and he didn't speak. It wasn't long afterwards that I was told he'd died — but there was no question of my going to the funeral. The aunts, like my parents earlier, seemed always concerned to shield us — or just me? — from adult worry and sadness. I suppose that was right.

On Sundays, while Auntie Rittie came to church, Auntie Emily often stayed behind to cook the Sunday lunch. I washed up afterwards, or helped wash up, in the shallow stone sink. It wasn't very convenient but there were no dishwashers then. After that, the aunts retired to the drawing room, one each side of the fireplace, and did the *Sunday Times* crossword, followed by a snooze. (The drawing room was generally reserved for Sundays and parties.)

Dick was never expected to help wash up. Those were the days when even career women had these quaint notions of the male role – or lack of it! I noted this without much rancour. But I *was* cross when the tiny garden was shared out. The first year, Dick was allotted the one sunny corner, quite a nice-sized triangle by the front door. I had the cold shady strip under the wall. This was on the grounds that he was the elder and next year we would switch. That sounded all right, didn't it? But next year, 'Dick has done so well with his garden, it would be hard on him to change and Bay doesn't really mind, does she?' Well, I'm afraid Bay did, as she saw her horticultural plans evaporate.

After this I gave up on gardening. My dank strip would grow nothing but Solomon's seal, and I still don't care for it! Dick also got first go with all the coupons which then came with Rowntrees' cocoa and could be redeemed for various boxes and tins of chocs and biscuits. My turn would come next, when he'd collected enough to send up for something. It didn't, of course. Naturally enough, he set his sights on the most coupon-expensive offer – and by the time he got anywhere near, the war came along and all coupons etc. (except ration coupons!) stopped, like so much else, 'for the duration'. This all sounds as if I was seething with frustration and injustice. I suppose I must have felt some, to have remembered such details. But I simply can't recall it. It was just another aspect of the separation between my brother and me, which I certainly had felt deeply – but then left behind, or at least, on hold. Once, though, we'd have shared those coupons.

Anyway, the aunts, the dear aunts, were so good to us both in so many ways, no child should have felt hard done by. They had longer terms and less free time than we did but they still devoted to us much of what time and energy they did have. They took us on expeditions into the Derbyshire dales, walks on the moors picking bilberries and round Wyming Brook and Redmires. We went further afield by bus – once, memorably, to Eyam, the plague village.

Everyone should know the story of Eyam, a peaceful, quiet village – until a box of cloth for the tailor arrived by carrier from

London, together with some second-hand clothes. Very welcome, it might have been, since clothes were substantial and costly. Those were the days when people itemised their second-best coats in their wills! But in London, the Great Plague was raging and very soon it was raging in Eyam too. The village lost nearly three-quarters of its population of less than 400. The plague would have spread further but for the vision and leadership of the rector, William Mompesson, his wife and the nonconformist preacher – and the unselfishness and self-discipline of their flock. They sent messages far and wide to keep away from Eyam, appointing places on the open hillside where food could be left, without any physical contact. As far as is recorded, no one ran away, though scarcely a family, if any, escaped the plague, including Mompesson himself, who lost his wife. It's a moving and inspiring story.

But I digress. To return to the aunts. They organised all such trips by public transport, since we never had a car. They also gave wonderful parties for us, spending the whole weekend making jellies and trifles and scrumptious cakes, organising games and puzzles – and never forgetting prizes. After a solid week of other people's children, you'd think they'd have had enough; but no, on they went, and the parties were unfailingly successful.

When invitations to school friends' parties came along, they took endless trouble to be sure I had a nice party frock and those bronze pumps with crossed elastic, which were then essential party wear. They combed the big stores for remnants and searched out dressmakers to provide the velvet cloak which was also absolutely obligatory for small girls' parties at the time. They could be bought ready-made, of course – but that cost a lot more.

When I was 12, the last triennial Sheffield Music Festival before the war took place. Berlioz's 'Te Deum' was to be a major event – conducted by Sir Henry Wood, no less. It calls for a treble choir, so Sheffield council schools were asked to nominate boys and girls for audition and Auntie Emily entered me. I remember it so clearly – my very first audition, in an echoing upper room in a vast Victorian school near the city centre. The City Director of Music, intimidatingly large, sat behind a table – and we were called in, one by one, to trill a few scales and sing something of our own choice. I sang Psalm 23 – 'Brother James' Air' – because I loved it and so did Auntie Emily. It was also an unconsciously shrewd choice, because it really sings itself. Anyway, I was selected. (It was a good omen for many subsequent auditions. To my astonishment, I never failed one.) We rehearsed away:

> *Judex crederis esse venturus,*
> *In te Domine speravi,*
> *Non confundar in aeternum . . .*

I have it by heart to this day, so we must have been well drilled by the Philharmonic Choir's chorus master, Dr Frederic Staton. Then came the final rehearsal with the full choir and Sir Henry Wood himself. We expected to be overawed. We weren't, anything but. If his aim was to make us relaxed and confident, he certainly succeeded, and he inspired us and made us laugh into the bargain. I remember that rehearsal so well but, curiously, not the concert itself. I know it was a success, I know the aunts came in support; but I can't remember anything about the evening. I expect I was too drunk with it all! I've sung in choirs ever since – at school, in the Oxford Bach Choir and in the (London) Bach Choir, at home and abroad, until age and weakening eyesight and hearing made it a bit difficult. So I resigned from the Bach Choir after 38 years, having survived every triennial audition – and I miss it still. It has added immeasurably to the quality of my life. It has been a lifeline in the darkest days of deep domesticity and periods of political perplexity. There's absolutely nothing like it for rising above the 'long littleness of life', being just one small part of glorious music and emerging uplifted and refreshed. And it all started with Auntie Emily getting me that first audition.

Though growing apart, Dick and I did still share Bill-dog. We always had, after all, before we ever went to Africa. And agreeing that pets were Good Things, we added others. How complaisant the aunts were! We had a pair of Dutch rabbits . . . Naturally enough, we then had a pair of Dutch rabbits and six baby rabbits. Then we thought guinea pigs rather sweet, so we acquired three guinea pigs – a large tortoiseshell one, a small black one and a middle-sized fawn one. We had a tortoise in the garden and a family of white mice in the basement kitchen – and the sink was full of newts. I was put off the white mice by their naked tails, and even more when they produced babies – and ate them! Mismanagement on our part, I expect. We had all these pets at the same time. I don't remember any tragedies, apart from the white mice, but we must gradually have given our surplus stock away until we were down again to the mother rabbit, an extraordinarily fierce creature called Lopsy, and two or three of her offspring. They had the run of the backyard, with a hutch in the outhouse for warmth and sleeping. It was very secure, we thought – until, one day, Lopsy was found with a gash and alien fur in her claws, and one of the babies in a dreadful state with several patches of fur torn off his back. We assumed a cat had got in to the yard, attacked the baby and been fought off by Lopsy.

The aunts came to the rescue. The little one was brought into the house, his wounds anointed with Acriflavine, and he was nursed and cosseted, grew new fur and made a perfect recovery. We called him Jimmy and he became completely domesticated. He never made any mess, except in the same corner by the kitchen sink, so he had a litter tray there. He loved great old Bill-dog and would sit between his paws for hours or, occasionally, perch on top of his head. He was kept firmly out of the drawing room and never ventured upstairs but he considered the dining room his own territory and would jump up on the chairs to check what was on the table. Once it was chrysanthemums. Jimmy yanked a couple out of the vase and sat there munching the flowers, his mouth adorned with a fringe of bronze petals. Another day he investigated the tea tray. I heard a bump – and there was Jimmy, sitting on a chair in a heap of sugar, having a lovely time. The basin was upside down on the floor.

By the time the war came, Bill-dog had died, full of years; and the rest of the pets had either died of old age or were found new homes before we finally left Elmore Road.

THE FOURTEENTH BEAD

High Days and Holidays (1934–1938)

The aunts had a great sense of occasion. They never missed the chance for a celebration, however modest. Birthdays were an obvious opportunity, red-letter days for every member of the family, because apart from the birthday cake (and a party at the weekend if we wanted one) they had invented the delightful custom of 'unbirthday' presents, so that no one in the house should feel left out, not even the dog!

They were very good at remembering our parents' birthdays *in time* to get letters and packets to them. It needed forethought, for post could take up to six weeks in those days and without the aunts' prodding, we'd always have been late. At Christmas, I don't remember that we made a big thing of the tree – but we did have pillowcases – or rather, bolster cases – at the end of our beds, keeping up the fiction of Father Christmas. Church was an essential part of Christmas, of course. We went up to St Thomas's as usual, listened to the Christmas story, fresh every year, sang lustily and came back to a late Christmas dinner and an even later Christmas tea. In between, the aunts would never miss the King's Christmas broadcast – nor did we. At teatime one year, the Christmas cake carried a novel decoration – a silver ocean liner. Perhaps it wasn't exactly Christmassy, but it was a cheering symbol, representing the ship on which our parents would soon be coming home. But they didn't come. It wasn't long after that that the war broke out – and any plans there might have been were put on hold. I don't think there were any concrete plans anyway – but the little ship was still a hopeful symbol; and I've still got it.

Once, we were all invited to a Swedish Christmas feast. There was a Health/Therapeutic Institute, the Edgar Allen Institute, where Auntie Emily went for treatment for rheumatism and became very friendly with two Swedish practitioners. They had been to see us and now wanted us to share their Christmas traditions. I was much struck by the decorations, especially straw 'goats', actually reindeers, a very Swedish Christmas symbol. I still have the one they gave me that Christmas and bring it out again every year. (You can get them now at Ikea – but they're poor examples.) There was another novel custom which made me stretch my eyes. We were invited to load our plates with *every* goody we might want as soon as we all sat down. Whether this was to save the trouble of handing round, I don't know; nor whether it was a general custom in Sweden or an idiosyncrasy of Miss Allgülander. I thought it was a great idea but it certainly wasn't the way we had been brought up! On the face of it, it might seem a shocking incitement to greed but actually it was rather inhibiting. You couldn't pretend to yourself or anyone else, that you weren't eating all that much if it was all on your plate at once, now could you? Anyway, it was a very jolly party, with lots of laughter, scarlet and gold predominating on the table and around the room and altogether the epitome of Christmas cheer – positively Dickensian.

On another lovely Christmas Eve, the aunts were a bit behind-hand with their preparations. Very uncharacteristic – there must have been some reason. As a result their local presents weren't ready in time for the post, so in a burst of extravagance, Auntie Emily hired a taxi and she and I went round Sheffield playing Father Christmas ourselves. Enormous fun. We couldn't stay long anywhere but were feasted and toasted wherever we went. It's lovely to get a nice surprise but believe me, it's even nicer to find yourself *being* a nice surprise!

Another year a group of us, all girls living round about, thought we'd go carol-singing – properly, with a lantern and a fiddle, which one of us could actually play. I suspect it was her parents who arranged a route where they knew we'd be welcome, no doubt a wise precaution. So we sang our carols from house to house and enjoyed ourselves enormously. We hadn't expected to be welcomed with mince pies, lemonade and everything nice, wherever we called; I guess we were singing a bit flat by the end, but no one complained.

Holidays

We were at home for part of the school holidays, of course, with the aunts still teaching and not at hand to plan expeditions. I don't think that was any problem. Day after day, I would take the tram down to the public library, where I had a ticket and a supplementary ticket, both allowing me two books at a time. I'm amazed to recall that at one stage, I read school stories almost exclusively, boys' and girls' alike. I was beginning to think about boarding school myself, especially as some of my friends were trickling away from the High School in that direction. These books weren't exactly substantial, not like Scott! I would bear four back home, read them and return next day for four more. At least it kept me from boredom and mischief. (Actually, I didn't and don't bore easily.)

Partly fired by riveting descriptions of cricket matches in the boys' school stories, I suppose, I also began to follow cricket avidly in the papers and on the wireless, as I had once 'followed' racing in Pretoria and Johannesburg. So I knew when the Australians were coming to Sheffield to play Yorkshire at Bramhall Lane. Was it 1936? I think I was 12. I took myself down there to watch. I don't remember how much a ticket cost – perhaps someone, seeing this lone child, bought me one. The all-male crowd was extraordinarily kind and I was handed forward to land in the very front row right opposite midwicket. I could scarcely have had a better view. And that was how I saw Bradman bat (he made 57 that day) and Hedley Verity bowl. He died of wounds in Italy during the war. Herbert Sutcliffe opened the batting for Yorkshire and a young Len Hutton made an early appearance. And I lost my heart for at least ten minutes to the Australian, Jack Fingleton, who was fielding deep, just in front of me, and gave me one dazzling smile. But the revelation of that day was the delight of watching excellence and being aware of it. Every stroke that Bradman made seemed to have the inevitability of perfection, while Verity's bowling action was poetry. It wasn't just cricket, it was an aesthetic experience. I think I was perfectly happy that day. But I can't tell you who won in the end!

The aunts took us for two more seaside holidays like Prestatyn (before the outbreak of war put an end to such jauntings), both in North Wales.

One August, they joined with friends to take a bungalow at Rhosneigr on Anglesey. These friends had a son and a daughter about our age and I expect the aunts thought the companionship would be nice for us all. As it turned out, we weren't really soul-mates. Not that there were any arguments, we went our separate ways quite amicably – and the grown-ups got along fine. The bungalow was some way from the town, in a rough field sloping down to the lake. We looked across to a scatter of palatial mansions on the far side – the holiday homes of rich industrialists, we were told. One, I believe, belonged to the Palethorpes of sausage fame. Very nice too – the sausages and the holiday home! A rowing dinghy was provided with our bungalow, as the best way to the shops was by water, rowing across the lake and up to the end by a channel, through high reed-beds full of waterfowl and their nests. When we got there, every cottage garden seemed to be overflowing with hydrangeas spilling out all over the walls. It was a magnificent sight.

Auntie Emily, the botanist, took advantage of this holiday to teach Dick and me something about wild flowers. With sound psychology, she produced an attractive work – *The Children's Book of Wild Flowers and the Story of their Names* in two volumes – which she offered as a prize to whichever of us could find the most different species, which she would identify. As a result we walked the hedgerows, which were proper hedgerows then, roaming all over the island as far as our legs would take us. The competition was friendly rather than fierce, as we both got really keen and in the end our collections were just about level, both around the hundred mark – so we got a volume each. Such an astonishing richness and variety – I doubt you could still find so many today.

112

There was one achievement on that holiday I couldn't possibly forget. I learned to ride a bicycle. I didn't have one of my own and I don't know whose it was. It was a boy's – much more tiresome to get on and fall off than a ladies' model! And the only place to learn was in the rough field round the bungalow. It was not only rough, that field, it was dotted with rocky outcrops and generous clumps of nettles. And I can say with feeling, that if you have a choice between staying on at all costs or coming off among stones and nettles – you very soon learn to stay on.

Another year, we took rooms in a large old farmhouse, 'Ty Newydd', near Llanystumdwy, where Lloyd George was born. Many years later, I believe, Ty Newydd was the house he bought and lived in till he died. Although they would never divulge their politics, it is quite clear now that the aunts were good Gladstonian Liberals. Naturally we all duly visited Lloyd George's birthplace – a little stone cottage on the road towards Criccieth. It was very simple and genuine, not dolled up for tourists, without any souvenir shop that I remember, though I seem to recall a postcard or two.

We were very well fed on the farm and there was plenty around to interest us, including a splendid old tithe barn and a small river, a hundred yards or so away, splashing and burbling through trees and over rocks – most picturesque. (I recognised it in the background of a TV series on Lloyd George a few years ago.) Then the farmer's wife, Mrs Williams, had a *caed* lamb – bottle-fed and very tame and strokeable; I wouldn't have minded adopting it. There were only two guests besides ourselves, the Allens. They were a kind couple *and* they had a car! They took me for a wonderful drive one day to see Lake Bala. I still mean to go back there sometime – meanwhile *One Man and His Dog* occasionally features it on TV. We took a bus to Beddgelert, with the grave of the quintessential Faithful Hound, Gelert – very much to my taste. But the famous Swallow Falls at Betws-y-Coed, said to be magnificent, struck me as rather tame. I'd been brought up on descriptions of the Victoria Falls, where my parents had spent their honeymoon. They walked along behind the vast curtain of water, only getting slightly wet from the spray. Can you still do that, I wonder? Mother lost a diamond brooch there but when she went looking for it next day without much hope she was met by a native, who said to her: 'You look for this?' – and gave it back to her. She always bridled, I remember, if anyone called the natives in Africa dishonest. 'Only when corrupted by white men!' she would say, tartly.

Dick and I were closer again on holidays, and leaving the aunts to enjoy a bit of peace, we would walk into Criccieth and the sea. It was a peaceful, pretty little town, the bay quite unspoilt, there was swimming – and there were canoes. A pity they were mostly beyond our means.

We *could* afford to patronise the new milk bar, the first we had met, in the old lifeboat house just by the shore. Milk shakes were a revelation – utterly delicious. There was a bookshop nearby too which was always a magnet. It was here that I bought one of the very first Penguins – *Hamlet* – for sixpence, and discovered, like so many before and since, that it is indeed 'full of quotations'!

Further down the coast there was Harlech and a grander castle. Of course we had to sing 'Men of Harlech' at the tops of our voices but no one seemed to mind. It seems astonishing now how few other visitors there were in the middle of the summer holidays. I suppose fewer people could afford a summer holiday then. And almost no one in our world holidayed abroad. To do so and write it up was a certain passport to a slot in any school magazine.

Our wanderings were a bit curtailed when Dick developed an appalling toothache. When it got really unbearable he went grim-faced to the local dentist and had it out. He asked for it back, brought it home to the farm and took great and disgusting delight in planting it on the tea table, filling it with sugar and saying: 'There now, you blighter, ache as much as you like!'

The New Forest with Auntie Mother – and bridge!

That summer too, 'Auntie Mother', our grandmother from South Africa came to visit her Derbyshire relations and to holiday with us. She took rooms in a house on the edge of Brockenhurst, directly across the road from the New Forest. It was quite a

114

small house but comfortable and we had excellent food. Dick and I spent most of the time out of doors. He was still keen on collecting moths and butterflies, and used to go out at night and sugar the tree trunks. I didn't care for that much, nor for the killing bottle, though he assured me it didn't hurt them. But most days, fortified with good picnics, we roamed for miles and miles through the forest rides, out on to heathland, singing a popular ditty:

> Ten little miles from a railway station,
> That's where we'll settle down,
> Ten little miles from a railway station,
> Ten little miles from town.

till suddenly we found ourselves scrambling over a regrettable railway embankment, which rather spoilt it.

But we rambled on, hoping for deer, treating the ponies with respect – and very soon learned to keep our picnics well concealed. I don't know why we didn't get lost.

Now and again we went on expeditions with Auntie Mother. We 'did' Beaulieu Abbey, long before the motor museum; we went to Buckler's Hard, which was then gloriously quiet and undeveloped, and of course the Rufus Stone. I took a picture of that with a Brownie camera Auntie Betty had given me. It is not very good.

The evenings were a distinct contrast. Auntie Mother's idea was to give us a good holiday, and she succeeded. But she couldn't forgo her daily bridge. Our landlady was recruited, though bezique was really her game, and Auntie Mother gave us all a crash course in auction bridge. Contract bridge was only just coming in. It was too new-fangled for her. We played every night. Just occasionally we played bezique too, to please the landlady. I scarcely dared say I preferred it. By the end of that holiday I was playing bridge quite well for my age, said Auntie Mother. Never since!

Many years later, during my short Foreign Office career, I was inveigled into a game in Belgrade with the Brazilian Ambassador, the very aristocratic Italian Minister – and another I forget. I had rashly admitted to having played as a child, they were all bridge fiends and they needed a fourth. In vain did I protest that I really couldn't play. They thought I was just being modest and I was sat firmly down. After a couple of hands, they smiled, pained but indulgent. 'No, Miss Ludlam, you do not play bridge,' the Italian said kindly, 'You were quite right!' Well, they had been warned.

When we finally escaped from the bridge table in Brockenhurst, I would read in bed till I fell asleep. No limits as it was holiday and no school tomorrow. I read Scott – it might have been *Ivanhoe*. Then I read *Emma*, leaving only *Persuasion* to come. And then I embarked on *Tess of the D'Urbervilles*. It was a mistake. It horrified me. It put me off Hardy for life. It's true he loved the countryside – but not people. I thought then he must have been a dreary, depressing old man. He didn't spoil a lovely holiday, though. And perhaps I ought to try him again.

When she'd delivered us back, Auntie Mother was to have an operation in a nursing home in Glossop. How much more convenient, she always said, if we were fitted with zip fasteners. The operation went well, anyway, and she returned to South Africa. We used to write but we didn't see her again, I'm sorry to say, though she lived to a good age.

THE FIFTEENTH BEAD

The Vicarage, Crewe Green:
A Second Home (1934–1939)

Where on earth do I start? It's only in trying to describe it that I begin to comprehend what the Vicarage at Crewe Green was for me and what the people who lived there did for me. I took it all for granted at the time.

The Vicar was the Rev. Harry Collins, Uncle Harry, married to Auntie Betty, who was my godmother. That was our only connection. Neither was any relation.

Auntie Betty's father, the Rev. Mr Woolley, had been Vicar of the aunts' parish church in Sheffield. She and my aunts had become close friends and they frequently spent holidays with her when the Woolleys moved to Field House in Sandbach. When she married Uncle Harry, her father's curate, and they moved to Crewe Green, the visits continued; and when I appeared on the scene, I was welcomed with them. Crewe Green Vicarage soon became more than just a holiday perch – it was a second home. There was no limit to the kindness and generosity of Uncle Harry and Auntie Betty. And they never seemed to think it was anything out of the ordinary.

Crewe Green was scarcely a village – rather a scattered rural parish then, though only a mile or so beyond Crewe station, on the Sandbach road. Thanks to Crewe Hall park, 5 miles round, the town of Crewe stopped abruptly at the station and there was virtually open country until one reached Crewe Green church. The church stood in the angle of the road and a lane off to the right, which skirted the churchyard and led past a picturesque farm and the Vicarage gates on its way to – was it Haslington? Through the gates, a long straight drive led to the front door and round to the stable yard. It was bordered by woodland, heavily planted with daffodils and tulips, glorious every spring and profitable too! When they faded, I could supplement my pocket money by dead-heading at a halfpenny a dozen.

The Vicarage was a substantial Victorian house, with mock-Tudor overtones. The outer and inner halls were tiled in multi-coloured mosaic, a wide staircase rose with shallow treads round three sides of the hall to a broad landing and bedrooms of a comfort I had not known.

I slept in a shining brass bed in a big double room overlooking garden and fields. There was a large bathroom adjoining and clean towels every other day, which impressed me no end.

Every morning, I would be woken by Joyce (which was her surname), who would come in, draw back the curtains and tell me the time. I was always 'Miss Cicely', even at ten. It embarrassed me at first – but how soon one gets used to such things! Too easily, probably.

Downstairs in the drawing room and dining room, stone mullioned windows reached nearly to the floor. Both were lovely light rooms with what estate agents like to call 'double aspect'. There was also a door from the dining room leading through a little lobby directly to the garden – very useful in summer.

I spent hours in the study across the hall. It looked straight down the drive – a very useful 'early warning' feature – and was lined to shoulder height with oak glass-fronted bookcases (early Minty), filled with books, not exclusively theological and including all the classics I'd ever heard of and quite a few I hadn't. Leather armchairs were grouped round the fireplace and here I curled up and lost myself in literature. In my mind, that room is always associated with Scott, whom I loved far more than Dickens, for instance, particularly *The Talisman*. I couldn't tear myself away from it except for meals, which were obligatory!

Opposite the study, the green baize door led past the back stairs to the maids' bedrooms and on, endlessly it seemed, through kitchen and scullery and larder and pantry, out to the stable yard, very much as it was in Victorian times, but with cars instead of horses.

After breakfast every day except Sunday, a bell was rung for Prayers, usually in the study, sometimes in the dining room. But the dining room could be distracting as one could gaze out at the garden. Everyone in the house came to Prayers. Uncle Harry would start with a reading, always Psalm 121 when anyone was about to travel, as when I or the aunts were going home. After the reading, we knelt at our chairs for prayers. Only once did anyone interrupt. It was in the dining room and Ada, a Cook of Character, was indeed gazing out of the window. She suddenly rapped loudly on the window. 'There's Spot Fair making a mess on *our lawn!*' she expostulated. Spot was the dog from the farm next door. Service was resumed without comment!

At first, I went to Crewe Green with one or both of the aunts but later I usually went alone, changing trains at Manchester. The aunts soon stopped worrying that something might go wrong. I was always met at Crewe. The dark blue Lanchester (FM 8004) would be waiting on the forecourt with Geoffrey, the chauffeur, at the wheel. There was always room to park in those days.

Crewe Green made a wonderful change. Once you get there, the Sheffield countryside is beautiful, varied and dramatic. But at home, we had only a tiny garden and a backyard, even if it was well populated with animals. Ever since Africa, I hankered after wide open spaces.

At Crewe Green, I could run mad in a large garden, feed the hens, collect eggs and help pick fruit. Or, through a gate at the side, I could hare down two or three fields to a stream banked by wild garlic and celandine in spring – and sometimes guarded by cows I was never quite sure of. Across another field, one came to an iron fence and a gate into the woods surrounding Crewe Hall itself, empty and deserted. The family had moved to another of their homes after a tragedy connected with the lake, I believe. The woods were green and silent. I never went through them alone, lovely though they were. I don't *think* I was influenced by the 'Teddy Bears Picnic', which had just come out!

We did visit the Hall though. It was a typical Victorian mansion, highly decorated, and I thought it very romantic. Inside, it was echoing and desolate – cobwebby, too. But there was an intriguing little railway in the basement to carry food from the kitchens to the dining room! I suppose it was once the height of sophistication in getting food to table still reasonably hot.

The house was forlorn but the walled kitchen and flower gardens were still maintained, I suppose to supply the family. They were kept in excellent order by the head gardener, Spence, but his real passion was for dahlias. You went through an archway, swooned with the scent of heliotrope, and met a border – or rather, a multicoloured explosion – of giant and cactus dahlias. I've never seen such a display since. Behind this was a series of smaller hedged 'rooms', each devoted to a single variety of pom-pom dahlia. These are more fashionable nowadays than that exuberant border. I thought them all ravishing. Away from the formal gardens, I came one day on the rhododendron grove – a long, grass ride between banks of rhododendrons in bloom, a full 20 feet high on either side. They were only the common mauve ponticums, which are out of favour now but they were magnificent too.

Auntie Betty appreciated the dahlias but was really more interested in the tomatoes. Compared with Spence's tomatoes, she said, others 'weren't worth eating'. It was her standard dismissal of inferior food. At breakfast, she would examine each piece of toast minutely to see which was browned exactly right, not too little, not too much. Either extreme made it 'not worth eating'. Not that she liked 'fancy foods' – good, plain fare was her choice. I remember an outing to Chester, when she squandered the glorious opportunity of lunch in Brown's restaurant by ordering prunes and rice pudding! I was shocked.

Food was certainly plentiful at the Vicarage – good English beef and lamb, and home-grown vegetables and fruit. I had a good appetite but had quite a tussle resisting second and third helpings, because I was 'a growing girl'. Lunch on Sundays seemed a trifle boring because it always consisted of cold meat from Saturday's joint, with salad and jacket potatoes, followed by bread-and-butter pudding, which cooked itself in a slow oven, like the spuds. This was so that the whole household could go to church unflurried. I approve of that now; and even then, there was always fresh home-made lemonade on Sundays.

Every Tuesday, Auntie Betty would drive over to Sandbach, where she ran the welfare centre. She began this when she was still living in Sandbach, I believe, and carried it on faithfully for over 40 years, all through the war, when it became ever more important and demanding. This was in spite of the fact that she was not fit. By the time I knew her she was already finding walking difficult, though she tried various treatments and 'cures'. But she made herself keep going, walking down the fields with me as far as she could. Eventually, she was more or less chair-bound but, like my aunts, I *never* heard Auntie Betty complain. She was lucky, of course, in having domestic help and in being able to afford, in her own right, the comforts of life.

She had a highly developed sense of the ridiculous and was capable of relapsing into giggles like a schoolgirl. I never knew another vicar's wife get a fit of the giggles in church but she certainly did on holiday in Wales once, when some extravagance of the preacher set her off. We both nearly disgraced ourselves; just as well no one there knew us.

In a vicarage, you would, I hope, expect views of right and wrong to be unequivocal and I think they were. But they were never trumpeted and I heard very little, if any, righteous indignation. Both Uncle Harry and Auntie Betty were tolerant of human peccadilloes and different points of view. 'Oh no,' they might say, 'I can't agree with you there,' but never with anger; and I never heard an unkind remark there or at home in Sheffield. That came later, amongst my contemporaries!

Uncle Harry had been an army chaplain in the First World War – I don't know the precise cause but he emerged with very poor eyesight indeed. He could not read newsprint or normal books. All his service books for church were outsize print, and even then, he needed a large magnifying glass. Naturally, he knew the regular liturgy by heart. At home, Auntie Betty would read to him a lot; and so did I, when I was there. Sometimes it could be tiring and I didn't always find the *Church Times* as interesting as I might now. But if he sensed I was getting bored (and I wish I had hidden it better) he would never press me to go on.

He had an unusual gift, partly, I suppose, through having to depend so much on voices to recognise people. If there was a speaker on the radio, for instance, and a photograph in the *Radio Times*, he would listen for a while and be able to describe their main facial features while we compared the photograph. He was uncannily accurate. But he couldn't drive, of course, nor ride a bicycle. It didn't stop him getting round his parish, though. He would stride out briskly on his visits nearly every day, twirling a stout walking stick and hailing anyone he met on the way. He often had to peer closely to see who they were but I never saw him with a white stick.

It was at the Vicarage that I witnessed the only proper Sunday school treat I ever did see, just like the ones I'd read about in Victorian children's books. Trestle tables were put up on the cobbles in the stable yard, sheets spread on them and mountains of cakes and scones and jam and buns and jellies and goodness knows what else. The children had paper hats and streamers, balloons were burst and − after grace − an uproarious time was had. There were games in the garden afterwards, and everything went with a swing.

At the beginning of each summer we marked out the tennis court. This meant first finding the metal corner markers, embedded in the grass since the year before. Extraordinary how elusive they could be, when one knew, after all, more or less where they should be. Then we put in pegs, with string between them to mark the lines. Then came the fun of pushing the marking wheel, which rolled through a trough of whitewash along those lines. I can't begin to describe the mechanism. I've just tried and had to cross it out. It was very simple and most satisfying to operate.

In the summer of 1936, there was a great children's tea party to celebrate the Silver Jubilee. It took place in the grounds of some great house. Could it have been Crewe Hall, just for that occasion? We all got a commemorative mug, which I still have (minus its handle, alas!), and it is inscribed *Crewe Green, Crewe*, so it may have been the Hall but more likely somewhere near Sandbach. I remember a wide terrace, children's races on the grass below and a pageant too in the evening, which suggests that the flourishing Sandbach Amateur Dramatic Society was involved.

Crewe Hall was occupied again during the war; first, I think, by a Scottish regiment – in kilts. I came down the drive one day and met one of the officers by the churchyard gate. He was dark and dangerously handsome and kilts are *so* romantic – and he saluted me! I was a young 15 by then and nearly swooned with romantic exultation!

Later a coloured American regiment came and aroused a lot of interest. Uncle Harry invited their chaplain to preach – and to supper afterwards. I can't say I remember the sermon but he was very entertaining at supper. He suggested we might like his corporal to sing when they had their church parade. Uncle Harry agreed, of course. The corporal turned out to be Josh White – before he became so well-known. He sang us Negro spirituals, his voice rolling out and filling the air, then sinking to a whisper ... very dramatic. It wouldn't seem unusual now; but then, the combination of the war, the little country church, the unfamiliar phalanx of coloured soldiers, the presence of US troops at all – it all seemed bizarre yet it was very moving.

A couple of years after I had become so much at home there, Auntie Betty and Uncle Harry adopted Elizabeth. She was 11 months old, gorgeous – and I loved her on sight. She had a Norland nanny and a proper day nursery. I immediately decided to get my Child Nurse badge at Guides next term and spent a lot of time in the nursery. The nannies changed. Privately, I thought the first two a bit unmelting. But the third was a Princess Christian-trained nanny, Nanny Carey. When I had my own family, my sanity was saved by having the help of Eleanor for just two days a week. She too was Princess Christian-trained. Were they naturally warm and loving – or was it included in the training? Both, I feel sure.

I went with the Collins family on seaside holidays too, once to Anglesey again, to a house overlooking Trearddur Bay, with a delicious field behind it, where we gathered mushrooms for breakfast almost every morning.

Another time, we went again to Prestatyn – this time to a commodious house just behind the sand dunes. On these occasions, Auntie Betty took Nanny and Cook as well. Cookie, who succeeded Ada, was a sweet-faced lady who was very deaf indeed and used an ear-trumpet, the only one I ever saw seriously in use. She stayed for years after Uncle Harry died, devoted to Auntie Betty and Elizabeth, as they were devoted to her. It's very hard to be profoundly deaf but she seemed to manage it better than anyone I ever knew. She was a lovely lady.

I still went to stay at Crewe Green all through the war, thankful to escape air raids before we left Sheffield. Elizabeth eventually went away to school and I went to Oxford. Nothing changed the welcome, comfort and stability I felt there. It was not until I started work in London and didn't get long school holidays or vacations any more that my visits inevitably became few and far between. At the same time, Uncle Harry, always so cheerful and energetic, living in the 'sure and certain hope', became ill with cancer. I didn't know how ill he was but he died soon after I joined the Foreign Office. It was the first grief I really felt. My childish theory of being tougher after the age of 21 proved quite wrong.

So Auntie Betty and Elizabeth left Crewe Green Vicarage and went to live in Alsager. Hospitable as always, Auntie Betty put me and all my four children up more than once on our way to and from holidays in the Lakes.

I don't know whether I want to go back to Crewe Green. It must have changed so much. Looking at the Ordnance Survey map, there are roundabouts and dual carriageways where I remember only country lanes.

THE SIXTEENTH BEAD

Sheffield High School (1934–1938)

After Mother left early in the autumn term of 1934, I concentrated on school. The hiccups of the first term were behind me, Molly W. had left anyway. And I *wanted* to be happy there.

What did I enjoy most and remember best?

There was the annual book list, which we got at the end of the summer term for the school year ahead. We bought most of our own textbooks from A.B. Ward, Bookseller, then at the top of Hounsfield Road. I saw the whole operation as the most enormous treat. Imagine it, by myself, shopping for books! We were in duty bound to get second-hand copies whenever possible, so it was a question of getting there early and finding the best copies. But oh, the joy! when a book was on the syllabus for the first time and only new copies were available. I would bear my books home, stroke them, cover them, oh so neatly, in brown paper – and read all the English ones in advance. One year, late starting because of chickenpox, I learnt the whole of Act 1 of *The Merchant of Venice* by heart to while away the time. The pleasure in just possessing all those books! Do children nowadays experience this? There were no paperbacks then. The first Penguins came out two or three years later. Now the world seems awash with books; many of them tatty, both in form and content. But I treasured my school books and the few others I was gradually acquiring. The aunts had strong views about caring for them – indeed about caring for everything. Never bend a book backwards, I was taught; hold it supporting the

125

spine; avoid putting grubby thumbs on a page, rather turn the pages gently by their edges; even a clean thumb would leave a mark! Well, yes. Think of fingerprints. So I went and bought my books, I loved them and each school year began with this great treat.

Then there were games. Organised games are supposed to be a burden in some circles nowadays, I gather. I never really shone at any ball game, except now and again at hockey – but field afternoons were still red-letter days. We did have ideal conditions. We walked up from school to the end of the Manchester Road and caught the bus to the playing fields, high up above the Rivelin valley. The view was splendid, the air exhilarating and there was all the space in the world to let off steam. This was the site for hockey and for Sports Day. I shone then at high jump – scarcely believable now. The netball courts were more prosaically sited within the main school grounds. I actually once made a junior netball team. Disaster! We went to play an away match against Normanton Grammar School. They were a tough lot. We lost by something like 27 to nil! A bitter memory. The humiliation was indescribable at the time, though later it seemed hilarious.

An annual affair in the autumn term was the *Star* doll show. If I remember rightly, the *Star* newspaper provided schools with dolls for dressing. We took one each home and returned them dressed before the end of term. Then there was a show in school, followed by a grand one in town of all the dolls from all the schools, before they were distributed at Christmas to poor doll-less children. This might have been done through the NSPCC but I was never very clear. Nor was I much good at sewing but Auntie Emily was and helped to do my doll proud.

I missed the Guides when I left the High School. I was in the Poppy patrol and rose to be patrol second, would you believe? Our motto was 'Dare to do Right'. Not a bad one – especially tacked on to the Guide Law. But apart from striving for badges (even a Needlewoman one) I most enjoyed tracking in the countryside. And there was Empire Day, which was celebrated then with pride and modified pomp. Our company, together with other Guides and Scouts, looking our very smartest, joined in marching past the saluting base in front of the City Hall. I don't think I ever knew who was on the saluting base.

In the summer of 1936, there was a school camp under canvas in a field in Stratford-upon-Avon. The field is probably built over now, as it wasn't far from the centre. In the evenings we sang songs round the campfire and ate our smoky sausages and dampers. That alone would have been excitement enough to our unsophisticated souls. But the real magic came by day. We visited Shakespeare's birthplace, of course, and Anne Hathaway's Cottage and New Place. We went to Kenilworth Castle, where we pondered over Amy Robsart's fate. *Did* she fall or was she pushed? We went to Warwick Castle, where the witty guide told us that the secret passage originally emerged at Bramhall Lane ground in Sheffield. And we went to no fewer than four plays at the then new Shakespeare Memorial Theatre, which I loved. Writing to my parents, I noted its comfort and spaciousness 'enabling the fattest of adults to pass along the row without the seated being obliged to stand up'. Within that one week, we saw *Hamlet*, *Twelfth Night*, *The Taming of the Shrew* and *Romeo and Juliet*, Peter Glenville playing Romeo. We'd 'done' the notes on the *Taming of the Shrew* at school — and what a difference it made. We actually understood the jokes and found it hilarious. But it was, of course, *Romeo and Juliet* which had me mooning through the Stratford streets intoning over and over again, 'Oh Romeo, Romeo, *wherefore* art thou Romeo?' It took me days to get over it! I collected postcards and made a book of the trip for my parents. They kept it. It's still intact — just.

The final highlight of my time at the High School was the school play in my last year there, the year we did *Pride and Prejudice*. It was produced by a splendid lady called Miss Outram, who was closely connected with the Sheffield Repertory Theatre. I was already into my second or third reading of *Pride and Prejudice*. I had a nineteenth-century parasol from Aunt Jessie and was given to prowling round at home, draped in bits of lace and twirling this, pretending to be Elizabeth Bennet. So I did hope for a small part. In fact I dreamed about it, literally. I dreamed I was in the school cloakroom changing my shoes to go home, when someone came in and said: 'You're to be Elizabeth Bennet.' What a disappointment to wake up! However, whether you believe it or not, I *was* in the cloakroom a week or two later, changing my shoes to go home, when a friend came rushing in and said: 'The play list's up – and you're Elizabeth!' Obviously I thought she was joking – but she wasn't! I have to declare I'd never have made an actress. But well coached and steeped in Miss Austen as I was, wearing a proper Regency costume and a very fetching red wig, it was ... words are failing me. I suppose I did live the part. The one stumbling block was when, after reading Darcy's letter explaining about Wickham, I had to declaim alone, front stage: 'Oh I have been blind, wretchedly blind. Vanity not love has been my folly.' I was creased up with self-consciousness but Miss O. persevered. The evening was by all accounts a great success – anyway, our version was much closer to Jane Austen than the recent TV version! Miss Austen's Darcy would never have been so lost to all sense of propriety as to dive fully clad into the lake in his own park, nor could Miss Elizabeth Bennet have countenanced such conduct, which must go beyond the bounds of what is seemly! Admittedly, however, our acting might not have been quite as good.

My time at Sheffield High School was nearly over. I was happy there but less happy at home, due to the continuing friction between Dick and me – and my own teenage tantrums by now. My closest friend was leaving for Wycombe Abbey and the idea of boarding school began to seem very attractive. In the holidays, I still devoured school stories from the library, boys' and girls' alike. It sounded just the thing! But to go, I needed a scholarship. I was a year late for almost everywhere except Cheltenham. Needless to say, it was Auntie Emily who combed the reference books to discover this and Auntie Rittie who wrote to my parents to put it to them. The aunts were always *encouraging*. They never said: 'You won't manage' – or 'It's too expensive'. They said, 'Well, try!' or 'We'll see what we can do.' And if it couldn't be managed, whatever it was, that was that. You always knew they'd done their best. On this occasion, they persuaded my parents and I have little doubt offered to contribute themselves financially, *if* I won a scholarship. I had just won a prize at school, perhaps a good omen? So the aunts duly sent for the scholarship regulations and I was entered. And, wonder of wonders, I succeeded.

THE SEVENTEENTH BEAD

Cheltenham Ladies' College (1938–1939)

The name seemed quaint until one got used to it, and I'm sure it does now. It's historical, of course, dating from 1853, when the school was founded by a group of six local mid-Victorian gentlemen by means of 100 shares at £10 each. They had ideas ahead of their time, one being the need to provide a first-rate education for girls on a par with what was available for boys. A revolutionary aim! Miss Dorothea Beale, was appointed 'Lady Principal' five years later, after a spell at Casterton School for the Daughters of Clergy – the original of Charlotte Bronte's Lowood, I believe. Perhaps it was too rigid for Miss Beale!

Miss Beale was an outstanding figure in the development of education for women. She achieved an international reputation and the college developed phenomenally during her 50 years as Principal. Miss Buss, a distinguished contemporary, did similar service through North London Collegiate School. I dare say you may have come across that well-known jingle?

> Miss Buss and Miss Beale
> Cupid's darts do not feel.
> How different from us,
> Miss Beale and Miss Buss!

I don't know about Miss Buss but I don't think the hint of deprived spinsterhood is anything like Miss Beale. She was much more human and I should imagine, totally fulfilled. Her influence, both

129

academic and spiritual, still brooded benignly over College in my day. She epitomised the best Victorian values of academic thoroughness and integrity, a sense of responsibility towards the less fortunate, and a deep Christian faith.

I arrived to take the scholarship exam in the spring of 1938 and was put up in Fauconberg House. This was the first of the boarding houses actually bought by the school, for £3,000 in 1865. It is a substantial Regency building at the corner of the college site – very convenient and now much enlarged. I had already met the housemistress, Miss Gem, whose sister was a great friend of Auntie Betty. No 'house-lady' had anything to do with teaching or the scholarship exam; but just having met her helped me feel a bit less shy.

The girls themselves made me feel at home too. But I was over-whelmed by the College building. There was a lot of it – there's even more now. What I knew was confident high Victorian in style and decoration; the pre-Raphaelite influence of the latter part of the nineteenth century was everywhere, though I didn't realise it at the time. I was most impressed and not a little intimidated by the Marble Corridor linking the first Great Hall, Lower Hall, with the later and larger Princess Hall (after Queen Alexandra as Princess of Wales). Black and white marble squares, with floor-length windows to the garden all down one side, could it really have been 100 yards long? It felt like it; and what with the statues in niches and commemorative stained glass here, there and everywhere, to say I was impressed would be an understatement! When you reached it, the Princess Hall proved to be a monument to pitch-pine. Some might call it ugly, were it not for the scale, the two tiers of galleries all round and the painting of the *Dream of Fair Women* over the proscenium arch. This was painted in 1902, approved by Miss Beale but shrouded from view in my day for some inscrutable reason, rumoured to be modesty! Whose idea could that have been? I goggled away at all this, which is why I cannot remember a thing about the actual exam, or the journey there or the journey back home. What I do remember is the letter saying I had won the top scholarship, but kindly explaining that I wasn't quite clever enough for the maximum cash possible. It was enough – the fees were a hefty £162 a year!

What a flurry of preparation followed. A clothing list arrived which made me gasp. I'd never had so many clothes. It involved a trip to London with indefatigable Aunt Emily, because the uniform was supplied by Madame Forma in Dover Street. She was formidable indeed and devastatingly ladylike. I seem to remember a sort of drawing room on the first floor, nothing so plebeian as a shop! I expect there was also somewhere in Cheltenham itself but London was easier from Sheffield. We stayed at the Kingsley Hotel in Bloomsbury, the first hotel I'd stayed in since Amanzimtoti. I met again and this time approved grapefruit for breakfast. We did a bit of sightseeing. There was then an ABC tearoom in Bridge Street, opposite the Houses of Parliament, and I have a very skewed snap of Big Ben taken from the first-floor window.

Back home, I displayed my uniform on the marquetry table in the drawing room and everyone who came to the house had to come and admire! What a bore I must have been. I needed three non-uniform frocks, which I learned to call 'mufti' – very Raj. We changed into mufti, you see, when we got back to our houses and we had glacé kid court shoes (uniform) which also went with green silk frocks for formal College occasions. Goodness me, what a wardrobe! Auntie Betty gave me my overnight case. It was a buck-hide one from Finnigan's in Bond Street. I remember it because it was £25, which I wasn't supposed to know – half a term's fees! It was indestructible, lasted my time at Cheltenham and Oxford, served both my sons at St Paul's – until a Newcastle burglar stole it a few years ago. I rang Finnigan's to ask its replacement value. They immediately recognised the model from my description and could do one for £750. There's inflation, if you like!

I arrived again at Fauconberg House in September 1938 and loved it from the start. Miss Gem was one of the generation of cultivated Edwardian ladies, of whom I have met a few and admired all. She had an unforced dignity, a calm confidence without a hint of complacency. It was impossible to imagine her put out of countenance – or, in modern parlance, losing her cool – yet she was not cold. She was a splendid housemistress. The Matron was rather less splendid and rather more irascible but she added a spice of unpredictability.

If the 'Ladies' College' seems dated now, so do our domestic arrangements. We did not have dormitories in Fauconberg but bedrooms. The largest held five, others four and a few for older girls were smaller still. Ages were mixed, with the eldest in charge. Curtains round each bed gave us privacy when needed but were drawn back at night and during the day. Besides a bed, we each had a laundry basket under it, a dressing table/chest of drawers – and a washstand, complete with china bowl, soap dish and large pitcher of cold water. In the mornings, maids would bring shining brass cans of hot water, one each, and leave them outside the door as the rising bell went. The junior fetched them in. We bathed at night, three or four times a week, punctually at our allotted time and briskly! Ten minutes flat was allowed before the next person would be banging on the door. Bedrooms had to be left tidy at all times, all clothes put away – and *all hairs* combed out of hairbrushes, on principle but also out of consideration for the maids who had to handle them when dusting. Infringement of these rules earned a black mark; and that earned the black looks of one's room-mates as there was a termly room prize at stake. A late developer, I had only recently started to wear a bra and was too embarrassed to enter it on my first laundry list, so I left it in the laundry basket! Can you imagine a more daft expression of shyness? I was much more embarrassed to find a black mark against my name on the bedroom list for all to see: 'Soiled bra left in laundry basket.'

A team of hairdressers came at regular intervals. We would leave our brushes and combs in a large basket on the way down to breakfast, and collect them again, all clean, when we got back in the evening. We'd be called from prep in turn, have our hair washed and repair to various gas fires round the house to dry it and carry on with reading or learning prep. That was the theory; more often we chatted.

The hairdressers also made a ritual visit at the beginning of each term to check for any head infestation, to put it politely. Everyone came to school by train then and it was not unknown for Nasty Things to be picked up en route.

Good grooming was inculcated in a dozen ways and with a lot of help. The hairdressers kept our hair in good order, our hairbrushes and combs were washed for us, our shoes were polished daily by a small man in the basement cloakroom. How amazing that we did our own mending! One did mend stockings then, lisle they were – or silk for best – before nylon arrived.

Fauconberg was linked to the college by a covered way leading directly to the large two-storey high Music Room at the end of the Music Wing. Once the home of the kindergarten, it was still called 'Kindy' and served as our playroom, party room etc. But in the mornings two house prefects armed with clothes brushes checked everyone individually for holes, ladders or crooked seams in stockings, sagging hems and hairs on clothing. Hairs were brushed off but ladders etc. meant going back to change. Once checked and only then, we went on through the Music Wing into College.

It's hard to credit, looking at film of today's schools, real or fictional, that there was a universal rule: no talking at any time on corridors or stairs, no running, no taking stairs two at a time. And it was observed. Eagle eyes of gym staff and prefects spotted infringements, your house was plain from your tie and a voice would call: '*Stop* running, Fauconberg!' Every girl in the school also had a termly rating for deportment – carriage and neatness. You scored 15, 10, 5 – or, deep disgrace, –5. It seems astonishing, even to me, that the most prized inter-house cup was the Deportment cup. The overall effect was good but it did attract criticism as encouraging 'a poker back and a waddle' – rather like walking races! At the time, all this didn't seem restrictive – indeed, it was very sensible. The logistics of getting 800-odd girls from rooms all over the buildings into the Princess Hall for Prayers punctually each morning were formidable. So was the execution – all within 20 minutes.

The 'lines' started soon after 8.30 in strict order. A look-out at the door of every form room ensured that as soon as one form had passed, the next followed on immediately. Steadily and inexorably they went, down stairs, along passages, round Lower Hall and up the Marble Corridor, for all the world like the soldier ants of Tanzania. Halfway down the Marble Corridor, the senior forms came down the central staircase, joining in to make a double line. Exalted personages, college prefects, stood at strategic points, checking any tendency to run, whisper or slouch etc. It was known as point duty, like policemen – and policemen they were. There were always some visitors to Prayers. In those days they arrived from the street by St George's Archway at the end of the Marble Corridor. The prefect on duty there could feel the draught as the door to the street behind her opened and would call: 'Stop the lines' in ringing tones. Stop they did, the visitors crossed safely to the stairs up to the visitors' gallery and the lines resumed their surge into the hall.

Members of the choir could escape unobtrusively at this point too and make their way up to one of the four choir galleries. There was never a hitch in this performance. When the war came and relatives in the forces visited, they were known to watch open-mouthed, later comparing the discipline of their own troops unfavourably. It may sound regimented – it was! But what a boon in an emergency. Parts of the building were a warren; one little stair from a cloakroom was in fact called the 'bunny chute'. To be able to clear it so fast and so smoothly must have been reassuring.

In contrast, there were no bells at any time. Clocks were synchronised and lessons stopped and started on time. If you had to move rooms, that again was done in silence – until you got there. I think it did contribute to a calm and purposeful atmosphere.

This was most evident in the library. You had to be fairly senior before graduating there. It became my favourite place – the best place to work in that I have ever known. Stained-glass medallions in the windows, statues of philosophers, all with a particular significance, the ranks of books, many of them valuable – and the silence – all combined to create an atmosphere where one could pause, consider, reflect and conjecture. The stock of books was exceptional. From its beginning, Miss Beale herself had collected from second-hand catalogues countrywide and she had good contacts. Ruskin was a regular correspondent and gave several volumes, as well as two valuable manuscripts – a C12 manuscript of the four Gospels and a C13 Arras Breviary. Dr Jowett of Balliol was another friend, who sent two copies of his translation of Plato – one for Miss Beale and one for the college library; and there were countless others... A policy of bringing beauty and light into what would now be called 'the learning environment' had underpinned the expansion of the buildings towards the end of the last century and was nowhere better exemplified than in the library. Miss Beale is quoted as saying: 'What we desire for you is that you should live, not in a mere material atmosphere ... Pictures, windows, statues ... all tell us of the life of God in the soul of man.' No wonder it was a good place to work.

Back at the house, we came down to earth. Bodily rather than intellectual sustenance took precedence. We were well fed, without frills. We sat at long tables for meals, each headed by a house prefect, who served. Once, it is true, a padlock was scooped out of the rice pudding – but I don't remember any other mishaps. There were small conventions. You must not ask for anything and Heaven forbid that you should reach! You looked after the needs of your neighbours. If they were negligent, you could say, 'Mary, would you like some water?' – and if she were not as thick as two planks, she would get the message.

'Waste not, want not!' You were expected to finish what was on your plate but not to take too long about it. There was an escape route. The tables had side drawers, hidden by the table cloths. When the dining room was being got ready for the the house dance, Miss Gem was pained to inform us that remnants of rejected food had been found in those drawers – even bits of dusty jelly! We all tried to look duly appalled. No one could leave the table until everyone else was ready, so the last to finish would find ten pairs of eyes turned accusingly and impatiently in her direction. I'm afraid this did encourage gobbling – a bad habit which persists.

After lunch, the denizens of the junior study queued up for their sweet issue. At the beginning of term, we all brought a supply in a large tin labelled with our name. These were stowed in a cupboard under the back stairs and the sweets doled out daily by the house prefects. Two every day, and six on Sunday. Then we retired to our beds for a statutory 20 minutes' rest and read. One otherwise dull girl was famous for always managing to fall fast asleep. How often since have I thought of her with envy! Then it was up and back to school for games or whatever.

There were three house studies – a cross between sitting rooms and prep rooms. The junior study was the largest, the senior was smaller and the prefects' study, which also housed the house library, was very select and provided an armchair each! In the junior study, we each had a locker and shared a few worn but comfortable basket chairs round a gas fire. On Sundays, we did our mending here and wrote our statutory letter home. Both were checked, the mending to see that it was done properly, the letters to see that they were done. They were *not* read or censored!

There were house prayers every evening in the drawing room – a fine room overlooking the quadrangle between us and the oldest college buildings. A hymn, a reading, a prayer or two – and any notices. And on Sundays we went to morning service at the nearest church, St Matthew's, a short walk away. Never in a 'crocodile'. College did not approve of crocodiles; we were expected to be intelligent enough and well-behaved enough to go in twos or threes, never more than three and never straddling the pavement. St Matthew's was a large, cavernous church, where Fauconberg house took up a block of pews on the left of the central aisle. There were arcane customs toward the end of term like kicking the pew one Sunday, or leaving a button undone or something. I can't say I ever remembered. It was pretty pointless and already going out. I do remember the arrival of a new curate, who had the unfortunate habit of starting each prayer with 'Oh, God . . .' What, you may say, is odd about that? Nothing at all. The trouble was, he was so explosive about it. 'Oh *God*!' he paused. It was more an expletive than a supplication. Girls en masse are prone to giggling and he tested us sorely.

On Sunday afternoons after letter-writing and so on, we went for walks – sometimes round about, sometimes further afield up Leckhampton Hill. Leckhampton Hill in the snow . . . so lonely, so lovely. I was moved to write a poem for the college magazine. It got in, too!

Some grand and formal visitors arrived at the house one weekend and were shown round by Miss Gem. It seemed they were prospective parents – but decided against, because they had seen us going out in our twos and threes and feared the girls were encouraged to be too independent! We took it as a compliment.

With far fewer cars and many girls from long distances, it was the exception rather than the rule for parents to visit during the term, even at half-term. We didn't suffer! There were house expeditions, by coach with picnics. In spring, Miss Gem was happy to tell us that we had been invited to see the daffodils in Newent woods and, with the owner's permission, we could each pick some. We must be sure not to be greedy – that would be an abuse of his kindness. She must have put it very well because we did see the point. When we got there, there were hosts of them, little Lenten daffodils, like Wordsworth's. We picked – I think with discretion – and back at the house, there were boxes and packing for us to send some home. In the summer term we went to Sapperton woods, where there was a wide valley, and a stream through the middle, half-hidden by kingcups, and a fallen trunk or two to cross it by. No one fell in.

On Sunday evenings, the drawing room came into its own. We gathered there, while Miss Gem read to us and we stitched away at our 'St Hilda's work'. She read beautifully. I think it was there I first heard John Buchan's *Thirty-Nine Steps* and *Prester John*. St Hilda's in the East, in Bethnal Green, also founded by Miss Beale, was one of several similar settlements in the East End of London at the end of the last century, the best known probably being Toynbee Hall. There was real poverty then – and our puny efforts were bent towards providing warm children's clothing. The college provided the material and the finished garments were sent to St Hilda's in the East for distribution. A few years later I used to help there after work on Mondays, when I was at the Treasury and then the Foreign Office. But it has inevitably changed almost out of recognition from Miss Beale's day – even from mine.

When there wasn't work, there were games. I rejoiced to learn cricket but only shone as a fielder and that by accident. A ball hit me. My reflexes were instant. I clasped my knee in agony – and caught the ball. 'Very plucky bit of fielding,' said an onlooking parent. He turned out to be a county player, my reputation was made and I was put in the house team to field close in – horribly close. Silly point – very silly at times.

In the autumn term we played hockey, and in the spring term, lacrosse. Hockey was all right. I could run quite fast up and down the left wing, which wasn't a popular position, and I rather think I made the college 3rd Xl! Lacrosse was unpredictable, with no boundary lines and all those sticks waving in the air. One waved in my face and chipped a tooth. A tiresome game but graceful to watch, they say. Not my kind.

It was a happy first year. I liked being busy. The organised, stable life suited me very well and I wasn't short of friends, though I was a year young for my year and the rest were all well-established by the time I arrived. But I never felt isolated. There were none of the ghastly initiation rites one heard of in boys' schools, nor do I remember bullying in any form – not even malicious teasing. I was the only new girl that year in what was called Upper College (i.e. School Certificate year and above). And that year, new uniforms were introduced for Upper College – bright green Harris tweed skirts with white silk blouses. Existing uniforms were white blouses and navy djibbahs, like gym tunics without pleats and better cut – quite smart. These could be worn for another year. So I stuck out a mile wherever I was, the *only* girl in a green tweed skirt. I don't remember ever being made to feel the slightest embarrassment. Which says a lot for the prevailing standard of kindness and good manners – which amount to much the same thing, after all.

The school year drew to a close with School Certificate exams. They seemed to go all right. I was very lucky in quite liking exams, and anyway we were never encouraged to make a fuss about them and call it stress.

Then it was the summer holidays of 1939. No seaside holidays that year. Talk of peace and talk of war, uncertainty and disruption. We came back in September to a very different scene.

138

THE EIGHTEENTH BEAD

The Last Pre-War Summer Holidays (1939)

We were still on holiday when war was declared. Sheffield schoolchildren were already being evacuated in anticipation and Aunt Emily was to go with her class. Dick, now 18, was awaiting call-up – but I was a problem. Aunt Emily got permission to stitch me on to her class for the time being. So I arrived at the LMS station with a luggage label pinned on me for identification, a gas mask in a cardboard box hanging round my neck and a bag of iron rations, just in case. We had a tin of bully beef, a packet of biscuits – and two other items I forget. One might have been chocolate.

Aunt Emily was called away. All the other children knew each other and were a bit younger than myself, so though we smiled willingly, we were shy of each other and I felt very much alone. We were shepherded on to the train and eventually arrived and were driven by bus to a village hall or parish room or something at New Ollerton. There we were decanted for allocation to billets. It was a rough-and-ready procedure. Volunteer 'hosts', 'billatrixes', 'landladies' – whatever – arrived and stood at one end of the hall surveying the invaders – us! Then they began to pick the ones they liked the look of. The local billeting team registered names and addresses, ticked off lists, and gradually our group dwindled. As I said, I was older than the rest, taller and probably gawkier. Not a tempting proposition. The larger the evacuee, the more likely to cause problems, was in their minds, I expect. One by one or two by two, all the others were chosen until I was left standing alone. It

139

was the playground nightmare of not being picked writ large. Thankfully, after a pause of ages (probably a couple of minutes) a kindly couple said: 'Oh, we'll have her,' and bore me home. It was a smallish council house in a nice estate, from what I could see in the dark, spotlessly clean and welcoming. But I was desperately shy, lonely, homesick and very miserable. I tried not to show it; my hosts were trying hard to make me feel at home but I just longed to go to bed and cry, I'm afraid.

Then there was a knock at the door and behold! Aunt Emily had arrived with the billeting officer. Once she and her class were settled, she had tracked me down. I was reallocated on the spot, to everyone's relief. Aunt Emily's class was to join the school at a village called Kneesall and they were all billeted thereabouts. She and another teacher were at Church Farm, just by the church, and hearing about her stray niece, the Vicar, Mr Evans, had offered the evacuee place in the Vicarage. So there I landed – in an attic at first, hastily furnished and a bit bare. But it was late now, everyone was tired, I nibbled a biscuit from my rations and got into bed.

Before I went to sleep, I opened an envelope which Auntie Emily had given me, saying it was something to stop me feeling afraid. It was a card with St John, Chapter 14 set out in a border of flowers. 'Let not your heart be troubled, neither let it be afraid...' I started learning it by heart – and fell asleep. It did help.

The next day was Sunday 3 September and I went to church with the Vicarage family. Auntie Emily met us as we came out and told us, standing by the church gate, that war had been declared. I felt quite blank. What would it mean, now it had really come? No one knew. The aunts remembered zeppelins in the 1914–18 war. Air raids were expected or we wouldn't have been evacuated. But no one really knew. Just as well.

I stayed at Kneesall Vicarage till the end of the holidays, moving down from the attic to the regular spare room. There were three children, Brian, my age, Mary, a bit younger and Martin, who was only two or three. They and their parents soon made me feel at home – I was so lucky to fetch up there. The Vicar of Corby and his family, the Goodriches, dropped in one afternoon. I think 'my' family was out, so I officiated and gave them tea. Margaret and I met again at Oxford, recognised each other at once and have been friends ever since. Her brother Philip became Bishop of Worcester; we have met again too.

That first autumn of the war saw little action. People started talking of a 'phoney' war and the expected air raids didn't happen. They happened all right later! But meanwhile, quite a few evacuees drifted back home and by the time I came home for the Christmas holidays, it was to Sheffield, and both my aunts were back teaching there.

Inevitably, when I went back to Cheltenham at the beginning of term, things had changed.

THE NINETEENTH BEAD

CLC in Wartime (1939–1944)

We went back to Cheltenham in the autumn of 1939 to a completely different scene. *All* the college buildings except Principal's House and the swimming baths on the field had been taken over. We learned later that the redoubtable Miss Popham had been warned the Christmas before that this would happen in the event of war but was bound not to divulge it – which must have made forward and contingency planning difficult! One large house, Lilleshall Hall in Shropshire, happened to be available anyway and was retained. But when war was declared on 3 September, there was barely a fortnight to finalise arrangements for the accommodation and teaching of 500-plus girls! As far as I recall, term started on time and the school remained the *Cheltenham* Ladies' College.

Nearby stately-home owners helped. The year below us went to Cowley Manor, with marble and onyx bathrooms and Peter Scott murals to lift their spirits. A younger block went to Brockhampton Park, with my own Miss Gem. Still younger children went to Seven Springs House, rather nearer. But post-School Certificate forms stayed right in Cheltenham in an assortment of large houses hastily converted. Former house loyalties weakened as the new houses grouped classes and years together, which was probably good for us. It was a bore from my point of view, as all my close friends were on the science side, heading for medicine, and landed in one called St Keverne. I went to a vast white block of a building, Pallas, in a wide, quiet road known as The Park.

The housemistress came from another former house. She and I did not always see eye to eye. I am sure she was a Good Woman; and I'm pretty sure I was a Tiresome Teenager. She was a pontificator – indiscriminately, whether the matter was of high or infinitesimal importance. She lectured us forcefully but boringly when we turned our noses up at what she called 'jolly good fish pudding'. It was revolting. And she lambasted some poor girl who spilled its pink sauce on the table runner. Future spilling culprits would be fined sixpence, that being the cost of premature laundering. Inevitably, there was a future culprit, right at the start of the week too, when fresh runners had just been laid. She was duly fined. But her crime remained for all to see. The runner did *not* go prematurely to the laundry! This didn't seem to me to match the high ethical/moral tone so regularly taken by Miss R., and after four days, when the stained runner was still there, I raised the point publicly. What temerity! I had a little interview with Miss Popham thereafter but she was surprisingly sympathetic. She was a clear-headed and logical lady; I felt she saw my point and, I suspect, shared it.

To give Miss R. her due, she was more thoughtful, more spiritual even, than her manner suggested. She turned a tiny attic room in Pallas into a prayer room for any who felt inclined – and quite a few did. And there was a 'silent' room next door to retire to when the hurly-burly of the general common room jarred. I think of her gratefully for these. Anyway, we all agreed that everyone would be happier, especially me, if I went to join my scientific friends the following term. By then, the government was more flexible, the shape of things was clearer and Miss Popham was able to reclaim the college site, including my own Fauconberg House, so I and my friends in St Keverne all went there and stayed there for the rest of our time at Cheltenham.

Teaching was remarkably little disrupted in this first term of war. The Field substituted for College as far as possible. Luckily it was very big! The Baths stood at one entrance. They were big too, and, boarded over, provided room for some classes, study cubby holes in what had been changing cubicles – and even a study for Miss Popham in the towel room. Behind the Baths, on the Field itself and linked by duck-boards, we found a great wheel of army huts, each providing two classrooms – just like the World War I army hut of my first term at Sheffield High School. Books and other supplies from the College stores arrived as needed by any transport available, including a baby's pram used to ferry books from the library. With no Princess Hall, nearby Christ Church was lent for Prayers.

It still seems remarkable that this administrative nightmare was handled with so little fuss that we were aware of. There must have been problems behind the scenes for everyone. But I can recall absolutely no hand-wringing, hair-tearing or complaining. Staff and girls alike were all too conscious of far bigger problems elsewhere. And that was nothing special either – simply a reflection of the national mood.

After all the reorganisation, the government never did move into the College buildings, which Miss Popham got back by the end of the term – and she went on to retrieve some of the boarding houses as well. Some were able to come back from their temporary homes in the countryside, though the School Certificate (O level) year stayed out at Cowley Manor for four years, with special buses ferrying them in as necessary.

Otherwise, I believe there were mixed-age houses again, but Fauconberg, in the College grounds, remained as a senior house. We didn't get our Miss Gem back, though. We had a brisk lady who had, I think, been a journalist. She was efficient but perhaps not born to be a housemistress. She tended to favouritism – there was a little clique of favoured girls, one of whom was a close friend of my own; but she didn't seem to bother beyond them.

She made one minor but comic miscalculation in offering us yams! There was rationing, there were shortages. We knew all that, but yams was going too far. Miss X was *very* cross. Unlike Miss Gem, she did lose her cool. 'There are 600,000 people starving in Europe!' she blazed at us. (Why exactly 600,000?) Well fine! we thought, they would be most welcome to our yams. No one ate them, we never saw any again and I fear Miss X lost a bit of face. I don't think she stayed my time out as I associate house prayers latterly with Miss E., a gentle lady who, untypically for College, was also on the teaching staff. She could get muddled,

144

once finishing prayers with '... Father, Son and Gholy Host ... oh, my dears, I'm so sorry!'

We were fond of her and it was altogether a happy house throughout my last two years. I enjoyed most classes, working for what was then Higher Certificate. But living amongst so many scientists, I conceived the idea that perhaps I was missing my vocation and was really born to be a doctor too. Instead of being told not to be silly and get on with it, my timetable was studied and I was slotted in to zoology classes as a start. My enthusiasm began to cool when we dissected hens. Should my hen have come to this pass? She had obviously been in fine laying fettle. Eggs of gradually diminishing size were queuing all the way up the 'delivery channel'. Interesting in its way – but not really me. We were then forewarned about dissecting human corpses – which would be part of the medics' course, not so far ahead. This was enough. I confessed that I didn't think I should go on. I was not patronised, nor scoffed at – but told that I had probably made the right decision, because I really did have some ability in languages. How wisely my temporary aberration was handled.

The Higher Certificate course reclaimed full attention, French and German being my main subjects. But it was Latin which possibly gave me most delight on the one hand and most training in intellectual rigour on the other. We had a truly inspired teacher of Latin literature. Miss Rackham wore long tweed skirts, she was wild of hair, eager of gait, and glittering of eye, like the Ancient Mariner. But hers was the glitter of enthusiasm. She would stride into the room clutching an armful of books and pitch straight into Virgil's *Georgics*. She loved her subject; she made sure we did too. 'Just think of it,' she would say, '*Exiguus mus!* A fieldmouse of course. Can't you *see* the little creature?' She conjured up formidable Roman ladies from Livy – the '*ingens agmen matronum*' – '*agmen!*' she would say, 'drawn up in battle formation! Those awesome Roman matrons!' And she pointed out, to our pleasure, that that overworked motto '*Labor omnia vincit*' is incomplete without the next word – '*improbus*'. Work may conquer all – but how tiresome! She would forget to set prep, forge out of the room, then turn to suggest a piece almost as an afterthought. 'Just scribble it out,' she would say, adding invariably, 'on any old sugar-bag' – paper, like so much else, being in short supply.

On the language side, Miss Clarke, the senior classics teacher, was a total contrast but equally memorable. Her stature was diminutive, her personality anything but. The moment she entered a classroom, she dominated it. She wore button boots and long skirts, her hair was scraped back in a bun and she never, ever raised her voice. She never needed to. The hallmarks of her teaching were integrity, accuracy and thoroughness, all of which she expected in every piece of work, exposing the lack of them remorselessly. Many years later, I was asked to address an audience of Cheltenham Old Girls and some staff at the Public Schools' Club in Piccadilly. I was to tell them all about being a political wife – not a very demanding challenge. Nevertheless, I quailed to see Miss Clarke in the audience. However, she rose at the end to give the most charming vote of thanks! I was deeply touched, not to say, flattered. A late photograph in her *History of College*, shows a gentler, smiling face and softer hair than I recall. Small, splendid Miss Clarke! She no doubt relaxed after retiring from all those girls.

We were fortunate in most of our other teachers too. Miss Cleave strove to convey the atmosphere as well as the language of France, since we couldn't go there, and was very keen on pronunciation. I can see her now, striding up and down delicately enunciating: '*peu à peu le feu s'éteint*.' And again, '*Dinah dina, dit-on, du dos d'un dodu dindon*,' every vowel distinct. Like Miss Rackham's her love of the literature was infectious – the poets of the Pléiade, the classical clarity of Racine – even the sentimental Romanticism of such as Lamartine. Would that every child in the country could experience such teaching.

There were other teachers – two new ones, perhaps displaced by the war. The style of one was rather different. Her concept of teaching seemed to be to dictate notes expressing her own views, which she expected us to copy down – and presumably learn by heart. Very different from the shared enthusiasm and the encouragement to think for ourselves that we were used to. I don't know about her background but there was a tragic certainty about the other, the most unforgettable soul of all. This was Miss E. She

146

came from Germany – and she was Jewish. In my last year, I had two or three lessons a week with her, one to one. I did not enjoy them. We didn't yet know the full horrors of Hitler's Jewish policy although there were rumours. Miss E. had escaped – physically. But she found life an enormous effort. I can never forget her hands. Her nails were bitten right down to the quick. They were a terrible sight; and she had a nervous habit of clicking them together throughout the lesson, probably unconsciously. What nightmares she must have endured, what grief, perhaps for people she loved and had left behind. None of us knew for certain. I was torn between involuntary disgust at the sight and sound of the gnawed and clicking nails and sympathy for what I dimly per-ceived. It would be comfortable to be able to claim that sympathy outweighed disgust but it would not be true. At 17, I couldn't handle it. Poor Miss E.

'Madame' Hill, a later 'refugee' from France, was a different proposition altogether. She had run a finishing school in Paris until pupils evaporated with the war. She escaped as the Hitler hordes advanced. Miss Popham offered her a role, presumably thinking (rightly) that the senior girls might not be the worse for a little instruction in deportment/social graces. We had observed Madame Hill's progress down the Marble Corridor – she couldn't be missed. Tall and stately, her hair was beautifully coiffed, and a long black cloak swung from her shoulders as she sailed along, an example to us all. We were intrigued by the prospect of these lessons.

She came to the house on weekend evenings, her visits pure delight! We learned how to enter and leave a crowded room, not slinking round the door but opening it calmly and wide, even when late. If you try to sidle in inconspicuously, people would say to themselves: 'Look at her – she's late!' If you followed Madame Hill's advice, the reaction would be: 'Dear me – I wonder what can have detained her!' Should you have occasion to move your chair at a party, you did *not* move as one piece, clutching your chair to your behind. You rose smoothly, one foot behind the other, stepped behind the chair to lift and move it and sit again, never, but never looking behind as you did so. One foot a little behind for balance, feel the edge of the chair on the back of your leg and sink gracefully down. We learned to bow the head to an acquaintance across the street – not shout 'Hi!' Imagine a large flat book projecting from the top of your head and follow the track of an imaginary spider from the near corner above one eye to the diagonally opposite corner. It's a very elegant inclination, I assure you. Madame Hill taught us how to make conversation to a difficult or taciturn dinner companion – stressing that, if you're at that sort of dinner, it's your duty. I've often used her tip. It works! *And* she taught us the court curtsey – just in case. The left arm of the large Chesterfield sofa was the King – curtsey. Then execute three sweeping sideways steps and sink into a second low curtsey to the right hand arm – the Queen. Never gush at people. Saying extravagantly to overstaying guests as they leave: '*Must* you go, *can't* you stay?' conveys all too easily the opposite: '*Can't* you go, *must* you stay?' Her demonstrations were hilarious; so were the characters she conjured up for us: 'Snodgrass' (for all men) and 'Lady Knockemstiff' linger for ever in the mind.

We had good visiting lecturers too, mostly, I guess, before the war hotted up. There was Amy Johnson, the intrepid aviator; and a gripping slide lecture on the Incas of Peru. A pity I can't remember the lecturer! Less gripping, I fear, were three Lent Lectures – *all* on the first three verses of the First Epistle of St Peter. I'm sure they were erudite but, oh dear, how hard those wooden chairs in the Princess Hall were by the end of each! Fidgeting and coughing were not on. You did not cough in the Princess Hall. If you did so in Prayers, Miss Popham would pause, looking pointedly in your direction. Then, 'If you cannot control your cough, you may get permission to miss Prayers. If you come to Prayers, you do not cough.' We did not cough.

Cabinet ministers were known to come to Speech Day. (Not Prize-Giving – Miss Beale had not approved of prizes.) They went down rather well. Lord Swinton, I think it was, who endeared himself by quoting a weary headmaster: 'The more I see of the average parent, the more I admire the average boy – or girl, of course,' he added courteously. Sir Archibald Sinclair told of the absent-minded Scottish minister who offered up prayers 'for King George, Queen Mary – and all the other Clydeside steamers...' What a solemn thought that after nearly 60 years, I remember the jokes but not the substance of the speeches.

148

In wartime, house expeditions were a thing of the past. But senior girls had bicycles. I bought mine for 30 shillings (£1.50) from Chi, the Chinese girl who had left Fauconberg to get home to China. Providing we went in fours and left a note of our route, we were free to explore the Cotswolds at the weekends. What bliss that was. The countryside was still unspoilt, there were very few cars and it was all peaceful and relaxed. The only hazards were the occasional army convoys. Then we attracted a certain amount of attention but it was all in good part. And what energy we had! We got as far afield as Bourton-on-the-Water and the Slaughters and the Swells. One weekend we went to visit friends at Cowley Manor, a bit closer to home. They were delighted to show us those marble bathrooms and the more spectacular Peter Scott murals. We duly goggled and envied.

On Sundays, we could cycle in pairs the 8 miles to Gloucester Cathedral. Dr Herbert Sumsion was the organist – and also our Director of Music. He took the choral class, the musical highlight of my week – not to be confused with the choir, which was all right and we did learn to sing psalms properly but it didn't compare with Choral Class, where we sang real music in parts, Herbert Sumsion conducting. If he knew any of us were planning to come to Gloucester the next Sunday, he sometimes invited us up to the organ loft for the service. Pamela and I (we are still in touch) let him know we were coming, you may be sure!

The next Sunday happened to coincide with the opening of the Assizes, and the cathedral service involved pomp and circumstance and processions aglow with legal and ecclesiastical robes. The organ loft afforded a dress circle view. Herbert Sumsion, kind man, would also let us choose the recessional voluntary on these visits – and we had asked for Bach's 'Sheep may safely graze' – having just discovered it. Everything went smoothly until the sermon. The venerable Bishop of Gloucester had the idiosyncrasy of giving at the knees every few minutes and we were watching, fascinated, to see how low he might go and still bob up again – until Dr Sumsion murmured in my ear, 'I forgot the music for "Sheep may safely graze". I haven't looked at it for a while. I'll just go home and get it.' And without another word, he left the organ, he left the loft, he left us and the cathedral. Panic set in at

149

once. The sermon had already been running a good ten minutes. Supposing it ended? We hastened to the organ. The music for the next hymn was up. What would happen if we took a manual each? The Bishop seemed to be speeding up. We 'practised' silently, trying not even to look at the intimidating ranks of stops... At the last moment, the rightful organist returned, to be fallen on with furious whispers of reproach. 'You needn't have worried,' he said mildly, 'I knew the Bishop was good for twenty minutes at least.' All the same, it was a damned close-run thing, as Wellington said of a rather more serious crisis. Then we were soothed by Bach's 'Sheep', thanked our host no less warmly for the fright – and cycled back for lunch.

The war was never far away. Quite rightly, we were not allowed to forget it. The first term we were drilled by a ladylike officer of the MTC, the Motor Transport Corps. This was at Well Place, a small group of hard tennis courts belonging to the college, now a car park, I think. There we also learned the principles of the internal combustion engine, which would have been very useful for any of us heading for the MTC. Another term, a police sergeant visited us in the gym to instruct us in ju-jitsu – self-defence against an invader? We enjoyed that, though. Even now, if an assailant were so obliging as to warn me in advance and attempt to stab me – from above down to my shoulder – I could disarm him and perhaps break his arm. Well anyway, I'd know how to in theory.

Other things loosened up. For the first time, we fraternised with the Boys' College – that is, we had joint play readings and joint debates. These were always on our own ground, now I come to think of it. The debates took place in the Cambridge Room extension of the library – a fine setting. But the boys were far better than we were. Unless we were absolutely sure of all our facts, our speeches tended to lack conviction. The boys suffered from no such inhibitions. Our one exception was Siriol Hugh-Jones, who came to us from St Paul's. She was brilliant anyway and always effective. (She died tragically early, having already made a mark in journalism.) We even had a joint dance once. In my memory it was a stilted affair in our own Kindy, the large Music Room attached to Fauconberg. (But later, our Head Girl married the Head Boy of the Boys' College, so it can't have been that stilted.)

Finally, at the end of one term, we actually travelled home on the *same day* and the same trains. This had never happened before. We were solemnly warned that it was experimental and any repetition would Depend on Us and our customary impeccable behaviour. How times do change!

As the months went by and the Phoney War came to an explosive end, the mood became more serious. It had to, as we listened to the news and more and more of us had relatives involved. Triumphs or disasters were reflected in the daily routine, even in minor things like the musical appreciation class which a few of us asked for – and got. Our first project was an analysis of *Finlandia* when Finland fell. It seemed to be on the wireless continually. Sibelius then became all the rage, and we dived into the Second Symphony. What a difference good teaching makes. It became and remains one of my favourite symphonies – and one at least that I feel I understand.

The Nazi invasion of Greece had special impact. We prayed for Greece and for her people. The whole school learned the Greek national anthem – in Greek – and we sang it in Prayers. It's a stirring tune; I hope we did it justice. There was a Greek Week, when lessons were devoted to conveying some appreciation of Greek philosophy, poetry and drama and what it meant to our own civilisation. Three or four of us sang a little Greek dirge to accompany a dramatic piece, I remember – a wailing, mournful ditty.

We were strong on national anthems, our own included. All the Allies' anthems were played every night before the BBC news then. So when Queen Mary visited us from Badminton, where she was staying away from the London air raids, we naturally offered her the full treatment – all three verses of 'God Save the King'. Queen Mary was escorted on to the Princess Hall platform by Miss Popham. She looked exactly as she did in every photograph, upright, regal, the same gently floral toque aloft. She smiled benignly – and remained standing as the organ gave its customary gurgle and we all launched into the National Anthem. After one verse – she sat down. *We* ploughed on. Queen Mary perforce, stood up again. When we reached the end, she turned to compliment Miss Popham very charmingly – and said: 'What a beautiful organ!' Now the organ had been wheezing unhappily for as long

151

as any of us could remember and there was a permanent but poorly supported organ fund. Never mind – it was a kind gesture and we were immensely impressed by Queen Mary's 'presence'.

One night the war came closer. Many of us were used to air raid warnings, not to mention actual raids, during the holidays but this night the sirens sounded in Cheltenham. At Fauconberg, we gathered in the front hall, which had been designated as the best-protected bit of the building. We heard planes and gunfire, of course, as expected. Then a louder, closer plane. I was looking up the front stairs at the time – and on up the next flight to the very top of the house. There was a whoosh – an almighty bang and then sinister rumbling. I *saw* the walls at the top of the house sway quite distinctly – to the left and back to the right – and steady. It was indeed a well-built house! No one showed any fear or shock that I remember. Fear is so often in the anticipation rather than the event. Then there's no time for it. When the all-clear finally sounded, we had a hot drink and went back to bed. Next day, we discovered that a land mine had fallen on the back of one of the college houses – Bayshill, not half a mile away. By the grace of God, it had not yet been returned to college and was standing empty. The plane was thought to be a stray, returning after one of the Bristol raids and offloading surplus 'cargo'.

Life went on. I stayed an extra summer term beyond most of my year, with the aim of winning a State Scholarship on a second taking of Higher Certificate. Apparently I'd narrowly missed one the year before, and it was thought worth a try as I needed the money if I was to get to Oxford. (This was before student grants came in.) I was lucky. I did get one, and a County Major Scholarship from Sheffield, again thanks to my aunts sending in an application. Then college discovered a university scholarship at Oxford, open to those reading German as their main language. So I was posted off for that, hastily changing from French and German to German and French. There were only four or five candidates – the others were men. I stayed at Lady Margaret Hall, where I already had a place, and took the papers in the Taylorean Institute. Again I was lucky.

By the end of my time, I had become quite grand, Head of Choir, a committee prefect and Deputy Head Girl – and all that.

What was good about 'all that' was the briefing we got – the insistence on responsibilities before rights and service before self-service; never to think of others as 'you' and 'them' but 'we' and 'us'. It wasn't smug and self-conscious – it was simply imparting what was expected. There was a small service in an upstairs chapel in one of the oldest parts of college then, for newly appointed college prefects. I wonder if there still is. I hope so.

By the last term, most of my friends had gone and I was ready to leave. But I had had four happy and secure years – in spite of the war. I gained enormously from the start and there had been benefits at home too. Without regular mutual irritations, Dick and I began to like each other's company again. In the holidays we would spend hours, late into the night, playing Monopoly, the latest craze, in his eyrie at the top of the house. Sometimes the aunts joined in – downstairs! And I'm sure they appreciated the peace and harmony, whether playing with us or not.

But before I left Cheltenham, we had also left Sheffield, Dick was in the RAF and Aunt Rittie had retired and moved to Brierley, where Aunt Emily, still teaching, joined her at weekends.

Brierley

Brierley was then an unusually pretty mining village on the edge of the South Yorkshire coalfield. Auntie Emily took lodgings in Sheffield during the week until she too retired and joined Auntie Rittie there a couple of years later.

They rented the single-storey wing of a substantial stone farmhouse right on the edge of the village, as it was then. It was set at right angles to the main house, the back, without windows, forming one side of the farm forecourt. All its windows looked out over fields and there was a long, narrow garden running quite a way up the hill, separated from the field by a wavy vandyked hedgerow. Auntie Rittie, now she had time, loved this garden, especially the snowdrops. She was the family letter-writer, faithfully reporting the first sighting every year. The cottage boasted a bathroom made out of what had been a landing. This resulted in the curiosity of a wide flight of stairs leading up from the bath to a blank wall,

153

originally a passage to the main farmhouse. Very useful it was for storing suitcases etc. There was a good-sized sitting room, off which opened two small bedrooms. The kitchen/dining room was cosy but there were no mod cons. The oven was a coal range; you tested the temperature by sticking your hand in. I learned to cook on it, though. It's perfectly practicable – we're spoiled rotten nowadays! You heated irons by the range too – and spat on them to test the heat.

There wasn't much room for me, especially after Auntie Emily retired, but I always enjoyed being there and, by then, I was older and it didn't seem to matter. Anyway, I was coming and going, never staying for very long at a time. I did have my twenty-first birthday there – overwhelmed by the doctor's gift of a bottle of sherry. Hard to come by and it made me feel I really had come of age. He had become a good friend to the aunts and a regular visitor.

The aunts never wanted for company in Brierley; they had the gift of attracting and giving friendship. Auntie Rittie hadn't been there long before she seemed to know everyone. She took over collecting National Savings, walking from one end of the village to the other. The far end was round the small pithead and the Co-op, where everyone's ration books were registered. Then the road wound down, past the old Hall, the church and the doctor's surgery. There were a few substantial cottages and more scattered buildings till they petered out at the farm field. An alley at the side of the church led to two fields opposite us; we walked through them to church or as a short cut to the Co-op – but I expect they're 'infilled' now. Nearly opposite to the farm and the cottage, there was a small general store, then the road rose to the common, with a row of poor cottages on the right – and four definitely superior modern houses right on the edge of the common. I never met their owners. I don't know if Auntie Rittie did but I used to collect for her sometimes at the poorer cottages. They couldn't give much but they always had something: 'Must do our bit.' And I was always offered a cup of something and regaled with stories of Mrs O's gallstones and her latest operation. She seemed remarkably robust and cheerful in spite of it all. A bit further on, standing isolated on the other side of the road, was the pit manager's house

– and here we met the Lindsays and Jill, aged three. The Lindsays were endlessly kind to the aunts, then and even after they had moved back to the edge of Lodge Moor on the outskirts of Sheffield. They would bring the car over to take them for a drive, which was a rare treat then. Fifty years on, I am still in touch.

THE TWENTIETH BEAD

Home and Away in Wartime (1939–1944)

Reams have been written on World War II, better and better-informed. I can only give a personal account of growing up through those years.

My family didn't experience the worst horrors of war. Of course we were affected – everyone was. The war never went away. If they hadn't been bereaved themselves, it wasn't long before everyone knew someone who had lost close relatives or friends in air raids or on active service. But we were lucky. Dick was called up and was in the RAF but his eyesight confined him to ground duties. Whatever he may have felt, his family was relieved. We didn't lose anyone close to us, we weren't in the London Blitz, I was too young to join up and I never experienced violence directly. Not that we were cocooned in complacency or ignorance. We knew what was going on across the Channel, through the wireless and newsreels at the cinema: straggling columns of civilian refugees in Belgium being machine-gunned from the air – some lying dead, their pathetic bundles scattered. Unforgettable images, though we have become punch-drunk with even worse horrors since.

My aunts were always calm – but I was frightened. Like everyone else, we tuned into J.B. Priestley and Churchill on the wireless. Would national morale have been what it indubitably was without them? Their styles were different but both were inspired and inspiring. To get a flavour of Churchill in the darkest days, visit the War Cabinet Rooms and hear the recordings. To us who remember, it's extraordinarily evocative.

Air raids

Sheffield didn't suffer on the scale of London, but as a centre of the steel industry, it certainly had its share. And an air raid is an air raid and bombs are bombs, whether many or few. The shopping centre below the cathedral was blasted out of existence and the industrial areas, towards and beyond the railway lines, where some of the poorest lived, were devastated. Auntie Rittie, returning with difficulty from Heeley Bank, came through some of the worst-hit parts but would never elaborate. Understatement was less likely to 'spread alarm and despondency'. Air raids became a fact of life.

As soon as war was declared, our cellar stairs were reinforced and the space beneath was our air raid shelter. Tucked in there below ground level, the coal cellar protected our rear, the food cellar defended our right flank and the disused kitchen was a comforting buffer zone between us and the backyard. We felt safe from all but a direct hit. Well – some of us did. The wailing, insistent banshee siren keening up and down the chromatic scale was alarming in itself. Moaning Minnie indeed. It was followed all too soon by the sound of approaching planes and gunfire. Then the whistle and crump of falling bombs.

It was at home on holiday that I heard the sirens for the first time. I admit, without shame, that I felt abject terror. You know the expression, being 'sick with fright'? Perhaps you think it's just a figure of speech. It isn't. That night I was literally sick with fright, even *before* the bombs started dropping. I rushed into the old kitchen and was sick in the sink where our newts used to sport. Dick, soon to be called up, was much more stoical. After that first exhibition, I calmed down, helped by my aunts' example – I never knew them to show fear – and because habit accustoms you to most things, even air raids. If a plane came over close and low, 'It's one of ours,' Aunt Rittie would say soothingly. German engines produced an intermittent, hiccuping sound, while ours were smooth and steady – so we believed. We were some way from the main target area; we heard the explosions but they weren't often close enough for us to feel serious reverberations. We were lucky. Ironically, I was far nearer the land mine in Cheltenham than I ever was to a direct hit in Sheffield. And there was always tea! The aunts, who believed in tea as a panacea for all ills, turned each air raid into a sort of tea ceremony.

As the evening wore on, 'Shall we have a cup of tea before the sirens go, dear?' one of them would say. No sooner had we drunk that, as often as not the sirens did go and down we went to the cellar.

'Just put the kettle on, Emily,' Auntie Rittie would say as we settled down, 'and we'll have a cup of tea before the bombs start.' So we did, and then ignored as best we could the menacing droning overhead and the bumps and bangs and crashes.

Then, as the first wave of bombers turned for home: 'What about a quick cup of tea while there's a lull,' Auntie Emily would say; and up went Auntie Rittie and made another pot.

At last came the steady comforting note of the all-clear. 'All-clear!' they would say together. 'Now for a nice cup of tea before bed!' However did our tea ration last out?

Visits to Crewe Green became especially welcome and going back to school brought quieter nights too. But I'd listen to the news carefully to check that the Broomhill district of Sheffield was all right.

Towards the end of the war, rockets – 'doodlebugs' and V2s – had succeeded the Blitzkrieg. I was older and more blasé – or hardened – and found these less alarming. But of course I didn't live in London. I came up from Bletchley once and stayed overnight somewhere near Warwick Avenue. The warning went and a doodlebug came chugging over like an airborne motorbike. If the engine cut out directly overhead, you could relax. The thing would plane down before exploding at a safe (for yourself) distance. I was tired that night and more irritated than scared by the warning. After the first doodlebug had gone past, I remember getting up and half dressing, saying idiotically to myself: 'Well, if I'm going to be blown up, I'll be blown up decent!' And I went back to sleep.

158

On another visit the occasional V2 was exploding on London. I was with a friend in Shaftesbury Avenue when one landed not too far away. No warning this time, no minatory engine noises, V2s arrived too fast for that. There was just a sudden, whacking great explosion. 'That was fairly close,' we said to each other and went on our way. You can't be frightened of something if you don't know it's coming!

War Work

'Doing your bit' was a part of life. There wasn't much one could do while still at school but we did knit away at 'comforts' for soldiers, sailors and airmen. We were allowed to knit during meals, looking like so many *tricoteuses* round a dining table instead of a guillotine. I achieved an enamel RAF badge for my efforts with mittens and socks. But our champion was an amazing girl called Pauline Scott, who, with an extra-long needle tucked under each arm and flashing fingers, could produce a sweater in a couple of days. A human knitting machine.

During the first holiday of the war at Crewe Green, I went along and offered to help at the NAAFI canteen at Crewe station. I was most welcome. I washed up for three hours until one perceptive lady realised I might have had enough and promoted me to spreading margarine for sandwiches. 'Not too much, there's a war on, you know! Put in on and scrape if off,' were my instructions. I never got to serve the soldiery the other side of the hatch as I'd rather hoped!

The next holiday I was staying with a schoolfriend in Doncaster, when we were asked to help out on the overnight shift at the station Forces canteen there. They had been warned to expect large numbers of troops, arriving late and hungry. They duly did; but with very few exceptions, they were not the cheerful, flirtatious soldiers we were used to. Clearly exhausted and in no mood for joking, they fell on the bacon and eggs. Extra supplies must somehow have been scrounged that night. Gradually they moved on, still uncharacteristically subdued, and we had time to clear up and listen to the late-night news. It was 1940. The news was

Dunkirk. Disaster and defeat turned into a kind of victory? That night there weren't many details. Perhaps the evacuation was still going on ... happier memory of Dunkirk resurfaced – drinking hot chocolate in the square with Mother and Dick; and kind Mr Drabble pointing out the shell marks from the First World War – the 'war to end all wars'.

More cheerfully, there was a Forces dance on that visit to Doncaster, presumably for troops stationed at Catterick or thereabouts. Gay and I enjoyed ourselves enormously. It was my first grown-up dance, probably hers too. But at the end we found we'd committed a sustained social gaffe by dancing all the time with 'other ranks' rather than officers. We liked them better! But it was not approved by our hosts.

Between Cheltenham and Oxford, I filled in part of the long gap as an au pair with a service family in Southport, helping with two small children. Their mother had already been widowed, her husband lost at sea. They were very nice people. But for the first but not the last time, I discovered that toddlers are exhausting; especially as the two-year-old, whose cot was in my room, greeted the dawn unfailingly with cheerful song ... Five weeks saw me worn out but I hope I was some use!

By chance Dick was stationed at Blackpool on his early RAF training, so I went to see him on my half-days, taking a few cigarettes and some nicer things to eat than he was getting in his billet – not difficult! We sat on the beach and chatted as we used to and he described the joys of overnight guard duty at the end of Blackpool Pier. I picked up sand to run through my fingers – and was left with litter in both hands. The promenade seemed to be full of little except stalls selling flyblown meat pies – *what* meat, one might well ask? I thought Blackpool a dump and I'm afraid Labour Party conferences there many years later did not change my mind. But 'there was a war on'; and I know lots of folk *love* Blackpool.

Hop-picking which followed was much more fun. With so many farm workers called up, there had been an appeal at school for extra help with the hop-picking at a farm in Worcestershire. It was September. The countryside was glorious, exotically red and gold and russet – not least from the apples on the trees everywhere. As for hops – well! We were so *slow*. We worked alongside gypsies who went at least ten times faster, though we improved a bit through the two weeks. The wasps were ubiquitous but I don't think we got stung – much. We were on piecework, so our earnings were modest. We lived/slept up a ladder in the loft of an old mill house, on straw palliasses – which were *not* comfortable. We gave ourselves sing-songs at night and it was all very good for us. The gypsies then were very picturesque. They weren't called gypsies but 'travellers' and they travelled in old-fashioned, beautifully painted wagons, with shining pots and pans hanging on the outside. Their encampment was in a field on the way to the station and they were very friendly when I wanted to take pictures with my old Brownie. They gave me poste restante addresses to send them copies; but they didn't want to know when I asked for help with my luggage as I struggled past on my way up the hill to the little station on my way home. I sent them the pictures, though.

When I got to Oxford, naturally and properly war work was a requirement. Although we were only there for two rather than three years as in peacetime, we were regularly reminded that the shorter course did *not* mean lower standards, so we worked quite hard. We were lucky to be there at all. It was something to be able to sublimate feelings of guilt by doing anything that might help the war effort. Fire-watching in LMH (Lady Margaret Hall) hardly counted since we never had anything to put out.

Civilian nursing services were stretched, so I started by helping with suppers in the men's surgical ward at the Radcliffe Infirmary – the old building in St Giles. It was harrowing. I was no Florence Nightingale. I was ignorant. I had no idea how ill any of the patients were and was distressed when I couldn't understand what one poor man was trying to ask me. I went to the nurses for help and was at first shocked by their apparent callousness. Then I realised how useless my weak and tearful sympathy was. The nurses, on the other hand, did what was needed without dissolving into ineffectual emotion. Perhaps that is the difference between pity and compassion, weakness and strength.

The next term, I went to help in the Red Cross Section in the New Bodleian Library, which dealt with books for prisoners of war. I was more use here and it felt really worthwhile. Requests would come from POW camps via the Red Cross and we would try to find the books and arrange for their dispatch. The variety of requests was endless and often entertaining. I remember fondly one Bombardier Rosebloom who asked for *The Individuality of the Pig*.

Talking of pigs, there's a dim feeling they figured somewhere in the LMH economy but maybe it was just in the collection of kitchen waste, potato peelings etc. Helping in the kitchens counted as war work too. I don't remember how many hours a week we were meant to do – but I jibbed at the kitchens when I was asked to 'hand finish' machine-peeled potatoes for the High Table. Everyone else put up with the odd eye left by the machine. Why not the High Table? How could that pose as war work? So I refused. 'There's a war on,' I said. 'Fair shares for all!' I added for good measure. I was bolshie by nature. The point wasn't pursued.

Staying with potatoes, they were the target of a spot of genuinely useful war work in the long vacation. Some of us stayed up for a bit of study without the distractions of term-time, and were recruited to help with our own potato harvest. Virtually all the gardens had been dug up for vegetables. 'Digging for Victory' it was called. The large field down by the river was a potato field. Had it been a hockey pitch? We never knew. But harvesting the spuds was an acceptable blow for Victory.

Operations were supervised by the excellent LMH Land Army giantess, appropriately named Miss Gardner. We were stationed at the perimeter of the field while a tractor trailing some devilish attachment churned round and round at speed in diminishing circles, flinging potatoes far and wide but mostly at us. As it passed, we were supposed to stuff them into sacks – but before we had bagged one lot, the tractor would be on us again. Physically speaking, I've never worked faster or harder. Hop-picking was restful by comparison. We finished it, though, and Miss G. had a heart. I seem to remember copious draughts of cider, the traditional harvesters' tipple, and very welcome too.

Clothes and Food!

There was a TV 'soap' recently about wartime life. The little I saw bore no relation to anything I remember. As to 'No bananas' — what did that matter? Bananas did disappear. How could you justify dangerous convoys to bring bananas? But it was hardly a serious privation. I don't think we gave them a thought. Oranges and lemons vanished too.

Rationing has been documented at length — not by me! Food came first, clothing, I think, later. Whenever it was, the mending habit instilled at school proved handy. We mended and turned and dyed and swopped. 'Mend and make do' was the slogan. Parachute silk, if you could find it, made superior underwear. I never did get any. You unravelled wool from the good parts of worn woollies and reused it. Extraordinary things became unobtainable, like proper string and brown paper, much missed by scattered families like ours at birthdays and Christmas. You hoarded what you had. You untied knots laboriously, *never* lazily cutting them, and rolled the string in neat little bundles for future use. Newsprint was rationed too, with the result that newspapers, much reduced in size, had room only for real news and essential information. Not a bad idea at all, though I wouldn't want to forgo Libby Purves. I cannot honestly say that any of these things caused hardship, let alone 'suffering'. They didn't. But it was disappointing to get a parcel from Mother in Africa, with a slot neatly cut out of the side and only one belt left of two cotton frocks. That was very unusual, though.

As to food, of course catering was more difficult, whether for family, school or college. And queuing became tedious. But we didn't starve. What's more, "Fair shares for all' meant what it said and that was a very good thing too. Dried eggs and dried milk made their appearance — unless you kept hens or a cow. A dried-egg omelette is not exactly haute cuisine or Delia Smith but it could be palatable and, anyway, 'Don't you know there's a war on?' was the standard answer to petty complaining.

When I got to Oxford, we did do a minimal bit of managing for ourselves. Our 'tea' parties were pretty basic. I think we drank mostly cocoa, made with National Dried Milk at that. I don't remember coffee. If there was any it wouldn't have been genuine. Our brews weren't delicious – but they were enough for conviviality and late-night gossip. Tea was rationed and milk for it scarce. If actually invited to *tea* you took your own milk. At LMH, we put out a jam jar on a trolley in Hall every morning and collected it at lunchtime – with 1 inch of fresh milk in the bottom! Cream didn't exist at all until well after the war. I don't think we enjoyed our parties any the less.

Now and again we heard of 'corn in Egypt'. Oliver & Gurdon's cake factory in north Oxford sold unrationed lardy cakes (no eggs needed) on Fridays – if one got there early enough. So cycles were mounted and pedalled furiously to arrive before they sold out. The lardy cakes were delicious the first day – after that, there was a sad deterioration into rather dull dough.

Honey, unlike jam, was not rationed. We heard of a bee-keeper in Stokenchurch, at least 12, or was it as much as 16 miles away? Four of us actually cycled there and back to get four or five jars each! Was it worth it? Well, others obviously thought so besides ourselves, because the beleaguered bee-keeper, having kindly sold us what we wanted, pleaded with us to warn our friends off. He was under siege! It would seem absurd to cycle so far for so little now – but things were different then and it was very gratifying to be able to take a couple of jars home to my aunts in due course.

Even more gratifying was the episode of the lemons. One of my LMH contemporaries was Elisabeth de Gaulle. She was in the same part of the college and we fire-watched in the same group. Watch was kept in shifts all through the night, with stirrup pumps and fire buckets to hand. Fire-watching in congenial company was no hardship. I recall an animated discussion about love and marriage, with us English girls sentimental and romantic over love and 'happy ever after' and all that. And surely 'arranged marriages' were abhorrent? 'Not at all,' said Elisabeth, with French practicality. 'My parents know far more about life and about men than I do. Of course they do. They are more likely to know who will make me happy than I am.' And she meant it. We were astonished. But who shall claim she was wrong? Consider our divorce rates. Years later, I visited Colombey-les-Deux Eglises and saw her wedding photo on a side table. I hope she

164

was/is always as happy as she looked there. At LMH, her room was virtually a Free French shrine, with the General and the Cross of Lorraine much in evidence. It was shortly after his return from Dakar on the West African coast that the General came to visit his daughter, very discreetly. I don't think any of us saw him and you wouldn't think he was easy to miss. But he brought Elisabeth a present from Africa – a case of lemons. Inspired man! These were much more precious than bananas. Elisabeth, dear girl, shared them among her friends and I got six. I made some lemonade with one (sweetened with saccharin!) and sent the rest to the aunts. Auntie Rittie saved up butter and eggs and achieved local fame with lemon curd – the Genuine Article – courtesy of General de Gaulle.

Oxford Otherwise

Social life and societies catered for every conceivable interest, not to mention rough games and rowing: they all went on but inevitably in a muted and limited way. I joined something called the Cosmos Society. I think it was meant to deal with international/current affairs. I was persuaded to give a talk on the 'History of the Jews and the Rise of Anti-Semitism'. Horribly topical at the time. I researched exhaustively and spoke exhaustingly and at exhausting length. Too late I knew I'd overdone it but hadn't the skill to cut it short. It must have been an eye-glazing evening for everyone – but there were probably only half a dozen sufferers at best. Much later I learned the speaker's rule: 'Start at the beginning, go on to the end – and then *stop*'. The last bit's the most difficult.

I didn't stay with the Cosmos Society, probably to the secretary's relief. I don't think I wanted to identify with any particular group at that time. I'm sure the political parties soldiered on but I wasn't engaged. I did go to one political meeting. Sir Richard Acland addressed a small gathering in some upper room or other, conveniently near to LMH. Was that why I went? It might have been. He set forth his idea of Common Wealth. It was all a bit vague and confusing though, and didn't catch on.

The Student Christian Movement was active, certainly in LMH. But again I resisted joining, though a regular chapel-goer. I was being ecumenical, sampling the range of churches in Oxford. I rather liked the Presbyterian St Columba's but suspect that an unworthy element of that was a clutch of stalwart young Scots from Trinity who came wearing kilts and dirks in their socks!

One Evensong at St Mary's University Church, Archbishop Temple came. The church was packed. I forget the text but never the stature and spiritual authority of the preacher. At the meeting afterwards, I managed for once to frame a question before it ended. A post-war War Crimes Tribunal was much in the air. Could such a policy be reconciled with the Christian doctrine of forgiveness? The Archbishop's view was that Nazi atrocities were so appalling that something of the sort would be essential to channel the flood of hatred and revenge which would be unleashed when Hitler was finally defeated; it had to be contained. It was a convincing argument. But the hatreds are still with us. So are war crimes.

On a lighter note, there seemed to be an exuberance of enthusiastic drama groups and play-reading clubs. There were earnestly trendy performances of obscure modern works in rooms with rafters and minimal scenery, where everyone was very serious and absorbed. I went along and tried to look as if I was too – but in fact I was bored to my toes. But then came John Gielgud's *Hamlet* at the New Theatre and that put the rest into perspective.

I suppose we all go through a stage where we need to conform to the herd in the most trivial ways. Smoking was fashionable in our generation. To us it spelled sophistication and maturity. It had to be Balkan Sobranie, of course, 'they' said. I tried but I didn't enjoy it, and when I went to the shop in the High where Balkan Sobranie were sold, my naïve prudery was shocked by the poster proclaiming: 'Soft and smooth as a baby's bottom'. How vulgar, I thought! Luckily for me, I didn't persevere with smoking in spite of my friends' useful advice: 'It gives you something to do with your hands at parties!'

Earl Grey tea was another absurd 'must'. When I slavishly tried that too, I wondered why. At home we had Mazawattee or Typhoo, good no-nonsense brews. I didn't like Earl Grey then and I don't now. I only mentioned these silly things because they seemed so important at the time. Perhaps they do have their function in the business of growing up – painless ways of developing independence. 'If you can say you loathe Earl Grey when all around you' etc., you are taking a first tiny step towards independent thinking when it matters. Or so I felt.

War or no war, music flourished and I joined one 'herd' I loved unreservedly. I auditioned successfully for the Oxford Bach Choir as a First Soprano. Monday evenings from 5 to 7 p.m. at the Sheldonian Theatre, with Tommy Armstrong (and occasionally Sir Hugh Allen) became the highlight of the week. We sang some stirring Parry motets, Handel's *Samson* and, most memorably, Beethoven's Mass in D. Amazing to think I was happy on top B then; I've gone steadily down the scale since. At that concert, I found myself directly behind the soprano and alto soloists, Isobel Baillie and Astra Desmond. That was a bit unnerving, but they turned and smiled so I relaxed.

There were several smaller singing groups, such as a madrigal group in Balliol, I think. A bit precious – and I didn't last long. Those of us reading German gave a German carol concert in LMH – a nice antidote to Germany's wartime image. There are such lovely German carols, quite apart from '*Stille Nacht*'.

I only remember one college dance, in St John's. The setting was marvellous – but one did notice the dearth of able-bodied young men other than a handful of medical students. The Doncaster dance, in a drill hall or shack, was nothing like as beautiful but much more fun!

The blackout didn't help evening socialising, especially after the Americans arrived at the Oxfordshire air bases. One was apt to run up against them in the dark streets and, though I never heard of any serious incidents, there were a few minor embarrassments and one never quite knew!

I loved Oxford. I was seriously tempted to claim the third year of my scholarships when peace came, as I could have done. But by then I was already in the Treasury and hoping for the Foreign Office. To go back rather than forward seemed like a negative step and it might have disappointed. I don't know whether I was right.

I'm sure we missed a lot by being there in wartime. But there was still the Bach Choir, even with only four tenors. There was still the countryside within easy reach. Cycling out beyond the northern bypass brought you to Elsfield, where, at the beginning of the Hilary Term, there were drifts of snowdrops in the woods and later on, golden catkins in the hedgerows and cowslips in the fields close by.

And there was still the river. In summer you could take a punt upstream towards Marston, moor by willows on the bank where the grass was like a lawn and lie in the sun and the peace. The peace has gone now, a sacrifice to progress.

There was, and still is, I hope, the choir on Magdalen tower on May morning. We went down by punt from LMH, *Lady Precious Stream* I think she was. In the dim light before dawn I mistook foam for the edge of the landing by the rollers at Parson's Pleasure and fell in. I fell in again while manoeuvring near the tower. Then, after a quick change at St Hilda's across the bridge, I jumped from punt to punt to regain our own – and fell in for the third time as two punts drifted apart. The applause was deafening! But then the sun hit the top of the tower and the singing began and it was well worth it. Afterwards we went to look at the fritillaries in Magdalen meadow and punted back for breakfast.

Most of the time I enjoyed the academic side. It was stimulating. It was inspiring. Fancy being able to work somewhere like the Duke Humphrey Library at the Old Bodleian! Apart from that, we had one inspired lecturer, Dr Stahl, and an inspired tutor of philosophy in Walter Ettinghausen (now Eytan). Thanks to the enthusiasm he generated, I got a 'pure' alpha in my philology finals, in spite of falling fast asleep in one of his tutorials. There were only three or four of us, so it was pretty obvious. If you put students into cosy armchairs at 2.30 on a fine afternoon, what do you expect? I woke up to find him laughing his head off and my very proper tutorial partner deeply shocked. Walter was a distinguished member at Bletchley Park – he has a chapter in *Codebreakers*, the book about it. He became a very good friend. Through him I got an interesting job when I too went to Bletchley. We still carry on a lively correspondence and were able to meet in Jerusalem a couple of years ago when I went with a St John's group to the Holy Land. After 40-odd years one might expect an initial strangeness. There

168

was none. It was a delight to meet again. But to return to Oxford days, it must have been my philology papers that tipped me up to a First. My own LMH tutor, writing to 'congratulate' me later, said: 'I'm sure we both understand it wasn't the most brilliant First.' What a sourpuss. I suspect she preferred my tutorial partner, who was indeed much more conscientious and dutiful but wasn't so fortunate. Ah well. You never can please everyone.

As we approached Finals in the summer of 1944, speculation about the 'second front' was rife. Germany had been defeated in North Africa, the Soviet Union was now an ally, and Italy was virtually out of it. I can't remember consciously longing for peace – but everyone had had enough of war. My closest friend's parents had been in Singapore when the Japs invaded. Her father, a judge, had been taken prisoner. A liner evacuating women and children to Australia had got away just before Singapore fell but never arrived. She was fairly sure her mother had been on board – and all the time we were at Oxford, she was waiting and hoping for some news. It never came.

The night before Finals began was a time for feverish revision. Some say it never works. I always found it to pay off. But this evening was disrupted by a distant, then gradually increasing throbbing until the whole night sky over LMH seemed to be shaking. We went into the garden. It was a clear night – a 'bombers moon'. Black and threatening against the sky, wave after wave of bombers were flying in formation directly overhead, south-east towards France. We knew beyond doubt that it must be the second front at last. It was. It was the start of the D-Day landings.

Some of us had relatives who would be going into action. One lost her only brother a little later at Arnhem, another lost her fiancé. No one knew what the outcome would be. All of us, I guess, felt useless and wished we were in uniform. It was an effort to concentrate on academic work. But that was why we were there – and one just had to get on with it. When I hear about student stress nowadays, I can't help wondering what they mean.

We did have one advantage over today's graduates. We didn't have to worry about finding a job. Not that we could pick and choose; we were directed. Joining the Wrens was popular – but shifting regulations meant that my age group wasn't eligible just then — and so, as a German linguist, I landed at the GCCS, otherwise known as Bletchley Park — and now 'Station X'!

THE TWENTY-FIRST BEAD

Bletchley Park (1944–1945)

Nowadays, what went on at Bletchley Park during the war is common knowledge. There have been documentaries, a book of eye-witness testimony (*Codebreakers*), a best-selling novel and a play. It's even become a tourist attraction.

This publicity is the very antithesis of its wartime image – or rather, non-image. The achievements of the codebreakers are now famous. They made the difference between ultimate victory and early defeat. It isn't necessary to understand the breaking of Enigma to appreciate that a high profile then, indeed any profile, would have spelt disaster.

My contribution was less high-powered – a lot less. I was a late and insignificant player, hardly more than a walk-on part, for the last year or so of the war. By then, I learn from *Station X* on TV, that there were over 10,000 people on site, working in shifts round the clock. I always knew there were a lot. It was an extraordinary population of civilians and all three services, with a scattering of Americans thrown in. There were mathematicians, of course, linguists, several distinguished academics – and not a few eccentrics who didn't fit into any category. The writer Angus Wilson was one. The social and intellectual extremes must have been as divergent as anywhere in the country. Given the numbers, the 'mix', the total lack of restriction of movement outside the perimeter and the magnitude of what was going on, it is nearly incredible nowadays that there was no breach of security through-

171

out the war – and for 30 years afterwards. I learned (also from *Station X*) that many of those doing routine jobs were unaware of Bletchley's central role. Maybe. I only know that I was very well aware of it and so were all those I worked with. But never a 'leak'! Is such security – and loyalty – imaginable in today's leak culture? Perhaps, if so much depended on it.

I arrived not long after Finals and the D-Day landings, an eager minnow, in Hut 8 hard by the lake. It was NID 6, Naval Intelligence. My first job was not as exciting as that might suggest – punching holes in photostatted documents and threading them on to blue tape. There was a forceful Scottish lady in the same room whose language turned the air as blue as the tape. After the initial shock, it did at least break the tedium. Two or three days later, my erstwhile tutor Walter arrived on the scene. I knew by now that he was there but still had no inkling of what he did. In fact he was head of the 'Z Watch', just upstairs, so we were among the first to know that the pocket battleships *Scharnhorst* and *Gneisenau* were leaving the Norwegian fjord where they'd been holed up for some time. Great excitement. That was the end of them.

I guess it was Walter who didn't think punching holes and threading blue tape really demanded a degree, let alone one in German. I moved to the tiny section dealing with captured naval documents, presided over by an entertaining and efficient Wren officer, Vivienne Jabez-Smith. (She has a chapter in *Codebreakers* too.) There was one other civilian from Cambridge and one Wren rating. In spite of not being eligible for the Wrens, I ended up working with them after all.

We worked a two shift system, 8.00 till 4.00 and 4.00 till midnight, changing round periodically. From time to time, lorries delivered sacks of captured documents to the end of the hut. They were often sea-stained and tattered, especially when they came from U-boats. It could be macabre and, war or no war, very pathetic. I still have a small, much thumbed little book *Das Feldgraue Spruchbuch*, full of heartening maxims; beautiful photographs in *U-Boat auf Feindfahrt* (U-boat on enemy patrol) and *Heimat* – the homeland, idyllic pastoral scenes. It didn't do to dwell on the fate of the original owners. Our job was to sort and translate technical handbooks, anything that described equipment, especially new gadgets, and compile accession lists, classified as far as possible, for the Admiralty in London. Seriously important folk came whistling down when we discovered sketches, installation and maintenance instructions for the original *Schnorchel*, the improved periscope, in effect, which made U-boats even more deadly. *Schnorchel* and snorkelling has a more friendly connotation now. German degree or no, finding the English equivalent of naval technical language needed more than a dictionary to make technical sense. A small and erudite research section helped, so did the *Manual of Seamanship* – and the inherent interest of the subject. I became fascinated by torpedoes, acoustic types especially; by de-gaussing equipment (against magnetic mines) by echo-sounding devices – in fact by submarines generally. All old hat and out of date now, I expect. (I was myself immensely privileged to launch our last conventional submarine in 1966; and to have a trip to sea in her years later. And once, in the Rope Walk in the old Chatham Dockyard, I scored Brownie points by knowing that what looked like a giant gym mat was in fact a collision mat.) Work was definitely interesting and the company congenial.

There was life outside the hut. Naturally I joined the Choral Society, run by Herbert Murrell, from the BBC Music Department in civilian life but then an Army Intelligence sergeant. We got a lot of enjoyment performing *Dido and Aeneas* with élan – and some talent, I think. I rather think we broadcast some carols near Christmas. Getting up and down to London on days off was easy; and on a late shift, the morning was free to be lazy – if one's billet was congenial – or to go swimming in one of the disused claypits in the neighbourhood, now filled with water. It needed care – they were very deep.

Billets, good or bad, made all the difference. It was a pity, therefore, that civilian personnel administration was pretty poor. Being charitable, one could say winning the war was infinitely more important. True. Or that the place became too big to be manageable. Maybe.

But consider the Billeting Office, which had commandeered virtually all the available accommodation by 1944 and dictated where one went. The Swan Hotel in Woburn Sands (requisitioned

173

for the duration) served as a temporary roost for batches of new civilian arrivals till a permanent billet could be found. When I went to ask about one, the somewhat off-hand Billeting Officer offered me half of a double room and double bed with a total stranger, to accept at once, unseen. It was all that was available. This I knew to be untrue. 'No,' I said. If there was nothing else, I'd find my own. That wasn't allowed, according to Mr G.

I went away. A nice girl from Kettering who'd also been in the Swan when she first arrived and had stayed in Woburn Sands knew that the other twin bed in her billet would soon be free and I'd be welcome. Back at the Billeting Office, there was affront. I couldn't find my own billet like that! (You'd think it would help.) Anyway, I had. But I needed a room in the hostel for two to three weeks. The hostel by the main gates was meant for even lower-grade clerks. I was Grade 1. I couldn't have a place, though there was room.

'You can't leave me without a roof over my head,' I said, quite calmly, I thought.

That boring man trumpeted about the shared bed place and said: 'I'm offering you a roof over your head.'

'I dare say,' I answered, as far as I recall, and stalked out.

But I got the hostel place and duly checked in. The warden, who had the reputation of being a dragon, greeted me with: 'Oh, so *you're* Miss Ludlam – the girl who told Mr G. not to talk rubbish.'

'Oh dear, did I really?' I said rather nervously.

But she went on: 'My dear, let me shake your hand. I've been longing for one of you girls to tell That Man where he gets off!'

So I enjoyed my brief stay in the hostel. Later, I enjoyed sharing with Edna from Kettering and a cheerful plumber and his family, the Faireys, in Woburn Sands. The bed was army issue planks, and *Music While You Work* blared out from the kitchen below from 6.00 a.m. till close-down – a bit tough when you've come off shift at midnight. To this day, I can't abide background music. But they were lovely people. Later, I went to live with Leonard and Jeanne Forster, Taffy and Meg in a picture-book thatched cottage in Aspley Guise, and that was pure joy. Leonard, a distinguished don from Cambridge, headed our NID 6 research section. They were

174

so kind to me — and very good for me. But no thanks at all to Bletchley's personnel department.

To raise feminist hackles, consider too that Bletchley, as a reserved occupation, received some able-bodied young men with the right skills. Two or three of my own Oxford year went there instead of one of the services. As *men* with degrees, they automatically entered the Administrative grade. As a woman from the same university, also with a relevant — and better — degree, I entered as a clerk. To fuss would have been inconceivable at the time. But when Germany was finally defeated, the Z Watch was wound up and three or four of its male staff came to work with us to cope with the mass of naval documents flooding in. I was asked to instruct people two or three grades higher than myself on the procedure. Fine. But I did think it was about time my grade went up a bit. Oh no, that was impossible. There was no satisfactory answer as to why, so I got myself a job in London — Assistant Librarian to the Printing and Allied Trades Research Association. And I resigned from Bletchley Park. It was obviously already shrinking, and by now, with the war with Germany over, there was a lot of disaffection among the lower civilian orders like me. It's catching.

'But you can't resign,' said our Administrative Officer, 'you're frozen.' (He meant, by the Ministry of Labour.)

'If they've got time to come and reclaim me, they're overstaffed,' I said, thoroughly bolshie by now. He gave up.

At a debriefing to stress the continued need for security, we were offered references. I declined. After the billeting nonsense, the blatant sex discrimination and, I suppose, like most people, a certain reaction after the tension of the past six years, I felt I'd had enough of the Civil Service. I was told a reference would stand me in good stead; it would be from the *Foreign Office*!

'If,' I remember saying, with more force than modesty, 'I can't get along without a reference from this place, I shall be very disappointed.' There was a distinct murmur of agreement and the rather nice woman doing the debriefing smiled faintly and said no more.

After Bletchley

I was getting along nicely in my new job in the City four months later, when a telegram arrived, inviting me to an interview with the Civil Service Commission about a job as (temporary) Assistant Principal in the Treasury! That was the grade which my male colleagues held at Bletchley but which was denied to me as a woman. My new Director was very kind and said I really shouldn't turn the opportunity down, especially in the Treasury, without at least going to see. So at Burlington House I faced four or five solemn gentlemen behind a long table.

'Why do you want to join the Civil Service, Miss Ludlam?' asked the Chairman, courteously.

'I don't,' I said simply.

'Then, er, why are you here?'

'Well, you sent me a telegram asking me to come, so I thought it was only polite,' I said.

He looked at me. 'May I ask,' he said, 'why you feel like this?'

'You see,' I said, 'I was at Bletchley Park.'

The light of comprehension dawned. I was obviously not the first to complain. In fact he said as much. I was assured that our experience was not typical of the Civil Service; that due to wartime security, Civil Service inspectors on the personnel side had not been allowed access, and that, if I gave it a try, I would find the real Civil Service very different. So I did – and I have.

It was coming home from the Treasury one day that I saw the placards announcing that the war was finally and officially over. I was getting off the 53A bus at the top of Baker Street. It was an odd sensation. This was what we'd been waiting and working for for six years. And I felt quite blank. My first conscious thought was: But what do we all do now? I'm not sure we've found an answer yet.

But the VE-Day procession was a great occasion. I had a ringside view of Whitehall from the old Treasury building. The crowds were vast, good-humoured – orderly! All the famous names of the war drove by to enthusiastic cheers – and a jolly touch, Nelson's column was draped in red, white and blue streamers, just like a maypole.

I got keener on politics about then. So did most people in the aftermath of the 1945 Labour landslide. Now and again I went down the road to listen to the House of Commons debates. It was while waiting on the benches before the Central Lobby and observing the comings and goings, that I saw a purposeful-looking young man striding past on his way out.

I have a tendency to talk aloud without realising it. 'There,' I said, 'goes an earnest young Labour MP.'

My neighbours giggled. It was, I am 99% sure, my first sight of my future husband, your father, your grandfather.

My time in the Treasury taught me a great deal on the personnel side; and it's an odd thing to say but I felt valued, a tribute to my bosses. After a year or so, I sat the exams for a permanent job in the real Foreign Office – the same exams for which, much later, I was to be an assessor myself for 20 years. I was successful and never regretted it for a moment. It marked the biggest change in my life since leaving Africa. And it brought me into contact again with that earnest young Labour MP – not *too* earnest, as it turned out.

At this point, I stop counting my beads. They become less distinct and I've gone beyond childhood, after all. But to maturity? Walter said, on one of our long walks around Bletchley, that very few people really grow up before they are 35. I don't think I did until I was about 60! But as I said at the outset, while childhood and youth pass in clearly defined stages, the rest runs together, less colourful perhaps; and memory, strangely enough, is less clear. The freshness of discovery has gone, life becomes more complicated – and altogether, it's better left alone!

So the beads stop – but the string which is life, goes on. For how much longer? Who can say. That's in the hand of God – and there I leave it.

177

EPILOGUE

My Father

In spite of everything, we never quite lost touch. Before the war and through it, we wrote constantly. It was usually my mother who wrote to the aunts, letter-writing being one of her few occupations. But whenever my father wrote, he added a special note for me. When the war came, there was some doubt as to whether we could keep up this correspondence but the introduction of air letters came to our help – and later, a photostat mini-version. They were remarkably reliable, if sometimes a long time coming.

My father stayed in Tanganyika after my mother left but was not successful there, and soon after the war ended, he moved back south once more to the Copper Belt area. He was a convivial man and I gathered from his letters that he found more companionship there. And again he had better luck. He sold a concession reasonably well and came back to England on the proceeds in the mid-1950s. Aunt Emily was overjoyed. Aunt Rittie had died a year or two earlier and she must have been lonely. Laden with presents, he stayed with her, then with us and then with Dick and his family. I'm afraid he upset Dick at one point by suggesting that he wasn't very adventurous! I don't think he can have meant it unkindly but poor Dick felt he had suffered from adventurousness quite enough, though vicariously, and he had a point.

So I met my father again for the first time since we waved goodbye in Mbeya in 1933. I was married with three children of my own by then, and they helped to break the ice; such a gulf of time couldn't help but make it a difficult meeting. He didn't stay long on that visit. Perhaps the money ran out due to the presents and to a trip to his old bird's-nesting haunts in Spain and the Camargue, which he couldn't resist.

It was only a few years later that he came again to spend the last years of his life with Aunt Emily, who was now living in Brighton. He took to Brighton and Aunt Emily's small circle of friends. On my frequent visits, they seemed very happy. I now had four children. I'm glad he was able to see them all. He took the two youngest on to Brighton Pier one day, where they tried every slot machine and every rolling coin trap in sight, not to mention gorging on candy floss. It's a moot point who enjoyed it all most.

But he died in hospital there not long afterwards. The last time I saw him, he was unconscious but I've always hoped he sensed somehow that I was there. After he died, Auntie Emily, following the Victorian custom, asked me to go and 'view the body' as she was too upset and too frail. But she felt it was right and proper, so of course I went. I can't deny it was an effort, but it was less distressing than I'd feared.

He lay composed and peaceful in the hospital chapel. But what I saw was not my father.

I am not sure exactly what theology teaches here. I only know that what I saw in the chapel was merely a shell. The soul, the essence of my father, was somewhere else entirely. And somehow, there was reassurance in that.

It was more upsetting to collect the few possessions he had taken with him into hospital. The nurses had been kind, explaining, on that last visit, that he was in no pain. The clerk, or whatever he was, at the counter where one claimed deceased patients' belongings was less sensitive.

'Oh yes,' he said, bored, when I gave the name. He walked over, took a plastic bag off a shelf and just tipped it out without a word, presumably for me to check. I couldn't. What was there, apart from a plastic soapbox and his shaving gear, were the childish letters and silly postcards I had sent him through all the lost and lonely years. Had they really meant so much to him? I never knew. He saved them till the day of his death – and I never knew, I never knew.

My poor father. I had had the busy years and distractions of growing up, of school(s) and wartime, of Oxford (when he managed somehow to send me £60 a term), of Bletchley and the Foreign Office and then marriage and a family of my own. All he had had of his children, after the early years, were letters. Inevitably he became a penfriend more than a father. Neither of us had had the opportunity to develop a proper relationship as I grew older and grew up. This loss affected him all his life and had its long effect on me too, though I only realised how much, comparatively recently. I don't think I succeeded in bridging the gap when he finally came back. I could have tried harder. Thank God I did keep writing.

When I got back from the hospital that day, Dick was there with Aunt Emily. We were close again then, for he understood at once about the letters and put his arm round me – and I was comforted.

After the Depression of the 1920s, my father was not a great provider, for all his efforts. But as a child I loved him dearly. I never knew anything from him but warmth and gentleness and a great sense of fun.

My Mother

After Mother went back to rejoin my father in the autumn of 1934, they moved to the Chunya area and were there for some years. But their mine failed and she eventually went alone to Dar-es-Salaam, where she worked in a government office during the war and later in the main bookshop there. She had good friends and by all accounts led a lively social life, which included the local amateur light opera society. There's a snapshot of her in the cast of a musical version of *1066 and All That* but it's not at all flattering.

She also had a wonderful surprise when Dick was posted there with the RAF. He got a rapturous welcome, as you may imagine, not only from Mother but from her friends too, who found him charming. It's sad, though, that there wasn't an opportunity for him to meet Father then. He had already gone south, a long way from Dar-es-Salaam.

I never had any explanation of my parents separating – if indeed they ever formally did so. Mother's departure was her attempt to contribute financially towards school fees and to help the aunts with the unexpectedly prolonged burden of providing for us.

I never knew my parents to quarrel but then I never lived with them both together after the age of nine. But Mother said they never did and I never heard either of them criticise the other, except perhaps for my father expressing muted reservations about marriage in general, when he wrote to me on my engagement. I dare say Mother shared those reservations but all she ever said was that Tanganyika was all very well, but it was a man's country – and by implication, not much fun for her. To my child's eye, it was fascinating. But looking at it from an adult angle, I don't think I could have lived there happily for as long as she did, without company or concerts or any entertainment other than four records and a scratchy old gramophone. No shops either. No new clothes, only mending and mail order – and that would take upwards of six weeks to arrive and no 'on approval' possible. The aunts' parcels were a godsend. I loved my year there, indeed I did. For me it was one long adventure. But not, I think, for Mother. And I suspect that ultimately it proved a disappointment for Father.

I half hoped they would come together again after the war but they never did; and I think my father lost most.

Mother came over for Dick's wedding in 1947 – the longed-for reunion. Sadly, she didn't seem to approve of us as we were. 'Doesn't she love us, after all?' I asked Dick in puzzlement.

'Oh, I expect so,' he said consolingly, 'but she seems to think we'd have been different if she had brought us up.'

Perhaps she did. But I don't think she could have done better than the aunts. We adjusted to each other, as one does, and were more relaxed by the time she went back, this time to South Africa. She resumed her original teaching career as Head of Music at St Mary's Diocesan School in Kloof (Natal), where the headmistress was an old friend.

When she retired she came back to England for good and lived in Kent, first in a picturesque rented cottage in Patrixbourne and then in Canterbury, in a little Georgian house in the Blackfriars area, until the steep and twisting staircase became a problem.

She sold that with Dick's help and was lucky enough to get a delightful flat in Eastbridge Hospital, an ancient pilgrims' hospice, right on the bridge in the High Street.

She was eligible for Eastbridge as an active worker for the Cathedral, a supporter of the Friends, one of the 'Holy Dusters' (she looked after Archbishop Tait's tomb) and, most remarkably, the organist for 20 years for Chislett Church out in the countryside. After she gave up driving, she went by bus, well into her eighties, and she never missed. Thanks to my son David, there is now a memorial to her there. She'd like that; and now I come to think of it, when he was only nine, she predicted that he would go into the church. I don't think she ever claimed to have the sight – but how did she know? It goes without saying that she was also an enthusiastic member of Canterbury Choral Society. I don't know why she would never come to any of my Bach Choir concerts, though she often visited us and Dick and Hilary in London. I gave up suggesting it in the end.

Her greatest grief was losing Dick to cancer before she died herself. She really hadn't bargained for that.

She was nearly 90 when she fell down a step in her flat and broke her thigh. I remember her in the hospital bed, telling me about it and saying: 'Damn! Damn, Damn, DAMN!' She was more angry with herself than anything. But she was never mobile again. She came to us until doctor, district nurse and daily nurse all said firmly this was no longer in her best interest, as she needed 24-hour nursing care. Luckily there was room in a 'Friends of the Elderly' nursing wing very close, and after an aggressive and difficult start, which they kindly didn't tell us about till later, she relaxed and seemed content, though increasingly vague.

We visited several times a week. Once, when I met her in the passage on her Zimmer frame, she looked at me enquiringly, then smiled sweetly and said: 'I *think* we've met before?'

'Yes, probably,' I said, 'I'm your daughter, Bay.'

'Of *course*!' said she, light dawning. And she burst into peals of laughter. It was lovely to see her sense of humour return, as it certainly did, even if memory fluctuated.

'Such a nice young man came and took me for a drive yesterday,' she said once. 'I don't know who he was.'

'It was my husband, Christopher,' said I.

She looked at me in astonishment. 'Your husband,'she said, making it sound like Edith Evans' 'Handbag'. 'I didn't know you were *married*.' Christopher was very good and often took her out. The next time he did, I'm glad to say she was perfectly clear about our relationship.

After her ninety-third birthday in August 1987, she began to fail and I went to see her nearly every day. In October, I had a walking weekend planned at Parcevall Hall in Wharfedale, with David and his family. By then, her doctor said I'd be better for a break myself and he'd ring at once if necessary. So I went.

We walked up Hebden Beck on one of those golden October days, just the kind of country and the kind of weather Mother loved. She was much in my mind. I wasn't surprised to get the doctor's call.

David drove, rather fast, to catch the next train from Leeds. But by the time we got there, I knew she had died; a call from the station only confirmed it.

Christopher met me at King's Cross with a stiff drink and we drove straight to the home. She was still in her bed, very pale and quiet and cold. I kissed her for the last time − and I don't think I can write any more.

POSTSCRIPT

1997

Two years ago, when an opportunity arose to revisit South Africa, I had some doubts. It's supposed to be a mistake to go back to scenes once loved and familiar. I suppose it has a lot to do with timing. To return too soon positively courts disappointment. One expects everything to be the same and of course it never is. After sixty years however, perhaps especially in South Africa, one really can't expect *anything* to be the same. There have been such fundamental changes and they have not exactly gone unnoticed. I would have to be prepared to see nothing at all of what I remembered, perhaps even to the point of doubting those memories and finding them dissolving into a vacuum. Which would have been desperately sad.

But still, here was a chance which wouldn't come again. So with some trepidation – I went. I went along with a Bach Choir tour, the choir I belonged to for 38 years. This meant no worries over accommodation or travel, excursions laid on and congenial company – not to mention the concerts.

The first stop was Johannesburg. The centre has certainly changed beyond my recognition. But, unlike Pretoria, we never did frequent the centre much. It can be a dangerous place now. Sheets of advice to tourists warned, among other things, not to stop at red lights if there were lurkers there. A nice balancing of risk! But our hotel was out of the centre and actually quite close to Parkview. So, with a hotel-vetted taxi and Jim the driver from

Soweto, two of us set off. Jim knew the way quite well. What astonished him – and me – was that once there, I could direct him without hesitation. There seemed to be no high-rise, concrete development and the road pattern had not changed. 58 Roscommon Road was there, opposite the school still, which also looked the same – apart from grass where we had had a dusty playground and were none the worse for it. If it hadn't been the Easter holidays, I'd have gone in and asked to see the classrooms I remember best. I'd have liked that. But it was all closed. So on to Kildare Avenue, where my best friend Winifred Till had lived at number 22; then down to the end of Emmarentia Avenue – and there was number 34 still. (There was no sign of the dusty lane we used to take to school though, with the grenadillas hanging temptingly over the fence.) Best of all, opposite number 34, was the golf course, still unbuilt over, still unspoilt, the scene of our happy childhood naughtiness! Even the line of willow trees, Dick's escape route from justly furious golfers, stood where they had so long ago. We took snaps of Jim and ourselves to prove it. Back past the school and, most surprisingly of all, the little parade of shops down near the Zoo Lake was still there, not noticeably modernised, or supermarketed, still human and friendly – but no fish shop, alas!

Such changes as there were, were sad but inevitable signs of the times. 58 Roscommon Road had lost its lovely garden to infilling – as far as one could see behind higher fences. 34 Emmarentia Avenue looked bigger and modernised but it was difficult to tell by how much. Our plain, open iron railings had been replaced by high walls and tall double gates barred a drive. As I approached these gates, wondering whether it might be seemly to introduce myself, two Dobermans came bounding down, stating very plainly that it would not!

But as a recompense, the Zoo Lake was much the same. More manicured perhaps – it would have been difficult to find a drain to crawl through! And the surrounding parkland was beautifully kept. On the far side, there were apparently boats for hire and a tea-garden. Here we repaired, parked the taxi and found a shady table. Mary and I had a cooling drink, Jim an ice-cream.

'Well,' I said to him, 'this is something we couldn't have done

185

last time I was here.' We both laughed. I had thought there might have been some constraint – there was none. Jim was definitely politically conscious – is it possible to live in Soweto and not be? He was interesting on the state of the nation and optimistic on the whole, although there have been troubles since. But he has been proved right on the Mandela succession and I hope his optimism about the future still holds.

The following day, he came again and took us to Pretoria (at a discount, too!). But Pretoria was less rewarding. It wasn't such familiar ground for Jim. We couldn't find our way round Arcadia or the school or Entabene where we had lived. So we drove up the hill to Union Buildings and these were as fine as ever, so were the gardens around them and the field below was still green and empty. But the view beyond also suggested a much more crowded and concrete suburb than all those years ago, which perhaps explained why we couldn't find our house and school.

So, back to the centre we went and to my first South African playground – Church Square. Alas! The pools on each side of the central steps were nearly empty and litter-strewn. A not very 'kempt' African was standing in one, while a couple of policemen tried to persuade him to come out. At least they weren't resorting to any rough stuff. Tourists teemed, souvenir stalls too, at the entrances; and the once immaculate lawns were trampled at the edges. In the centre, a vast brown stone memorial to Paul Kruger dominated. Even as children, and comparatively close to the Boer War, we were taught, rightly, that he was a great man. But this monument does him no favour, out of scale and style with the rest of the square as it is and really rather ugly! Others no doubt think differently – and it was still Church Square! The pavements around were pretty scruffy – though no more than some in London now; and round the corner, where my grandmother's commodious flat used to be, was a multi-storey car park. Oh dear! 'Sic transit...' etc.

So – that could have been a sad visit *if* my memories had been more recent. But how can one expect no change in sixty years? Ridiculous! A later visit to Melrose House, still wrapped in its Victorian dignity, restored the balance – and we glimpsed the Loretto Convent on the way by. This time I was *not* tempted to go in.

My snaps of Parkview came out well and I sent copies to Jim in Soweto, who wrote a most touching note back. I hope we can keep in touch.

Later we went to Durban. The sea front is now a modern sea front, much like any other and pleasant enough, but with nothing I remembered. Admittedly, we were never there for long. I couldn't find the old Grand Hotel and the splendid Zulu rickshaw men had gone.

I thought of visiting Amanzimtoti, further down the coast, but heard that it had been developed into a vast holiday complex — lots of concrete. True or false, I didn't dare go.

So I can still cherish untarnished the memory of the hotel/home, with its wide verandahs, the river estuary where one of us, at least, enjoyed fishing, the pineapple fields, the lane where I saw the green mamba, and the bay, without a building in sight, where the Indian Ocean rollers came smashing down on the empty beach and where the glow-worms shone at night from the grassy bank on the way home to supper.

I'm glad I went back. The Jesuits say, I believe, 'Give us the first seven years of a child's life and we have him for life'. This is when habits of mind are formed, and impressions are made which never fade. I spent more than half of my first ten years in Africa, at least, in part of it. Both of my parents spent most of their lives there, in Southern Rhodesia, now Zimbabwe, as well as South Africa and Tanzania. It was the family background and, presumptuous though it may be, I still feel an affinity — I always will. I am saving up to go back once more — to the Victoria Falls, where my parents honeymooned.